L.R. JACKSON

TAINTED LIBERTIES

BLACK ODYSSEY
MEDIA

WWW.BLACKODYSSEY.NET

Published by

BLACK ODYSSEY MEDIA

www.blackodyssey.net

Email: info@blackodyssey.net

Library of Congress Control Number: 2023919235

First Trade Paperback Printing: July 2024

ISBN: 978-1-957950-14-3

ISBN: 978-1-957950-15-0 (e-book)

Cover Design by Ashlee Nassar of Designs With Sass
To the extent that the image or images on the cover of this book depict a person or persons, such person or persons are merely models and are not intended to portray any character in the book.

All rights reserved. Black Odyssey Media, LLC | Dallas, TX.

10 9 8 7 6 5 4 3 2 1

Manufactured in the United States of America

Distributed by Kensington Publishing Corp.

DISCLAIMER

This book contains content relating to race, religion, sexuality, and more. It contains hate words as well as scenes that may be difficult to digest. It highlights many stereotypes that exist in our country, and although these are fictional characters, there are real people who share the same views as the characters in this story.

If this sounds like something that could be triggering for you, please do not continue to read.

If you choose to continue, please know this is a tough read. This book is emotional in every way, but keep reading. It does have a happy ending.

CHAPTER ONE

MARK

The conference room buzzes with anticipation as everyone tries to guess who was fired today. Glances around the round table show that we use the process of elimination to figure out who is missing. We heard the rumor this morning. The person was fired by email and was told their items would be shipped to them later. I scan the room desperately, trying to solve the mystery, when it dawns on me that my manager is missing. The door swings open when I ask about his whereabouts, and the firm owner walks in.

"Good afternoon," he speaks in a raised voice to quiet everyone down.

He waits until the room is silent before he continues to speak. "I know you all wonder why we're gathered here this afternoon. Unfortunately, the rumors are true, and we had to let someone go. As of this minute, Mr. Hollis will no longer serve as the manager of this team."

Silence fills the room, and everyone glances uncomfortably at one another. I am disappointed and can't believe what I'm hearing. Colin Hollis was an exceptional manager, and because of his leadership and guidance, I was up for a promotion as a senior designer this year. So, what could he possibly have done to get fired? I'm about to ask if they'll tell us what happened with him, but the conference room door swings open, and a tall, dark man wearing an expensive suit enters. He walks to the front of the room and stands beside the owner.

"I'd like you all to meet Andre Mays. He'll be the new head manager of the international team. Andre has extensive experience and a wealth of knowledge in the architecture business. He has helped design some of the most famous buildings in the world. Please help me welcome him."

Sounds of applause fill the room, but I'm barely clapping. I don't like him, and I don't like his kind. I never have. Who does he think he is barging in, wearing an expensive suit as if he can be as good as us? I don't care what his credentials are or how smart the owner thinks he is. I know better. I know how they think. I know how they act and what they stand for.

He introduces himself and gives his background, but I'm not listening. I'm too busy imagining him hanging from a tree with a noose around his neck, like the images my father used to show me. Times were extraordinary back then ... back when they knew their place. Back when they didn't have positions of power. Back when they could be controlled.

Now, they think they can run shit. Say what they want and take over the country like a sewer full of rats. I won't stand for this. I won't stand for him prancing around like he owns me and looking down on me like he's so much better. And I refuse to be managed by a nigger.

AMY

"We better hurry back before we get caught," I tease as I slip into my pants.

His brown eyes meet mine. "I bet you'd like that, wouldn't you?"

I smack his forearm lightly but hard enough to leave a red mark on his skin. "I'm not into voyeurism so, no. I wouldn't. Your mind is so dirty."

"Isn't that what you like about me?"

I smile. "Yes."

I'm grateful for how easy it is to slide into my scrubs as I tighten the drawstring in the front. The easiness of getting dressed and undressed allows me to continue my regular lunch dates with Sheldon. And by "lunch date," I mean sex. We've been sneaking around in the on-call room before and after his shift.

"You worry too much, Amy. It's been seven months. Have we ever gotten caught?"

"No."

"And we won't. Just relax."

My mouth curves upward in a devilish smile. Sheldon brings out a different side of me. One I've never shown to anyone else, not even my husband. I feel liberated with him. Vulnerable. Sexy. I can't get enough of his baritone voice and big, strong hands. It keeps me coming back for more, which isn't good because I could lose it all if I'm not careful. *We* could lose it all.

"I'll see you later?" he asks before giving me a peck on the lips.

"Yeah, see you later."

He places a pen inside the pocket of his white coat and slips out the door. I stay behind because it'll look suspicious if I walk out right after him. Before walking out, I rush to the mirror to ensure I look presentable. I run my fingers through my messy hair, attempting to smooth my black strands down as neatly as possible. Exhaustion fills my eyes, courtesy of the three orgasms Sheldon gave me. But there's nothing I can do about that right now. I check the time before grabbing the white pill from my pocket and pop it into my mouth. I swallow it, and then I open the door. The beeping monitors and announcements over the intercom greet me, reminding me I have five hours left in my shift. I pull the chart for my next patient and walk inside the examination room. The older woman smiles when she sees me. She's holding the hand of a frail man, and her eyes are red and filled with tears. I take a deep breath before I speak.

"Hi, I'm Amy. I'll be your nurse for the next few hours."

"Hi, Amy. I'm Marsha Gillard, and this is my husband, Frank."

I take a second to scan his chart, and stage four cancer leaps out at me. My heart breaks for both of them. "I understand Mr. Gillard has grown weaker these past few days?"

I walk over to check his vitals as she responds to my question. "Yes, he's barely eating or talking."

As I suspect, his vitals aren't strong, but I don't tell her. I leave that up to the oncologist, who's already been paged. He looks peaceful as he watches me check his heartbeat. The calmness in his eyes tells me he knows he doesn't have long. The worry shows me that he's concerned more about his wife than himself. She watches him and caresses his head, assuring him that he will be okay. "I'm right here, honey; you'll be just fine."

I turn to face her while reading his chart. I'm interested in the length of time he's been sick. When I find it, I speak gently. "Any other symptoms since his diagnosis three weeks ago?" She shakes her head. I offer a smile, but not a happy one. One more along the lines of compassion. "I know this must be hard for you both."

She turns to look at him. "Yes. I can't lose him."

"How long have you two been married?"

Part of my job is to separate the personal lives of patients from my job. If I become emotionally invested in every patient I have, I'll lose my mind. But this is different. This time, I'm curious.

"We've been married for over forty years," she replies.

That's a long time. It's an even longer time if the marriage isn't a happy one, like Mark's and mine. Her eyes swing to mine. "Are you married?" she asks.

"Yes I am."

She looks back at her husband, who's clinging to life. "Cherish it while you can. Because one day, one of you will leave this earth."

I take a risk and ask my next question, wondering if I want an honest answer. "Forty years is something to celebrate. Has it always been a happy marriage?"

She laughs lightly. "Honey, some days I can't stand the sight of him. But that's marriage. It's not meant to be unicorns and butterflies every day. It's two people choosing to love each other even when they don't like each other. My Frank isn't perfect, but he's perfect for me."

Watching how they look at each other brings tears to my eyes. Mark used to look at me like that. I used to look at him the same way. There was a time when I was head over heels in love with him. Now, not so much. Two kids later, I feel like I made a mistake marrying him, which saddens me. The loving couple in front of me is how I envisioned Mark and me, minus cancer. I look at the heart monitor before I scribble in my exam notes. When I'm finished, I glance at the time. "The oncologist should be in shortly."

She nods without taking her eyes off her husband. I don't know how many patients I've seen during my nursing career. There are way too many to remember. But sometimes, I encounter a patient that sticks with me. I find myself thinking about one even after they've long been discharged. This is one of those times. My mind swirls with curiosity. Do they have kids? Will he miraculously live longer than what the statistics say? If not, what will his wife do without him? My heart softens at the thought of Mark dying or being gravely sick. I love him and would never want anything to happen to him. He's the father of my children. He must sense that I'm thinking about him because my phone suddenly vibrates and when I check the message, it's from him.

Hollis was fired today. Can you believe they brought in some monkey as our new manager?

I don't respond. I've got more patients to see, and I won't allow him to ruin my mood with one of his racist rants. They're starting to become annoying. He hates anyone that doesn't look like us. Native Americans, Chinese, Spanish—it doesn't matter. He hates them all. But he especially has a hatred for Black people. I don't know why, and I never bothered to ask. He's my husband, so I go along with it. I pretend to hate Black people as much as he does, which kills me. How can I hate Black people if I'm sleeping with one? It's another reason I've got to be careful. If Mark ever finds out about Sheldon and me, I don't know what he would do, and I don't want to find out.

SHELDON

I pull into my driveway and turn off the ignition. I take a deep breath and give myself a moment to gather my thoughts before I head inside. Today was an emotional day. I lost two patients, and although it's not uncommon for doctors to lose patients, it's never easy. I slowly leave my car and drag my feet toward the front door. As soon as I walk in, my daughter runs toward me.

"Daddy!" she excitedly yells.

I scoop her up and give her a big kiss on the cheek. "How's daddy's favorite girl?"

"Good," she answers with a giggle.

Eva walks down the steps carefully, holding our newborn son, Sheldon Jr., and I can tell by the expression on her face that she's had a long day. She's wearing her usual outfit: baggy sweatpants, an oversized t-shirt, and a bonnet. My wife is beautiful: smooth brown skin, long hair, and curves in all the right places. God, I miss seeing those curves. And I miss seeing her doll herself up for me. When we first married, she made it a point to keep up her appearance. She got her hair and nails done every week. She wore sexy outfits for me and kinky lingerie. But those days are long gone. Sexy outfits are replaced with baggy jeans and t-shirts, and lingerie is replaced with long flannel pajamas. She doesn't keep herself up anymore and could give a damn about keeping the spice in our marriage. Her only focus is Bible study and church.

"Do you mind taking the baby?" she asks.

"I just walked through the door," I answer.

"So! I've been home with him all day, and I'd like to rest before Bible study tonight. It won't hurt you to help with your son," she fires back.

This is the reason I work late every chance I can. This is the reason we barely get along anymore. And this is the reason why I'm fucking Amy. Besides becoming a boring Bible scholar, Eva complains and nags like most Black women do. I've dated three in my lifetime, and all three caused me headaches. It's the same with all of them. They don't know how to stay in their place and submit to their men. That's why dating white women is so much better. They're easygoing, submissive, and know how to treat a man like a king. But I couldn't dare bring home a white woman. My parents would disown me.

My parents grew up in the civil rights era. They marched, protested, and fought side by side against racial injustice. I won't say they hate white people; just that they aren't fond of them. No. Who am I kidding? They *do* hate white people. A big chunk of my family consisted of members of the Black Panther party. Growing up, I was taught that white people hated us and were not to be trusted. I was taught that I must work just as hard and be twice as good to have the same opportunities that they have. Racism was discussed daily, and I watched my parents struggle financially, working jobs that paid little, all while blaming it on oppression.

"Before you start an unnecessary argument, did you ever stop to think that it won't be good for me to handle the baby until *after* I've showered and changed? I've been helping sick patients all day, Eva, and I'm full of germs."

She narrows her eyes and tightly presses her lips together. "I'll be in the nursery when you're ready for him."

I shake my head in frustration as I watch her climb the steps. This won't be the last I hear about this, and it makes me want to walk right back out that door. Eva just can't let shit go. She always must have the last word, and according to her, I'm in the wrong . . . about everything. Obviously, her church doesn't teach her the importance of submission. I don't know much about the Bible because my parents forbade me to read it. But I do know that there's something in there about wives submitting to their husbands.

"Daddy, I wanna go play with Shellon," Kamryn says as she wiggles out of my arms.

I chuckle. She still can't pronounce Sheldon's name correctly, and I hope she doesn't grow up calling him Shellon instead of Sheldon. I place her down, and she takes off running up the steps. I love my kids, and if I'm being honest, I doubt Eva and I would have lasted this long if it weren't for them. My thoughts are interrupted when my cell phone vibrates. It's a message from Amy.

Are we still on for tomorrow?

Yes, I reply.

I look forward to my time with her. At first, it was just sex between us. But as time passed, I started developing feelings for her. I wish things could be different with us. I wish we were both free and single so we could be together. I wish my parents weren't so pro-Black. And I wish society wasn't biased against interracial dating. Even if Amy and I could date, many challenges would affect our relationship.

She's very different from Eva. They're both gorgeous, but their personalities are like night and day. Amy is gentle and easygoing. She doesn't nag or complain. She sees me as the perfect man. Come to think of it, all my white exes saw me as perfect. With them, it was easy. We got along well. They weren't snappy and sassy all the time. And boy, did they know how to take care of me. They prepared my meals, washed my clothes, and spoiled me rotten with affection. They also did anything I wanted in the bedroom, unlike Eva, who thinks sucking dick or anal sex is disgusting.

I'm also sick of Eva's rhetoric that she doesn't need a man. Why would she marry me if she didn't need me? And what man wants to be married to a woman who constantly reminds him that she's okay with or without him? I like for my woman to need me. But in the Black community, finding a woman not on the independent train is almost impossible. They're taking this shit too far. They act like allowing their man to care for them is a crime. Maybe if more of them learned that they could still be independent *and* care for their man, the divorce rate wouldn't be so high, and there wouldn't be so many single mothers. I planned to marry a white woman, but unfortunately, none of my relationships with them lasted because I knew I could never bring them home to meet my parents. So now, I'm stuck with the type of woman I swore I didn't want.

Make no mistake; I love my wife. But I'm no longer *in* love with her. I don't desire her, and I hate everything about our marriage—especially her resistance to her role as a wife. For one, she's too opinionated. She has something to say about everything, and sometimes, I just want her to sit back and shut the fuck up while I handle things. *I'm* the man of the house, but she doesn't see it that way. Secondly, we agreed that she would be a stay-at-home mom, but now, she's changing her mind. How the hell can she have a career while raising our two kids? I almost lost my shit when she talked about sending the kids to day care so she could run off and work a job she don't need. I make enough money to support us comfortably. She should be at home, raising our children and caring for the house. *That* is her job. But she thinks otherwise. And we clash because of it. Eva thinks my expectations are unreasonable. She feels she's an educated, strong woman who can work, be a mom, and have a career. She doesn't think she should have to compromise, but I say, yes, the hell she does.

EVA

I place Sheldon Jr. in his bassinet, grab my Bible, and sit in the rocking chair. He's been fussy all day, and it's caused me to feel both frustrated and overwhelmed. I wanted to give Sheldon a piece of my mind just now, but I didn't want to argue in front of the kids. We've been doing much of that lately. He swears his job is the only important job on the planet. I know he saves lives every day, but that doesn't mean that I'm supposed to do nothing but stay home and raise his babies. I'm sick of him and his misogynistic ways. I had an exceptional career as a marketing director before we had Kamryn. I planned to be a stay-at-home mom until she turned one. That turned into five years, and then Sheldon Jr. came. My position was given to someone else, and now my résumé displays a five-year gap in employment. I want to return to work, but Sheldon wants me home barefoot and pregnant. We argue nonstop over it, and it's caused me to lose respect for him as my husband and as a man. What man wouldn't want his wife to have a career?

Proverbs 18:22 says, *He who finds a wife finds a good thing and obtains favor from the Lord.* It doesn't say, *He who finds a maid that caters to your every need finds a good thing.* That's what Sheldon wants. It's almost like he's child number three. "Eva, can you heat my dinner?" "Eva, can you iron my scrubs?" "Eva, the baby is crying!" I swear if I hear him call my name one more time, I'll end up on an episode of *Snapped.* He blames his lack of help around the house on his job. Don't get me wrong; he does work a lot. But so do plenty of other fathers who still help around the house. Sheldon is just lazy. He leaves his socks and dirty briefs on the floor, won't put the toilet seat down, and won't even bother to change the baby now and then. His view of being a father is to provide for and play with them. The day-to-day care is all on me, and all I want is a little help. I want him to pick up after himself, wash a dish, or feed the baby sometimes.

Our marriage is in the dumps. We don't communicate, are barely affectionate, and haven't made love in months. The fire that once burned between us is gone. I sometimes hear him masturbating when he thinks I'm asleep, which disgusts me. I know he has needs, but I'm here to satisfy them even if I'm not in the mood. I also suspect that he's sleeping with somebody else. He's been cold toward me lately and always on his phone. He's also working more than usual, which leads me to believe he could be sneaking around with one of his coworkers. He works with a staff of women, and I've seen how they look at my husband. Sheldon has a high sex drive and is into all kinds of things—things I'm sure every woman in that ER would be willing to do for and with him. I used to be that woman. Ready to do everything in my power to please him. But I'm a saved woman now. The church has taught me that a woman doesn't have sex to enjoy it. We have sex to procreate and to please our husbands. My job is to allow him to take me until he's satisfied, and that's what I do. All that other stuff he wants to do is unnecessary and very sinful.

The thought of sex reminds me to check my ovulation calendar. I grab my cell and open the app. I'm not ovulating, so it's doubtful I'll get pregnant if we have sex tonight. I have a sex schedule that I stick to every month, but we've both been so busy that we've fallen off track. I planned to have sex last night but got called to the hospital to pray over the pastor's nephew. So, today it is. I stand to my feet, dreading the idea of having to do this. If it were up to me, I could go the rest of my life without sex. It just isn't all that important anymore, but I know Sheldon likes it. So, I'm doing this for him. I look at Sheldon Jr. to ensure he's asleep before I leave the nursery. When I enter our bedroom, Sheldon is drying off with a towel.

"Where's Kam?" I ask.

"Taking a nap."

This is perfect timing. I've already showered, he's just finished his, and the kids are asleep. So I can get this over with quickly, just in time to get to the church for six o'clock Bible study. I pull the t-shirt over my head and toss it to the floor. Then I slide out of my sweats and panties. He turns around to face me.

"What are you doing?"

"What does it look like?" I take a step toward him and wrap my arms around his neck. His eyes search mine. "It's been three months, Sheldon."

"I know."

I place my lips against his, not feeling an ounce of passion. However, he stops me when I lean into him, slightly pushing me away. His rejection humiliates me, and anger sweeps through me. "What's wrong? Don't you want me?"

He shakes his head. "Not like this."

He walks away from me and grabs a pair of briefs and a T-shirt from the dresser drawer. I grab the pile of clothes lying on the floor and quickly dress before he humiliates me further. I take two steps toward him. "'Not like this.' What's *that* supposed to mean?"

"It means I'm tired of *scheduling* sex with my wife. It means I'm tired of you treating sex like a box to mark off your to-do list."

"Well, at least I try. You barely touch me anymore."

"Because you recoil when I do. You're never into it, and I feel like I'm fucking a corpse."

His words sting. And he must realize that he's gone too far because he attempts to sweeten his statement.

"I didn't mean that. I mean that you hate the thought of me touching you. You're either tired or not in the mood."

"Well, I'm in the mood now," I reply.

"No, you're *not* in the mood, Eva. You're doing this because you think you're *supposed* to. That doesn't work for me and certainly doesn't turn me on."

"I don't turn you on because you're too busy watching porn, wishing I'd do all those filthy things those women do. I shouldn't have to compete with that, Sheldon."

He whirls around angrily. "What else am I supposed to do? Walk around with a hard dick all day?" He exhales loudly before he plops down on the bed. "Listen, I'm tired. I don't have the energy to argue."

"Are you sleeping with someone else?" I don't know why I ask a question I don't want the answer to. Although I know we don't feel the same about each other, the thought of him with another woman crushes me.

His eyes narrow. "What? No." He pauses. "But would you care if I was?"

It's a tricky question to answer. I don't think I'd care if it was just a sexual relationship with a woman. She'd be doing me a favor by taking the pressure off me to have sex with him. But it's the intimate part that would crush me. He getting close to another woman, confiding in her, and developing feelings for her. I'm about to answer him, but Sheldon Jr. cries, interrupting me. Sheldon shakes his head as he rises from the bed.

"Yeah, I didn't think you'd care. I'll go get him."

He's gone before I can stop him. It disappoints me that he thinks I don't care about him because I do. I have two kids by this man. He's all I've ever known. Of course, I don't *want* him sleeping with another woman. It's just that I don't think I'd be that surprised if I found out that he was. My plans for tonight have been ruined. I suddenly don't feel like going to Bible study, but I know it's necessary. I need to seek guidance about how to continue in this unhappy marriage. When I go to church on Sunday, I'll ask the pastor to pray for us. I sit in the chair by our window and open my Bible to the book of Proverbs. I need to highlight a few passages before I leave. I'm feeling stressed, and this book has a way of calming me. It always gives me answers. And right now, I need answers. I don't believe in divorce; it's a sin. I don't want to leave my husband, but we're both unhappy and making each other miserable. It isn't good for our home, and I must think about my kids and what's best for them. I love Sheldon, and I know he loves me, but sometimes, it takes much more than love to save a marriage.

I take my seat next to Sister Clarice. She's waving a fan in front of her face, hoping to alleviate some of the humidity in the building.

"How are you, Sister Eva?"

"Good. A little tired, though. The kids have been restless this week."

Her mouth curves into a big smile. "God says to be fruitful and multiply. What a blessing your kids are."

I know the scripture she's referencing, and I take great pride in giving my husband two children. But now, I don't see us having any more. For one, we can't get on the same page sexually. He seems not to want it, and I barely want to give it to him when he does. And second, I'm already exhausted from caring for the two we have. I nod and smile.

"Yes, they are." Finally, I change the subject. "It's so hot in here."

"Whew, you ain't never lied. I'll be glad when the air-conditioning is fixed."

"I thought Pastor said we were close to reaching our goal for the building fund."

"We're short about $600. But I know God will provide," she responds.

"Yes, He will."

I grab a fan in front of me with a picture of the Holy Bible. I fan myself to cool down, and Sister Clarice looks around the room.

"Lawd, it's a shame what happened to Sister Bertha."

My head whips around, and my eyes land on her. "What happened to her?" I ask.

"You didn't hear? Chile, her husband dropped dead last week. They say he was having an affair with his mistress and died right on top of her."

I gasp while my eyes stay fixated on her. She don't look heartbroken or angry, for that matter. Instead, she seems as though everything is all right in the world.

"How horrible."

"Yes, it is. Word on the street is that he got churren by her too. I reckon he ain't never claimed them, though. That's why it ain't good to have bastard kids."

"That is such a shame. If that is true, it sucks that the children suffer," I reply.

"Um hmm. You didn't hear none of this from me, though."

"I can't imagine how devastating that is. Do you think she knew?" I ask.

Sister Clarice giggles. "Sweetheart, we women know everything. Even when our men think that we don't. I'm *sure* she knew."

My mind shifts to Sheldon and my suspicions about him having an affair. How would I know? The signs are there, but I have no proof. "But how can you know for sure?"

She cocks her head to the side. "Sister Eva, do you think Sheldon is stepping out on you?"

I pause. "I . . . I'm not sure. I just have a feeling right now."

She leans in and lowers her voice. "That's how it starts. As a feeling. You have to use the intuition God gave you."

"And what do I do if I find out he *is* having an affair?" I ask.

"There's nothing you can do. You made a vow before God."

"But the vows also say to be faithful."

"They do. But men will be men, sweetheart. No sense in you bringing unnecessary discord into your marriage by arguing about it. Just pray about it, and I'll also pray for you."

The pastor approaches the microphone, and the room goes quiet. I tune him out as Sister Clarice's words spin in my head. Maybe she's right. Maybe it's best to turn a blind eye to Sheldon's actions. But he's my husband, and we made vows. So, even if I discover that my suspicions are correct, it's not like I can divorce him. It's not an option because I refuse to go to hell.

CHAPTER TWO
MARK

I toss a loaf of white bread into the cart as I wait for my mother to grab the jar of jam. She places the jar inside and then picks up the loaf. She reads the label before she puts it back on the shelf and reaches for the potato bread instead.

"What's wrong with the white bread?" I ask.

"Nothing. But your father likes his sandwiches on potato bread."

"I see." I pick up the jar of jam. "No homemade jam this week?" I ask.

"Maybe. I'm not sure if I'll have time to make any. So I bought some just in case."

I smile. "I miss your homemade jam, Mom. I wish Amy would learn some of your recipes."

She grabs the jar out of my hand and places it carefully into the shopping cart.

"Amy is her own person, Mark. It's not wise to compare your wife to another woman, even your mother."

"I didn't mean it like that. I just meant that I miss your cooking, that's all."

"Well, why don't you and the family come over tomorrow for dinner? I'll make your favorite."

I nod. "I wouldn't dare miss your famous pecan pie. We'll be there."

She smiles before she turns around to continue shopping. My mom called me at work today to ask me to take her to the market. My father was fixing the carburetor on his antique truck and wouldn't be done in time to take her grocery shopping. I told her I'd gladly take her. I see my parents at least once a week but seldom spend time alone with Mom. She usually keeps herself occupied in the kitchen while Dad and I smoke cigars on the porch.

She finds all the items on her shopping list, and I pay for them when we reach the checkout line, but not without her resistance. She finally relents, and we leave the store. She waits for me inside the car while I load the groceries into the trunk. When I'm finished, I return the cart to the front of the store, climb inside the car, and start the ignition.

"Is there anywhere else you need to go?"

"No, sweetheart. I'd best be getting home to fix your father's supper."

"Okay then."

I put the car into drive, and the moment I press my foot on the gas, another vehicle pulls out in front of me. I slam on the brakes, causing my mother and me to jerk forward. "Son of a—"

I stop before I say the word in front of her. I place the car in park and hop out. The other driver hops out of his car, and I angrily approach him. "Hey, you almost hit my car."

"Sorry, man, I didn't see you," he replies.

"You need to learn how to fucking drive."

He cocks his head to the side. "I just apologized and told you I didn't see you, but it seems like you're looking for trouble. If you want to pick a fight, let's do it."

I take a second to size him up. He's not much taller than me, but he's more fit. Not that it matters because I'm sure I can take him out. But not here. Not in front of Mom. I don't respond. I turn around and walk away.

"Fucking niggers."

He yells after me. "What the fuck did you just say?"

I spin around, bold and unafraid to repeat myself. "You heard what I said."

He stalks toward me. "Say it again so I can fuck you up."

My anger gets the best of me, and I'm about to attack, but I hear my mother's voice behind me. I turn around. "Get back in the car, Mom."

She refuses. She stalks forward and gets in between us. "Stop this right now. Both of you."

He glances between my mother and me, confused. A second goes by, and he seems to calm down a little.

"Listen, lady. I made an honest mistake and apologized. But your son here wants to be disrespectful."

She looks at me. "Mark, let's go."

I'm fired up. I don't want to go. For some reason, I want this fight. Maybe it's the frustration from my workday or the fact that my mother could've been injured due to his reckless driving. But whatever it is, it has me on edge and needing a release. I take a deep breath and look my mother in her eyes. "Okay."

She turns to the other guy and speaks gently to him. "I apologize for my son's behavior."

He nods and walks away. When we get inside the car, I immediately say my piece. "You shouldn't have done that, Mom."

"I had to. You were acting out of control. What's gotten into you today?"

"You could have been hurt," I reply.

"We're in a parking lot, Mark. Not on Highway 46 driving sixty-five miles per hour. You overreacted, and you know it."

"You're *really* going to defend another man over your own son?"

"You're acting like a brat right now. I'm defending what's right."

"He pulled out in front of me."

"I'm not talking about that."

I scan her face closer until it dawns on me what she's saying. "What, because I called him a nig—" I catch myself. "Since when does that word bother you?"

"When have I ever said it *didn't* bother me?"

"But . . ." I take a minute to think about all the years the word has been used in my home. And come to think of it. I never heard my mom say it. "But Dad uses it all the time. He still does."

"Your father uses that word, honey, *not* me."

I'm in deep thought as I place the car in drive and pull out of the parking lot. As we hit the highway, my mind races. "Mom?"

"Yeah."

"Have you ever said the word?" I ask.

"No. And you shouldn't either."

I'm quiet as her answer sinks in. I wonder why she chooses now to be so vocal about it.

"I know what you're thinking," she adds.

"What?"

"You're wondering why I never corrected you before. You're wondering why I allowed your father to use the word repeatedly." I don't respond to her. Instead, I allow her to continue. "I have my reasons, Mark. Reasons you won't understand. Not right now, anyway. But one day, you will."

"What do you mean by that?" I ask.

"Nothing. Just forget I said anything."

Something isn't right in her tone. I feel she's hiding something from me and is too afraid to tell me the truth. "Mom, is there something you're not telling me? Is everything all right?"

She looks over at me and smiles. "Everything is fine, honey."

She hums the rest of the drive, and I'm anxious, wondering why my mother is suddenly speaking to me in cryptic messages. Memories of my childhood flash through my mind, and they're all the same. My mother is a woman of few words regarding men's business. While our father had his hands full raising three boys, my mother supported us, loved us, and was a shoulder to lean on whenever we needed her. But now that I think of it, she never spoke about sensitive topics. She never agreed or disagreed with my father's views, and not once has she ever spoken negatively about people of other races. How did I not see this before?

I pull into the driveway and put the car in park. Then I turn to my mother. "Mom . . ."

She holds her hand up. "Don't." She turns to face me. "We will pretend today never happened, and you won't ask me any more questions, okay?"

A flicker of pain flashes in her eyes. Something I've never seen and don't want to see again. "Okay."

"When the time is right, we'll talk," she adds.

She opens her door, and I do the same. I watch my dad kiss her on the lips as I remove her groceries from the trunk. He waves at me and continues to work on his truck. I wave back at him and watch my mother enter the house, wondering what secret she's hiding.

AMY

It's been three weeks since I saw my sister. There's no rhyme or reason for it. Sometimes, life gets in the way. But today, I needed to see her. I plop down on her couch and look around. "When did you take those pictures?"

She looks over at them and smiles. "Last month. It was a tough mountain to climb, but my team and I did it."

My sister, Viki, and I are complete opposites. I'm a married mother of two with a career, and she's a single woman with no kids who works odd jobs and goes on adventures. She lives on the edge and has done everything from mountain climbing, skydiving, scuba diving, and parasailing. She's two years younger than me, and I always gave her a hard time about how she lived her life. I used to tell her that she was too spontaneous. I told her she needed structure in her life. I told her she should do more besides working small jobs and traveling from state to state. But she seems happy as I look around at the pictures on her wall. She looks free and filled with excitement in each image.

She plops down beside me. "So, what's up, Big Sis?"

"Nothing. I left early and thought I'd stop by on my way home."

She takes a sip of her beer before she speaks. "I'm glad you did. It's been a while. How are my niece and nephew?"

"Good. It would be nice of you to stop by and see them sometime," I reply.

She shrugs. "I know. But you know that idiot husband of yours can't stand me."

Mark and Viki have never gotten along, which plays a huge part in our relationship and her relationship with my children. Her connection with them is almost nonexistent.

"That shouldn't stop you from seeing them."

"I know. I promise to do better," she responds.

I doubt it. She says she'll do better whenever I mention our relationship lacks closeness. But she never does. My sister is selfish. All she cares about is her life and what she has going on.

"You say that all the time."

She watches me for a second. "What's going on with you? You seemed bothered about something."

I am bothered about something. Something I don't feel comfortable talking to her about because I know she can't relate. "Nothing. Just a long day at work." I change the subject.

"How's Megan?"

She shakes her head. "We broke up."

"What? Why?"

"She said I'm emotionally unavailable. Can you believe that?"

Yes. I can believe it. When our parents died, I was ten, and Viki was eight. I dealt with it the hardest and showed the most emotion. Viki detached. We went to live with our grandparents, and although they tried their best to raise us, they had no idea what they were doing with two young kids. Viki became defiant. She was always in trouble and never followed the rules our grandparents put in place. She stressed them out, and I felt bad for them. Because of this, I did everything they told me to do. I followed every principle they ever taught me. They already had one kid they couldn't keep in line. They didn't need two.

Our grandmother taught us basic life skills she thought every woman should know. Cooking. Cleaning. Sewing. She stressed the fact that we're to act like proper Southern ladies. She believed that women are to be seen and not heard. Her generation didn't go to college or have careers. Their success was based on snagging a good husband who could provide and the number of babies they pumped out.

My upbringing plays a big part in my marriage. I'm meek when it comes to Mark. I don't make much of a fuss and allow him to make the decisions in our home. I may be a modern woman regarding education and my career, but I'm very much a soft-spoken wife who puts her opinions regarding my husband on the back burner. Sometimes, I speak up, but not that often.

"I thought she was the one," I continue.

"She was. But I don't have time to chase her down, you know? I've got a life too."

"So, you're going to let her go?" I ask.

"What am I supposed to do?" I don't answer her because I honestly don't have an answer. "Maybe relationships aren't for me."

"Don't say that," I reply.

"Married life may work for you, but it isn't for everyone, Sis."

She's right, and I'm in complete agreement. If my sister only knew that married life isn't working for me, either. I'm bored out of my mind, and I'm tired of the responsibility. Someone always needs something from me, and I never get a break. It's exhausting. Sometimes, I want to run away for a week and turn off my phone. She takes another swig of her beer and stands to her feet.

"I know why you're here. Let me guess; you ran out already?" she asks.

I nod with shame. She disappears around the corner, and when she returns, she hands me a small Ziploc bag of white pills.

"No more than one a day, Amy."

"I know. I'm a nurse, remember?"

"Right. So, why can't you get them from the hospital again?"

"I can't just steal Percocet and Oxycodone from the hospital, Viki. I could get caught and be arrested."

She folds her arms. "Well, you're taking from *my* supply. I make money off those."

"Yeah. Yeah."

I slide them into my purse to avoid taking one right now. I've already taken one today and have reached my limit. I've been using narcotics for a while now, and it's the only thing that helps me cope. These pills are perfect for me because they're better at being undetected. Marijuana stinks and makes your eyes droopy and red. Cocaine is too strong, and I have no idea how it will alter my mental state. When I take Percocet, I feel relaxed. I feel stress-free. Viki points her finger at me.

"This is the last time. If something goes down, Mark will blame me and make my life miserable."

I nod. "Okay. Thanks, Sis."

I'm met with the aroma of food as soon as I open the front door. I smile with relief that Mark has made dinner, and I can relax and unwind for the rest of the night. Mark and the kids are already seated at the table when I enter the dining room. He smiles at me as soon as his eyes land on mine. I love his smile whenever he decides to flash it. His straight, white teeth are a perfect contrast to his blue eyes. My husband is very attractive, with thick brown hair and a permanent tan, compliments of his Italian roots. But his demeanor often diminishes those good looks. He doesn't look approachable. Instead, his expression is always hardened, like he's angry at the world.

We met in college. I was studying nursing, and he was studying architecture. We were two nineteen-year-old kids who wanted to conquer the world together. He was fun back then. He enjoyed living life on the edge. But something changed during our junior year. He joined a club that focused on social issues and became more vocal with his views regarding race, sexuality, age, etc. It wasn't anything concerning at the time, not overkill like now.

We got married when we graduated, and he was dead set on making enough money to care for me. He was in the running for a junior architect position at one of the biggest firms in the city. They narrowed it down to him and one other candidate. But Mark didn't get the job. He later discovered the company needed to become more diverse, so they hired another candidate of a different race. I don't think that was the *only* reason they hired the other guy. But I couldn't talk any sense into Mark. His father made things worse by berating him for allowing a Black man to take his spot, and Mark spent every waking moment afterward trying to prove himself. By the time the kids came, he had secured another good job making great money. But his father never let him forget, which causes *him* never to forget.

I watched as Mark's attacks on people different from us became more frequent. I watched as he blamed the trouble of the world on other races. I told him none of it was right, but his father and brothers fueled his ego with the same thinking.

"Hey, how was your outing with Emma?" I ask.

"It was good. I picked up that case of water you asked for too."

It was sweet of Mark to spend some time with his mother today. He loves that woman to pieces. "Thank you."

Our son, Dylan, opens the fridge to get a Gatorade. "Hey, Mom."

"Hi, baby," I answer.

"He's not a baby. He's seventeen," Mark snaps before dumping a spoonful of mashed potatoes onto his plate.

"He'll always be my baby," I reply.

"Stop smothering him, Amy. You're gonna turn him into a fag."

I ignore him and wash my hands at the kitchen sink before sitting at the dining room table. He doesn't get to dictate how much affection I show my son. He's not the one who carried him for nine months and spent fifteen hours in labor. Just because he isn't expressive or affectionate doesn't mean I want my kids to be that way.

"Ireland, put your phone away. It's dinnertime," he snaps at our sixteen-year-old daughter.

"Sorry, Dad, it was important."

"I'm sure it's not that important. You can text Camilla afterward," he replies.

"How do you know I was texting her?" she asks.

"Because that's all the two of you do."

She rolls her eyes before turning her attention to me. "How was work, Mom?"

"Busy. How is Camilla doing?" I ask.

"She's having a crisis right now. Do you mind if I stay at her house tomorrow night?"

"Again?" Mark asks.

"It's the weekend, Dad. What else am I supposed to do on a Saturday night?"

"We're going to see your grandparents tomorrow," he continues.

"Can I go afterward, then? Please, Dad," she begs.

"Let her have some fun, Mark," I add.

He hesitates before answering her. "Okay."

Ireland lights up with excitement. As introverted as she is, I am happy she's making friends. It's something she's struggled with most of her life, and just when I'd accepted that she'll most likely be a loner, she met Camilla. It's only been six months since they became friends, but I hope their friendship continues. Mark and I have been dying to meet her, but Ireland won't bring her around for some reason.

Camilla attends a public school across town. She and Ireland became friends at a basketball game between her school and the private school that my kids attend. Despite our efforts, it's been impossible to meet this girl. Instead of asking us to drive her, Ireland takes the bus to see her. Ireland declined when we offered Camilla to stay the night at our home. I wonder if she's embarrassed that Mark will say something inappropriate.

I make eye contact with my daughter across the table. She looks so much like Mark that it's scary. Her brown hair hangs past her shoulders, and her blue eyes gleam under the chandelier.

Next, I shift my eyes to my son, who looks more like me with his black hair and brown eyes. Dylan is our genius. He's a straight-A student who is serious about his studies and an avid reader. He spends hours at libraries and museums and can answer any historical question you toss his way. Fear punches me in the gut when I think about the fact that my affair could cause me to lose my family. We're not perfect, but no family is. Mark may be a piece of work, but he's *my* piece of work. I signed up for this and knew my role in this marriage. I love my husband, and I love my kids even more. I'm proud of them and know Mark is also, even though he never says it.

"Busy day, huh?" Mark asks.

"Yeah," I answer.

"Did you get my text message?"

"Yeah, but I was busy with patients. What happened?" I ask.

"What happened is that they fired Hollis for conspiring with a competitor, and now they've brought in some darkie who thinks he's in charge."

"And he's your new manager?" I confirm.

"Yeah, and I'm going to resign tomorrow morning."

My eyes widen with surprise. I knew he was upset about what happened today, but I had no idea he was upset enough to resign. How can he allow his emotions to drive him to make such a rash decision?

"Is that a good idea? How can we keep up with our bills with one income?"

"We've got enough money saved until I find a new job, or I can sell a few securities from our portfolio."

"That money is for the kids' education, Mark. I honestly think you're overreacting."

"I'm not overreacting. I won't sit back and allow some nigger to think he's in charge of me; it just ain't right."

The kids pick at their food in silence while I glare at Mark. Anger is etched all over my face. He's not thinking clearly, and I want to throw this glass of cold water in his face to bring him to his senses. His job brings a lot of security to this family. He makes a sizeable salary. He has a company-paid pension, stock options, an annual bonus, and five weeks' vacation. And he wants to throw it away just because he doesn't like his new manager? I'm at my wit's end and too tired right now to convince him otherwise. Mark does what he wants to do, regardless of anyone's opinion or feelings, and I'm not in the mood to argue with him. So, I nod in agreement even though I disagree.

"Okay, if you think it's best."

MARK

Amy gives me a death stare from across the dining room table. I know she's angry, but she has no idea how stressed I am. She doesn't know how embarrassing this new work dynamic is. I work for one of the top architecture firms in Georgia. I'm one of their best designers and generate a lot of revenue. I was on track to becoming a partner, which would have been significant. But now that Hollis is gone, I don't know my future with the company. I break Amy's stare and pour myself a glass of lemonade. I hate it when she's mad at me. I just don't like to show it. I was raised to be the man of the house. I was taught to put my foot down, so my wife and kids don't run over me. So, I need to be stern with Amy and my children because showing emotion shows weakness, and Carson men aren't weak.

My mind takes me back to how I was with my wife. When I met Amy, I was a hopeless romantic. I did all the things needed to sweep her off her feet. I would buy her flowers and take her to dinner. I showered her with love and affection and ensured she knew I loved her. But all that changed when I brought her home to meet my parents. My father witnessed me head over heels for her and said I was soft. He pulled me to the side and told me I was going about the relationship wrong. He said that if I didn't tighten up, Amy would never respect me. He said my kids would never respect me. He made me realize that if I had any intention of marrying her, it wouldn't be my job to write her love letters and play pussyfoot with her under the table. My job was to earn a good living and pay the bills. My job was to make the decisions for the family and keep everyone in line. He said that was why he and my mother had been rock solid for thirty years. And there is no other marriage I admire more than my parents'. Dylan interrupts my thoughts.

"Dad, I'm entering a science fair."

"What project are you doing?"

"Climate control."

"Sounds interesting, and I'm sure you'll win. But I want you kids to remember we are superior. No other race can compete with us, no matter how much they try, do you understand?" I ask.

"Yes," they answer in unison.

"Stay the course, and both of you will be successful. And once you are, make sure you marry your own kind. Don't mingle with other races because they're beneath you."

"We know, Dad," Dylan says, becoming slightly irritated.

I continue my rant. "Also, watch whom you surround yourself with. Stay away from those faggots and lesbians. I don't like them either."

Everyone remains quiet when I finish. This isn't the first time I've lectured my kids, and I know it's probably becoming redundant. But they must know these things. It's important that I instill the same values my father passed down to me.

"May I be excused?" Ireland asks.

"Yeah."

Dylan rises from his seat. "I think I'll head to my room too."

They leave the dining room, and Amy takes a bite of her chicken, avoiding eye contact with me. Her face is tight, and I feel the tension rolling off her. "You're mad, aren't you?" I ask.

"Yes."

"I promise you that we'll be okay. I'll find another job just as good as this one."

"Sure."

That's her way of saying she's done talking about it, and I decide not to push. Not now, anyway, because tonight, I was hoping to do something I hadn't done in a long time. Romance my wife. It's been weeks since we've made love, and I'm sexually frustrated. I wanted to plan a special evening for her, starting with cooking dinner. I don't cook. But tonight, I took that task off my wife's hands. We were supposed to have a nice family dinner, then make the kids clear the table and do the dishes. I wanted to whisk her away upstairs, where I would draw her a nice hot bath, followed by a massage with soft music playing in the background. A few glasses of wine and kisses down her spine would seal the deal. But the night has gone off track, and I've ruined the mood. There's no way Amy wants to be close to me right now, let alone allow me to touch her. Not when she's this angry. But I'm desperate, so I try my luck anyway.

"How about we forget about the job situation and go upstairs? I have something romantic planned for us."

She slides her chair back and stands to her feet. "I'm tired. I want to go to bed."

IRELAND

"Did you ask if you could spend the night?" Austin asks.

"Yes, and they agreed."

"Good, because I've missed you."

"I've missed you too."

I grip the phone tightly, blushing at the thought of seeing my boyfriend. Austin and I have been together for four months, and I'm madly in love with him. I hate keeping him a secret, but my parents will never understand—especially my dad. He would flip if he knew I was in love with someone of Puerto Rican descent. Not only would he flip about Austin's ethnicity, but he would also flip about his age too. Austin is nineteen. Although that's not that much older than me, my parents won't go for it. It sucks because age shouldn't matter when you're in love.

"Hey . . ." His voice drops an octave.

"Yeah?" I ask.

"Bring that outfit I bought you, the lace one. I want you to wear it then."

"Okay, but we need to be quieter. We almost woke Camilla the last time."

"I'll try, but that's hard to do with you, baby."

I giggle. "Yeah, same here."

"I can't get enough of you. I can't wait for the day when we can lounge in bed as much as we want."

I take a deep breath before I dive into a more serious matter. "Me too. Any luck finding an agent?"

"No. Not yet."

"Austin, I can't be here too much longer. I'll start showing soon and don't even want to think about the consequences when that happens."

"Baby, I promise we'll have our place before then."

I sigh. "Okay."

"Don't worry. I got this. And once you're out of that house, he better not even *think* about trying to control your life. You and the baby are my responsibility now, Ireland. And as soon as you're old enough, I'll make it official."

I love how protective Austin is. I love how he looks after me and is always concerned about my well-being. It's something my father lacks, even though he swears he's the father of the year. My father thinks his job is to swear off boys and keep me innocent. If he had it his way, I'd still wear hair barrettes and play with dolls. He knows nothing about listening to me and supporting me. He doesn't take the time to teach me how a man should treat a woman. But he didn't have to because watching how he is as a husband and father shows me the kind of man I *don't* want to marry. Austin is different from my father. He listens to me. He supports my dreams and pushes me to be my best. He's kind and loving. And he's going to make a great father to our child.

"I gotta go. I love you."

"I love you too."

I end the call and place my hand on my belly, wondering if I'm having a girl or a boy. I wonder if I can provide a decent life for them. Austin doesn't make much money now, and I won't be able to work while I'm still in school and raising a baby. I quickly shake away my fears. We can do this. We have each other. Although we may not have money, we have lots of love. And that is what matters when raising a kid.

My finger hovers over Camilla's number as I debate calling her. She doesn't know that she'll be an aunt yet, and I want nothing more than for her to share in my excitement. She's my best friend, and I tell her everything, but I can't tell her this. Not yet. She wouldn't be happy about it. She thinks her brother is a lowlife. She always complains that he has no job or car and still lives with their parents. She calls him lazy and a man-child. She doesn't see him as I see him. She doesn't see how talented he is. He's a science-fiction author looking for his big break. Once he releases his New York Times Bestseller, the sky is the limit, and I'll be right by his side. We'll get married and raise our child together, and if my parents don't accept my husband and baby, we'll live a happy life with just the three of us.

DYLAN

My dad irritated me at the table. But it isn't unusual. He always finds a way to press my buttons. I'm sad most days. I have mood swings and barely function sometimes. I hardly sleep at night, and sometimes I cry for no reason. It takes a lot for me to be in good spirits. And I try my best daily to be upbeat and energetic, especially at home. Today was a good day for me. School went well because I got an A on a difficult test I had last week. I made a few new friends and am starting to gain some form of popularity. And lastly, I'm looking forward to attending a party I was invited to. I smiled today. I laughed today. And then . . . Dad came home.

We were enjoying our family dinner when he had to ruin it all by complaining about people who were different from us. It makes me sick to my stomach hearing the things he says. It isn't right, but there's little that I can do about it. But that will all change when I'm old enough to leave this dreadful house. I'll be eighteen in one more year, and then he can't tell me what to do or how to live my life anymore. I'll be an adult. I'll go from boy to man—a man who no longer needs to prove anything to his father.

I disappoint him, even though he won't admit it. But I see it all the time. I see it in his face whenever his friends brag about how well their sons are doing on the football team. I can feel his embarrassment whenever my grandfather asks if I've met a girl yet. My father doesn't think I'm boyish enough. He says I won't ever grow into his version of what a man is. He says Mom coddles me too much, and I'm two kisses away from being a faggot. He can call me whatever name he wants to, but he's ignorant and clueless. There are plenty of men who do all the things he thinks define a man. They cut grass, play football, have girlfriends . . . and still are gay. Everyone doesn't boldly express their sexuality. Some men keep it a secret because of people like him.

My dad doesn't and will never understand me. Instead of getting to know me, he tries to force me to be like him. His idea of spending time with me is sitting in front of the television watching a football game, but I don't like sports. Every Thanksgiving at my grandparents' house, my dad, grandfather, and uncles gather around to watch the football game. My dad tries to convince me to join them, but I decline. I'm much more comfortable talking to my mom, grandmother, and aunts in the kitchen. Football is stupid to me. It's a bunch of men running around in tights, knocking each other down for a ball. Listening to the women in my family is much more entertaining. I hear Grandma spill all the townsfolk's business, and my aunts bash their husbands. The women in my family get me. They accept me. I can be myself around them without fear of judgment or criticism. My thoughts are interrupted when my phone vibrates with an incoming call. It's Hansh.

"What's up?"

"Don't tell me you haven't left yet?" he asks.

"I'm leaving soon. Just give me a minute."

"What's taking you so long?"

"My dad unexpectedly cooked and made us have a family dinner."

"So, what time will you be here?" he asks.

"I'm leaving now."

"Cool. Ring the doorbell when you get here."

"Okay."

I end the call and quickly change my clothes. If I have any chance of hooking up tonight, I must dress to impress. I lock my bedroom door, shoot my mom a text, tell her that I'm working on my science project, and ask her to make sure no one disturbs me. I know I'm safe when she responds "okay" with a heart emoji. I hate lying to my parents. But if I had asked to go to the party, my dad would have said no, and Mom would have agreed with him to keep the peace. I slowly lift my window, climb onto the roof, and lower it slowly, leaving a tiny crack. I leap and grab the tree branch, then climb down carefully. When my feet hit the ground, I sprint across the backyard as I've done many times.

Hansh and I arrive at the party just in time. The house vibrates from the bass of the music. The rooms are packed wall-to-wall with people, and everyone has a red cup in their hand. Marijuana smoke floats in the air, leaving a smell so strong I feel it's making me high. It seems the entire school is here tonight. The advantage of attending a Catholic school is that we're portrayed as well-mannered, honest students. Our parents trust us and think we're good kids who never get into trouble. So, when we say we're going to a friend's house or the library, our parents rarely question it. But my dad does. He questions *everything*.

My classmate, Noah, approaches Hansh and me. Noah's father is a church leader. He served in one of Georgia's biggest churches before deciding it wasn't his calling. After Noah's mom died, his father said he needed to find his purpose. He said God wanted him to travel the world and preach the word of God. In addition, he felt that helping others would help ease the pain of losing his wife. So, he travels most of the year, leaving Noah and his older brother alone.

"I wasn't sure you two would show up," Noah says.

"There's no way I was missing this party," Hansh responds.

"You two aren't drinking?"

"I was just about to grab one," I reply.

Hansh and I grab a red cup from the drink table beside the Hennessy sign. I take a sip and immediately feel the warmth of the alcohol. I take a minute to look around. This is heaven on earth. So many men to choose from, all here for one reason . . . to hook up. Hansh hands me his cup.

"I see Troy. I'll be right back," he says.

When he's out of sight, Noah smiles at me. "I was hoping I'd see you here tonight."

"And I was hoping to see you."

"I've had my eye on you since the beginning of the school year. I never said anything because you're always with Hansh. Are you two a couple?" he asks.

Hansh glances at us while he's talking to his cousin, Troy. He watches us suspiciously, and I can tell he doesn't like us being so close. Although Hansh is my best friend, I can tell that he wants something more. He's hinted at it every chance he gets, but I change the subject and don't react to it. I'm not romantically interested in him. I like what we have: a strong friendship. He knows my deepest, darkest secrets, and I know his.

"Hansh and I are just friends," I confirm.

"Good. Now that we've got that out of the way, let's go upstairs."

CHAPTER THREE

MARK

Amy didn't say a word to me after dinner last night. I apologized to her before we went to bed, hoping it would smooth things over, but I was mistaken. She uttered an okay, climbed into bed, and shut her eyes. I tried to inch closer to her throughout the night, but she moved away each time.

I was restless. I kept thinking that maybe Amy was right about me overreacting. We have savings. Enough savings for me to quit right now if I wanted to. But what happens then? What happens if the savings run dry before I find another job? Amy and I have worked our asses off over the years to make sure we have adequate investments, sizeable savings, and money for the kids' tuition. We save every dime that we can, including our bonuses. The money is hers as well as mine, and I should have thought of that before I attempted to make a decision that affected us both.

Anxiety cripples me as soon as we arrive in my parents' driveway. I'm trying my hardest to forget what happened yesterday with my mother, but it's bothering me. Whatever she's hiding is too painful for her to speak about. So, I will do as she asked and forget about it. There's another reason I grow anxious. I love my parents and try to see them as much as possible because it makes me happy. But my father's endless, overbearing ways often overshadow this happiness. They're on the porch waiting for us, and as soon as the kids exit the car, they run toward them. Mom hugs each of them tightly while Dad looks on proudly with a cigar in his mouth.

"You guys made it just in time. Emma just took the chicken and dumplings off the stove."

I smile at my dad. "Good, 'cause we're starving."

He pats me on the back. "It's good to see ya, son."

"It's good to see you too, Dad."

After my mom hugs Amy and me, she gestures for us to enter. "Y'all come on in and eat."

I'm hit with nostalgia every time I enter my parents' home. Pictures remind me of my childhood, and the smell of my mother's home-cooked food reminds me of our nightly family dinners. After we've all washed our hands, we gather around the table. My mother says grace before we dig into the food.

"Mom, this looks delicious."

"Thank you, sweetheart. I made mashed potatoes too."

Amy beams with excitement. "I've tried thousands of times to make them the way you do, Mrs. Carson, and I still can't get it right."

Mom chuckles. "That's because I use a secret ingredient."

"I hope not too secret to share with me. Please tell me. Mark won't so much as touch my potatoes."

Mom chuckles. "I tell you what. Come over one Sunday, and I'll show you how to make them."

Amy nods, and I chuckle lightly. I love the relationship between my mom and Amy. They've always been close, and it pleases me that they love each other.

Dad starts to nitpick as soon as he's piled his plate with food. "You still at that big shot firm?"

"Yeah, Dad, I'm still there."

"I thought you'd be running the show by now. Have you gotten a promotion yet?" he continues.

"I'm working on it. I'll know when I have my annual review."

Amy glances nervously at me as she takes a bite of her food, and the kids eat silently as they wait to hear if I tell my dad about the possibility of me resigning. I have no intention of telling my father that my manager is a Black man or that I decided to quit. He would lose his mind if he knew and would berate me. The Carson men carry a legacy of white power. And when I say "white power," I don't just mean the pride of being a white man. I mean white power, as in the teachings of white supremacy, the segregation of other races, and the work to ensure that whites have advancements above all others. My father's father was a member of the Ku Klux Klan, or the KKK, as some call it. He and my father taught me that Black people are not equal to us and never will be. I was taught that we are superior and that the world would be better off without other races. Now, I teach my children the same.

Some may call us racists, but I beg to differ. We're proud of our heritage. We are people who want to stick to the laws of the original Founding Fathers and people who want to leave a solid legacy for our children. Out of my three brothers, my dad is the hardest on me. His expectations of me are unreasonable and unbearable, and I don't know why. It could be because I'm the oldest, but I've never questioned it. I try my best never to let him down.

His voice interrupts my thoughts. "'Working on it'? What's there to work on? You're doing your job, ain't ya?"

"Yes, I'm doing my job, Dad. But my manager was fired, and now I have a new one."

"Fired? What for?" he asks.

My mom quickly intervenes. "Russell, let's not spend our dinner discussing Mark's job."

My mother saves me! I'm relieved she's forcing my dad to change the subject because this was not a conversation I wanted today. She turns her attention to Ireland when my dad takes a bite of his biscuit.

"Ireland, you've grown to be so pretty."

"Thank you, Grandma."

"Do you have a boyfriend yet?"

"Mom, she's sixteen." The thought of my baby girl having a boyfriend makes me cringe. The idea of a boy kissing or touching her makes my blood boil.

"Age doesn't matter, honey. I met your father when I was young."

"Mom, things were different then."

"No, Grandma. I don't have a boyfriend."

"And she won't have one for a very long time," I state as I look firmly at Ireland.

Amy changes the subject. "Mrs. Carson, dinner is delicious as always."

"Thank you, Amy. Are you all ready for dessert?" my mother asks.

"Yes," the kids answer at once.

My mother has prepared her scrumptious pecan pie. She knows the kids love it, and she makes it every time we come for a visit. She rises from the table and heads toward the oven. As soon as she opens the oven door, the scent smacks me in the face like a cold winter's wind. It smells divine, and my mouth immediately starts salivating. She brings the pie to the table and cuts each of us a slice, starting with my father. When she places my piece on my plate, she smiles at me because she knows I've loved her pecan pie since I was a kid. Amy has tried to make it, but she's given up trying because she can't get it right.

I take a huge bite and close my eyes as I savor the taste of whipped cream, chopped pecans, and a gooey, sweet filling. I'm disappointed when I see no more left . . . until Mom whispers that she made a second pie for me to take home.

After dinner, Mom, Amy, and the kids do the dishes and tidy up the kitchen while Dad and I sit on the porch. He lights a cigar and passes me one of my own to light. Another Carson man's tradition. He doesn't know that I quit two years ago, thanks to being married to a nurse. I promised her I would never smoke one at home but that it was a tradition at my father's. We each sit in a rocking chair and smoke our cigars in silence, except for the sound of the crickets and the birds chirping. The silence is interrupted when he speaks.

"I don't know why you moved to that neighborhood. Ain't nothing like living here."

"I had to move closer to my job. How else was I gonna take care of Amy and the kids?"

"You could have gotten a job close to here. Close to your roots."

"I tried. There were hardly any jobs here—especially good-paying ones."

He takes a puff of his cigar. He's quiet, but I know what he's thinking. He believes that I think I'm better than him now. He believes I think I'm better than my family and the folks I grew up with. That's not true at all. I'm humbled. I'm grateful for the life I've been given. Had I stayed here, my only options would have been a mechanic or a farmer. And I wasn't going to settle for either of them.

"You just remember where you came from, Mark."

"I know where I come from."

He nods at my statement as we both watch a moving truck pass. It pulls into the driveway three houses down, and a Black man emerges.

"They just moved down the road in old man Leyton's house."

"No one has lived there since I was a kid," I reply.

"We haven't had a Black person live in this neighborhood in over fifteen years, and we'd like to keep it that way."

"I'm sure old man Leyton is turning over in his grave right now," I respond.

"You let one Black family move in the neighborhood, then they all come, and the next thing you know, we'll have Mexicans and those Arabs for neighbors."

My dad has a point. The same thing happened at my job. When I first started at the firm, all my coworkers were white. Then it started changing. Nothing overwhelming. Just a sprinkle here and there. But now, I work with one Asian, one biracial, and one Indian. I've learned to deal with it, but they've gone too far by hiring a Black man to be my manager. That's where I draw the line.

AMY

I'm high as a kite. Somewhere in the middle of dinner, I snuck to the bathroom and took a Percocet. It was the only way I could deal with listening to Mark's father spew ignorance. I'm usually on my best behavior when I'm around his father. With his pressure on Mark, I want to make my husband look good. Show him that Mark married well and is a wonderful father and husband. But today, I couldn't do it. I couldn't sit there smiling, nodding, and agreeing with his father. My head started to hurt. My hands turned clammy, and I became irritable—a clear sign that I needed a quick fix.

Things were so much better after that. I was able to sit through dinner with a smile on my face. I could interact and laugh at jokes simply because everything was funny. Emma kept glancing at me from across the table, and I started fidgeting, wondering if she knew that I was high. I shook away that thought because the pills sometimes make me paranoid. She couldn't know unless she has hidden cameras in her bathroom. I sit in the living room and watch Dylan and Ireland show Emma how social media works. I feel light, so light that I feel like I'm floating in the air. My eyes become heavy, but I manage to keep them open. I can't fall asleep in the middle of the day. It may raise suspicion.

"Are you okay, dear?" Emma asks.

I nod. "Yes. Just a little tired. Long day at work yesterday."

She nods. "You're welcome to take a nap in the guest room."

And give Russell the satisfaction of thinking I can't handle work, marriage, *and* motherhood? I think not. I can hear him now. *Back in my day, women hardly got any sleep between cleaning, cooking, and caring for the chilen.* "No, thank you."

She smiles and turns her attention back to the kids. I roll my eyes at the mere thought of having to sleep next to Russell. I honestly don't know how Emma has managed to be with a man like him all these years. But I guess someone could say the same about me being with Mark.

I grab my phone and decide to step away and call Sheldon. I know I'm playing with fire by calling him while I'm at my in-laws, but I'm bored. I walk into the bathroom and lock the door. Then I dial his number, and he answers on the first ring. "Hey."

"Hey."

"Everything okay?" he asks.

"Yeah, why?"

"Because you usually prefer to text."

"Well, I miss you," I reply.

A second of silence goes by before he responds. "You sound tired, baby."

I blush. "I love it when you call me that. Mark never calls me that."

"Have you been drinking?" he asks.

"No."

"You sound weird."

Now I get angry. "Nothing is wrong with me, Sheldon."

I don't mean to be sharp with him, but I didn't call for him to try to figure out if anything was wrong with me. I don't need him asking me why I'm talking funny. My purpose for calling him is to feel good. Taking my pills and talking to him gives me an inexplicable high. I hear the phone move around, and he speaks in a low voice.

"Hey, can I call you back? Now isn't a good time," he says.

"I hate being unable to talk to you whenever I want."

"Yeah. I feel the same way, but we both signed up for this."

I take a deep breath. "You make a good point. But you *do* miss me, right?"

"Yeah. I always miss you when we're not together."

I smile. "We're still on for later?"

"Yes."

He ends the call, and I take a deep breath. I was bold just now. We agreed that we wouldn't bother each other when we were home with our families. But I called him anyway. Call it drug courage, I guess. I check the time on my watch, hoping I don't have to be here much longer. When I hear the front door slam and Mark and Russell laughing in the kitchen, I smile, knowing we'll leave soon.

We're back home an hour later, and I couldn't be happier. I take a second to breathe deeply and unwind because that was a draining and exhausting situation. Words can't express how uncomfortable I am around Mark's father, so much so that I've often considered not attending any more of his family dinners with him.

Ireland is at Camilla's, and Dylan is at the library with a friend. As for me, I have plans to meet Sheldon this evening. My skin prickles with excitement as I shove a silk nightie into my oversized purse. I'm dressed casually in jeans, a fitted T-shirt, and sneakers. I tie my hair in a ponytail and forego wearing any makeup. I don't want Mark to become suspicious. He enters the bedroom just as I'm walking out.

"Where are you off to?" he asks.

"I'm meeting Tressa for happy hour."

"Who?"

"Tressa, one of the other nurses I work with."

"Oh. Are the kids gone too?"

"Yeah. Ireland is gone until tomorrow, and Dylan will be back later."

"Okay. Well, I guess I have the house to myself then. I'll fix that cabinet you've been on my ass about all month."

"Okay, thanks. I'll see you later."

"Okay."

I rush out of the room before he asks *where* Tressa and I are meeting for happy hour. It's not something he usually does, but I don't want to take the chance. When I enter my car, I take a second to text Sheldon, letting him know that I'm on my way and feel relieved when I put the car into drive.

Twenty minutes later, I'm knocking on the door of room number 214 at The Georgian Hotel. It's a hidden gem located right outside of the city. Since we're married, Sheldon and I try to be discreet. The door opens widely, allowing me to enter. As soon as I'm inside, he embraces me and kisses me. I break the kiss, and my eyes land on the half-empty bottle of wine behind him on the nightstand. "You started drinking without me?"

"Sorry, long day," he responds.

"It must have been. The bottle is almost empty."

"I know. But I needed something to take the edge off."

I plop down on the bed. "You're upset about something. You barely even like wine."

He sighs with frustration as he plops down next to me and rubs the tension in the back of his neck. "Eva wants to go back to work."

"Okay. And what's wrong with that?" I ask.

"She just had the baby a few months ago. It's too soon."

"Not if she feels up to it. Most mothers are cleared to return to work six weeks after giving birth."

"But we agreed that she would be a stay-at-home mom. Now, she's changing her mind."

"If it bothers you so much, won't you speak to her about it?"

"I've tried, and it's like talking to a brick wall. She's so fucking stubborn."

"Maybe she feels overwhelmed with the baby. Being a stay-at-home mom can be exhausting. I was home with each of my children for eight weeks and almost pulled my hair out. I think you should ask her *why* she wants to return to work."

"I did. She said she feels like she's losing her independence. She said she loved having a career and now feels like something is missing."

"Well, there you go."

"Amy, Eva won't have much time for a career between motherhood and her church schedule. We'll suffer if she does this. Her place is at home, and I don't know why she can't see that."

"Maybe she can cut back on her church activities to balance it out," I suggest.

"That won't happen. The church has become a priority for her. She attends Bible study, church meetings, and Sunday services every week. If she adds work to the mix, she may as well bring home the bacon and tell me to stay home with the kids."

"And there would be nothing wrong with that. Lots of fathers stay at home with the kids. Times are different now."

"I'm a man, Amy. Being a stay-at-home father is *not* what I signed up for nor a role I'll ever fill."

I don't see the big deal, but I know there's no use in arguing with him. So, I nod in agreement to drop the subject. "I understand."

"Did you go back to work after having your kids?"

"Yes. I didn't have to, but when I discussed it with Mark, he was fine with me being a stay-at-home mom. But, like your wife, my career was important to me. So, we agreed we could make it work."

"See, that's what I mean. You *discussed* it with your husband. You didn't decide on your own and blindside him with it. Eva didn't discuss anything with me. She woke up one day and said, "I'm going back to work.""

"Every household is different, Sheldon. Mark and I discuss everything. But I have friends who don't discuss things with their husbands."

He ignores my comment. "You get it, Amy. You know how to let your husband lead the home."

I think about his statement and conclude that he's right. But I didn't arrive here on my own. My grandmother raised me to be this way. She taught me that a wife is to be seen and not heard. I am to be my husband's peace and to avoid back talk. She was a Southern woman from Georgia, and that's how most women were raised. Sure, there are times I want to curse or yell at Mark. Sometimes I want to oppose his views and decisions, but I don't. I go along with every decision because he's my husband, and that's how it's supposed to be.

His hand trails my cheek slowly. "I wish I had met you sooner."

I smile. It's a sweet thing to say, but it causes me to reevaluate our circumstances. Maybe our wires got crossed somewhere in the past seven months, but I have no intention of this being anything other than what it is—good sex and a fun break away from my role as a wife and mom. Sheldon is speaking as if he's considered being in a relationship with me. Even if I weren't married with children, we couldn't be together, not in public anyway. Not with today's social standards. Interracial relationships are too much of a hassle. They're much too complicated, and I'm unsure if I want to marry a Black man anyway. Yes, I like him. And I like who he is in the bedroom even more. But he's a secret I'll carry to my grave. Sex is all I want or need from this relationship. Emotional ties are not part of the deal. Maybe it's my fault for allowing him to be open and personal with me about his crumbling marriage. Finally, I stand.

"How about we stop talking about her, and you relax while I shower and change into something comfortable?"

"That sounds good," he responds.

His hand reaches out to touch me, but I smack it away. "Not yet," I tease.

"Not even a little?"

"No. But once I come back, you can have all you want."

He grins, and I know his problems have dissolved ... for now, which is precisely what I intended.

"I'll be here waiting. Don't take too long."

DYLAN

Hansh and I lie across his bed, staring at the ceiling. We're both high off marijuana and hungry as hell.

"Crack the window a little. I can still smell the weed on your clothes," he says.

We smoked on the way to his house, and he showered and changed his clothes as soon as we arrived. But, unfortunately, I didn't bring a change of clothes to do the same. So now he's paranoid, thinking his parents will smell the weed on me.

Hansh is Indian. His parents were both born here and decided to adapt to the American way. They are good Christian people who genuinely love everyone, regardless of race, color, or religion. His father is a college professor, and his mother is a librarian. They seem like a loving family. But I sometimes wonder how they would feel if Hansh told them he is gay. He's known since he was seven, and that's a long time to keep such a big secret. I know because I have known since I was a kid. I guess he hasn't told his parents for the same reason I still haven't told my family. We don't want to be judged. America has come a long way with gay rights, but there's much disapproval regarding homosexuality. Carrying this burden is suffocating. I feel like I'm living a lie and want to be free, free to date, fuck, or love whomever I want without criticism.

"Where did you disappear to at the party?" he asks.

"I hung out with Noah for a while."

"You two went missing for a long time."

"It was a party. You're not supposed to stand around and talk all night, Hansh."

"I'm not stupid, Dylan. I saw the two of you go upstairs."

"Well, if you already knew, why did you ask?"

"Because I wanted to hear it from you."

It feels like he's interrogating me, and I don't like it. "What's the big deal?"

"Just be careful. I've heard things about him."

"Like?" I ask.

"Like, he's a whore."

"Aren't we all?"

"No."

"Hansh, we go to gay parties to sleep with men. If that isn't whoring around, I don't know what is."

"I haven't slept with many guys, Dylan, especially none at those parties. I like to look. It's eye candy for me."

"I can't say the same, but I'm single and can do what I want."

"I'm just saying, be careful. I care about you, and I don't want you hurt."

He watches me with a sort of tenderness. I'm not sure if it's the marijuana that has made him all emotional, but I'm sure his eyes are glassy, and he's close to crying.

"Do you think you'll ever tell your parents the truth?" I ask, hoping to change the mood.

"Maybe once I've graduated. How about you?"

"Never."

"Never?" he asks.

"Nope."

"Why not?"

"My dad would kill me. He hates fagg—" I stop myself from saying the word.

Hansh watches me with compassion. "Listen to me, Dylan. We are *not* faggots. That's a nasty word made up by people who are insensitive and cruel."

"I know. My dad has used it all my life, and I guess I've become immune to it."

"Your dad is an asshole."

"Yes, he is."

"What about your mom and sister?" he continues.

"I don't think my sexuality would matter as much to them."

The room grows silent as we both snack on a bag of chips. We're deep in thought, but neither speaks about what we're thinking. We're two teenage boys who have accepted that we're attracted to men. We've accepted that we're gay and that it won't change. We know the challenges that come along with being gay, and we know that once we come out in the open with our sexuality, we might lose family and friends. Will it be worth it? Will it be worth it to have family and friends turn their backs on us once we're finally free and out in the open with who we are? Or is it better to live secret lives? Whatever decision we make, I'm sure we're both aware that we'll suffer the consequences.

IRELAND

Dinner was terrific at Camilla's. I love the Puerto Rican cuisine her mother cooks and enjoy her family's fun and casualness. Camilla's parents came to America when she was seven years old. They still honor their traditional Puerto Rican roots, and I love seeing firsthand how different our cultures are. I don't care what my dad says. There is nothing wrong with learning about other cultures. Austin glances at me from across the table, and I briefly smile at him before taking another scoop of rice and beans.

"Ireland, you should invite your parents for dinner. We have yet to meet them," her mother says.

I've had every excuse in the world for why my parents can't meet Camilla and her family. My dad would snap. He would go off about how I shouldn't be hanging with illegal aliens from other countries and how they come here and steal all the jobs. It's not true in Camilla's case, but he won't see it for what it is. He'll only see she's another race, and nothing else will matter once he sees that.

"Sure, Mrs. Gonzalez," I reply.

"Yeah, it's strange I haven't met my best friend's parents yet," Camilla adds.

Austin watches me closely. He knows precisely why she hasn't met them, but he won't dare share it with his sister. I love my best friend, but I still can't find it in me to tell her the truth about everything.

"Maybe it's because she's embarrassed that you're a weirdo," Austin says to Camilla.

"Oh, shut up, Austin," Camilla replies as she rolls her eyes.

He winks at me as the two of them argue from across the table, and I'm grateful for his attempt to take the heat off me.

"Okay, you two. No arguing in front of company," Mrs. Gonzalez says sternly.

They obey their mother and quiet down. "Come on, Ireland; let's go upstairs," Camilla urges as she rises from the table.

I follow suit, and we go upstairs and into her room. She immediately connects her phone to a speaker and plays music for us.

"My brother is so damn annoying," she says.

"He's not that bad."

"That's because you don't live with him."

I may not live with him yet, but Austin and I will soon live together and raise a baby.

"When will you hook me up with your brother?" she asks.

"Who, Dylan?" I ask in shock.

"Yeah, he's single, right?"

"I don't know."

"Ireland, how do you *not* know if your brother has a girlfriend?"

"Because he's super private."

"Well . . . Can you introduce me? I've only seen the one picture of him that you showed me, but he's hot."

"Yeah, sure."

My answer satisfies her, but I'm unsure if I can pull it off. Dylan doesn't seem to be into girls. He usually studies at the library or hangs out with his best friend. His interests are museums, libraries, and documentaries. Most guys his age are girl crazy, but Dylan isn't the average guy. Girls always mention how handsome he is and ask me if he's single. But he told me before that he wanted nothing to do with any of the girls I tried to hook him up with.

"I think I'm ready, Ireland," Camilla says, snapping me out of my thoughts.

"Ready for what?" I ask.

"I'm ready to lose my virginity."

"Where did *that* come from?" I ask.

She turns over on her side and faces me. "Why should I wait? Don't you wanna know what it feels like?"

I already know what it feels like, but I can't tell her. "I'm not in a rush."

"Well, I am. I'm tired of being passed up by all the popular guys because I won't give it up."

We're interrupted by a knock just as I'm about to answer her.

"Mom needs your help downstairs," Austin says as his eyes meet mine.

"Uugg!" she says as she rolls her eyes and stomps out of the room.

As soon as she leaves, Austin grabs my hand and pulls me out of bed. He hugs me tightly.

"Do you know how hard it is to be around you and pretend we're not together?" he asks.

"I know, but it's best for now."

"When can we stop keeping this a secret?"

"Austin, we talked about this."

"I know. But I love you, Ireland. I don't want to hide it anymore."

My eyes swell with tears because I don't want to hide it anymore either. "Just give me some time."

"How much time?"

"I don't know. But soon."

He releases me and places his hand on my belly. "We can tell my parents. They'll let you live here with me."

"I can't do that."

"Why not?"

"I'd rather we not burden anyone with this. Let's stick to the plan and get our own place."

I can sense the frustration building. "What am I supposed to do until then? Continue to sneak around with you like we're kids?"

"What's that supposed to mean?"

"It means I'm tired of being a secret, Ireland. I'm an adult. You're carrying my child, and you need to stop acting like a little girl who's scared of her daddy and grow up. Either you want to be with me, or you don't."

"I do want—"

"What's going on here?" Camilla interrupts from behind us with her arms crossed.

Austin turns around, then looks back at me. He takes his place beside me, wraps his arms around my waist, and pulls me close.

"We have something to tell you."

CHAPTER FOUR
SHELDON

Amy left an hour ago, and after I showered, I stayed behind to clear my thoughts about my marriage. Eva and I already had problems after Kamryn was born, but we just had to go and make Sheldon Jr. Now, I feel obligated to stay committed. There are already too many single Black mothers in the world and too many African American homes that have been broken. That's not what I envision for my children. I don't want to be an every other weekend father. The type of father who sends a child support check every month and does the bare minimum. I want to be hands-on. I don't want to miss a moment in my children's lives. If Eva and I divorce, there's no way she would allow me to have full custody, and I would have to fight her for it.

Eva is a good woman. She's beautiful, intelligent, driven, and a good mother. But we met way too young and married way too fast. Eva's mother is religious, and she was strict when it came to her. I met her at the skating rink when we were seventeen. I was there with a group of friends, and she was there with her sister.

We hit it off right away. We were young and in love back then. We were living life to the fullest without a care in the world. But things changed when we got married and had kids. We didn't have fun anymore. We were more concerned about bills and raising them. Then Eva got saved. And that's when things took a turn for the worse. She put the church above everything—her marriage, kids, and herself. She tries so hard to be this pure, no-sin woman who tosses out Bible verses every minute of the day.

That's the problem with the Black church: always quoting scripture. Our ancestors were dragged to another country, ripped away from our religion, given a Bible, and preachers want us to worship the same God as those who stole us from our native land. I wasn't raised that way. My parents are Muslim and don't believe in Christianity. I was raised to believe Allah is the only true God. We didn't read the Bible or go to church. And we sure as hell didn't pray to a white Jesus.

As I got older, I pulled away from religion altogether. There were too many rules to follow for each of them, and honestly, as long as I believe there is a God, I think I'm all set. But my wife is super religious. She believes in the Bible and every scripture in it. She wanted to keep her virginity, and I promised her I would wait because I loved her. I laugh at that promise now. I screwed everything in sight behind her back. But I wanted her more than any of those other girls, and I proposed after a year of dating. We were married six months later.

The wedding process was a disaster. She wanted a traditional church wedding, and I didn't want that. I didn't want to be inside a fake church honoring vows to a fake God. But after seeing how much it meant to her, I gave in to her demands. After all, she was the bride. So, we had a church wedding and a lavish honeymoon in Aruba. Everything turned out perfect . . . except for the sex. I deeply regretted waiting until my wedding night to test the waters with her. It was far from romantic and far from satisfying on both our parts. It took time to get better, but it was amazing when it did. The chemistry and passion we had for each other was undeniable. We tried new things and kept it spicy in the bedroom. I was completely satisfied with our sex life. In fact, I considered myself one of the lucky ones. While other men complained that marriage changed their sex life, Eva and I were having the best sex of our lives. Well, more like my life since I was all she knew. But how quickly that changed.

When she rededicated her life to Christ, we had sex less and less. And when we did, it lacked the passion we once had. It was good, but not like it used to be and not how it should be between a husband and wife. I find her attractive, but we aren't sexually compatible anymore. Now, sex for us is me climbing over her and pumping a few times until I come. I doubt she comes at all anymore. She now hates oral sex because she says it's an abomination. The church has her thinking her only job is to look good as she lies there and allows me to take her.

My phone rings. It's my mom.

"Hi, Mom."

"How is my young king?"

"I'm good," I answer with a smile.

"And my grandbabies?"

"They're doing fine."

"Good, how's Eva? Still toting that Bible around?"

"Mom!"

"What? I'm just asking."

"We have to respect her religion."

"Yeah, well, don't teach my grandbabies that mess, and don't let her brainwash you with it either. We must praise Allah for everything, good and bad."

"Mom, she has a right to raise our kids how she wishes. She's their mother."

"It's a damn shame. That child stays in church more than the pastor does. Don't you go running behind her. Stay out of those money-hungry churches. They don't do a damn thing for the Black community except sell them false dreams."

"You don't have that to worry about."

"Good. Are you coming over for Sunday dinner?"

"Yes."

My phone vibrates with an alert from the bank. "Mom, I gotta go. I'll call you later."

"Okay, I love you."

"I love you too."

I open the notification and see a large withdrawal from our account. That can't be right. Eva and I agree that neither of us will withdraw $600 or more without consulting the other first. My initial thought is that it must be a mistake, but as I look closer at the details, I see the withdrawal was made in person at an ATM. So, I dial Eva to check with her first. I ask the question as soon as she says hello.

"Hey, I just got an alert from the bank. Did you withdraw $600?"

"Yes."

"Is everything okay? Did you or the kids need something?" I ask.

"No. It was tithe money."

I almost choke. "I'm sorry. Did you just say 'tithe money'?"

"Yes."

"Eva, we agreed to tithe one hundred dollars once a month. So why the hell did you give six hundred?"

"Don't curse at me, Sheldon. The building is humid. The air-conditioning is broken, and the church was short $600."

I make a fist and take a deep breath to prevent myself from punching a wall. "We have an agreement. We were supposed to discuss this before you decide to take the money out."

"I didn't discuss it with you because I knew you'd be unreasonable."

"UNREASONABLE?" I don't mean to shout into the phone, but I'm so angry I want to reach through it and shake some sense into her. I lower my voice. "What *you* did was unreasonable, Eva."

"No, it wasn't. Do you want me and your kids sitting in a hot church every week?"

I'm at a loss for words. My wife has officially lost her mind, and I'm starting to think that her church is more of a cult than a place of worship. "Get the money back," I demand.

"I'm not doing that."

"Eva, you go over to that church and get my fucking money back. Right now."

"It's *our* money, Sheldon. And God will bless us for this. Six hundred dollars is less than what we *should* be giving every week. We can afford it."

At this point, I'm beyond furious. "Fine. If you won't get our money back, *I* will."

I end the call and grab my clothing from the floor. Eva has crossed the line this time, and I won't sit back and allow that place to brainwash her into taking all our money. I'm going to that church, and I'm going to have a word with the pastor. And if he doesn't see reason, he'll never see my wife again.

"Sheldon, I haven't seen you in a while."

"I know. I've been working long hours, Pastor Walker."

"I understand. God has blessed you with the ability to change and save lives." He sits at his desk, and I sit in the chair in front of him. "So, what brings you by?"

"It's my wife."

"Is Sister Eva okay?"

His sudden concern about Eva makes me even angrier than I already am. Our marriage isn't going well, and I'm having an affair. But Eva is still my wife, and I don't take kindly to any man moving in on what's mine.

"Eva's fine. I take great care of *my* wife."

He looks taken aback. "I wouldn't insinuate otherwise, my brother. I guess I assumed something was wrong since you came all this way to speak to me about her."

"I came to speak to you about the money she gave the church."

He nods. "Ah, the generous donation to the building fund."

"Yes. I need our money back."

He's quiet as he digests my statement. "Sheldon, it isn't in our policy to return donations."

"Why not?"

"Because we don't keep cash on the premises long. Once the money is counted, we take it directly to our bank to avoid theft. The money has already been deposited."

I grip the chair's armrest, attempting to stay calm, but it isn't working. The money is long gone, and I can't do anything about it now. I could demand that they withdraw it and give it back to me, but I doubt they would. I stand, and he does the same. "Thank you, Pastor."

I start to leave, but he calls after me. When I turn around, he smiles at me. "It'll be nice to see you at service more."

I shake my head. "Not if it costs me $600 to attend."

CHAPTER FIVE

AMY

Mark fell asleep on the couch last night, and I admit I was relieved he did. I keep thinking he can smell the scent of sex on me. No matter how many times I shower or how thoroughly I scrub myself, I still get paranoid when I'm close to him. He was up early this morning, excited about going to the hardware store to buy the supplies needed to refurbish our hardwood floors. I thought it would be a good idea for him to take Dylan with him. It will give them the opportunity to spend some time together. Neither of them was happy about it, but they agreed anyway. I hate having to force Dylan to hang out with his father. But how can they grow closer if they continue avoiding each other?

I finish folding the last of Dylan's clothes in his room. I open his top drawer and place his folded T-shirt inside. Mark doesn't think I should do the kids' laundry, but I beg to differ. I like knowing that it'll be done correctly if I do it. When I placed the last of his shirts in the drawer, I grab my phone out of my pocket to call Sheldon. I'm home alone, so it's the perfect opportunity.

My phone slips from my fingers and falls to the floor, sliding under the dresser. I drop to my knees and put my hand under it to feel around. I feel something tiny. I know it's not my phone, but I'm curious.

I drag it toward me and pause when I stare at the flash drive. Did Dylan lose this? What if his science project is saved on it? I look around until my eyes land on his computer. I grab it and turn it on to find that it's been left unlocked. I shove the flash drive in and open the file. There are videos—at least ten of them. I press play, and my heart slams into my chest as soon as I do. Tears slide down my face as I stare at the images of men having sex. As I narrow in on the images, I realize I'm mistaken. These are *not* men. These are . . . boys. Boys his age. When the camera zooms closer to their faces, I realize one of them looks familiar. I gasp when it hits me. These aren't just random boys. The boy in the video is Dylan's classmate, Noah, and the other is my son. I shriek before I click the X at the top to exit.

This can't be real. How could I have missed this? Should I tell Mark? I shake my head immediately. No. Mark can *never* know about this. If he finds out, he'll kill him.

Suddenly, the front door slams, interrupting my thoughts. I take a second to wipe away my tears, but by the time I grab the flash drive, Dylan enters his room.

"Mom, what are you doing in here?"

"I . . . I was putting your . . . um, clothes away."

I'm stammering. As hard as I try to act unbothered, it's not working. He glances at the flash drive in my hand.

"Are you going through my things?" he asks.

"No. I dropped my phone and found this when I went to get it."

Before kneeling, I hand him the flash drive and find my phone under his dresser. When I rise to my feet, I can barely look at him.

"Mom—"

"Dylan, don't."

"What did you see?"

"I saw you and . . ."

I can't bring myself to say it. He slides his hand down his face. "Fuck . . ." He panics. "Sorry. Mom, you weren't supposed to see that."

I'm careful how I respond. I'm unhappy about what I've found, but this is my son. I want to yell at him, not because he's gay, bi, or whatever these kids call themselves nowadays. But because he's being careless. "Dylan, what the hell are you thinking, huh?"

He brushes past me and places the flash drive in his desk drawer. "Mom, please, do we have to have this conversation?"

"Yes, we do. Because clearly, you're not as smart as I thought."

"Why? Because I'm gay?"

I frown. "No, Dylan. Not because you're gay. You're my son, and I love you despite whom you choose to sleep with. But it's stupid of you to film it on video for the whole world to see."

He shakes his head. "It's not for everyone to see, Mom. Just me and Noah."

"Yeah? Well, what happens if Noah decides to show someone else? What happens if he betrays you and posts it online for *everyone* to see?"

"He won't do that."

"You don't know that. This was a reckless move. Not to mention, I saw no condom in sight. I thought we were past the safe sex speech at this point."

He plops down on his bed. "I know about safe sex. I just . . . I don't know."

"Jesus, Dylan."

It suddenly makes sense. His lack of interest in girls. His reclusiveness. The fact that he's so private. I should've known. I should've asked more questions. I should've assured him that I was there for him no matter what his sexual identity was.

"Mom, you don't need to worry. Noah and I are both free from disease."

"How do you know?" I ask.

"Trust me. I know. We agreed to get tested at the free clinic."

Relief sweeps through me, and I exhale the breath I've been holding. "Are you and Noah in a relationship?"

"Not yet. But we're working on being exclusive."

I have so many other questions. Questions about if Noah is his first. Questions about when and where this was filmed. But now, my senses are too overloaded to go into more detail. Dylan's eyes turn glassy.

"Are you going to tell Dad?"

His question breaks me. The fear in his eyes shatters my heart because I know why he's asked it. Dylan already feels his dad doesn't accept or love him. If he learned he was gay, Dylan would fear losing his dad forever. Mark and I vowed never to keep secrets in our marriage, especially when it comes to the kids. Maintaining a united front is the only way to prevent our children from manipulating us into getting what they want. But this . . . This is different. This isn't Dylan sneaking out to a party or using the car without asking. This news is life-changing for him and us. I don't want to keep this from Mark, but I need to. For all our sakes. "Dylan, you know your father and I don't keep secrets."

"Mom—"

"But," I interrupt. "I understand why you don't want him to know."

"Just give me some time to tell him."

I nod. "Okay. I'll let you tell him yourself."

His shoulders drop with relief. "Thanks, Mom."

"We're not done talking about this. I'm just too overwhelmed to finish the discussion tonight. But we need to talk, Dylan. I have so many questions."

"I know."

I kiss him on top of his head before I leave his room. When I shut the door behind me, I lean against it as the tears fall again. I hate this life for my son. A life where he feels he can't be himself. I hate that he feels he must hide things from Mark and me. I want better for my son. I want him to live his life unapologetically without fear of judgment. But sadly, that can't happen because if Mark finds out, Dylan won't just be judged by outsiders . . . but by his father.

SHELDON

Mom places one last kiss on Sheldon Jr.'s cheek, then hands him over to Eva. As she requested, I brought the family over for Sunday dinner, and she's been spoiling the kids all evening. My mother cooked my favorite meal: oven-fried chicken, baked mac-n-cheese, and her famous cabbage and collard green mix. I ate two plates. Eva can cook but hasn't done much of it lately. Between church and the kids, she complains that she's too tired. I've been eating frozen meals and sandwiches for the past two weeks. My mother looks me up and down, and I silently hope she doesn't ask me why I'm shoving so much food in my mouth.

After dinner, we gather in the family room to relax. My dad is stretched out on the chaise while my mom sits on the couch next to me. Eva sits on the love seat with the kids.

My mom pulls her locs back and out of her face, then turns to Eva. "Eva, how's your mother doing? I haven't seen her since the wedding."

"She's doing well, Mrs. Salaam."

"Good," my mother says with a smile.

"Sheldon, do you remember that teacher you had in medical school who gave you an F in his class?"

"Yeah."

"Well, he was fired yesterday over some racist tweets. I knew that cracker was racist. If it wasn't for your dad speaking to the board members, you might have never graduated. Thank goodness he was exposed. Who knows how many other students he could have failed because of the color of their skin."

"You can't trust them, none of them. All white people are against us. The system is set up to hold us back," my dad chimes in.

"I disagree," Eva says. "One of my closest friends is white, and I trust her."

Fuck! I shift uncomfortably in my seat as I brace for the altercation that's about to happen.

My mom folds her arms and leans back in her chair. It's a sure sign that she's about to wreak havoc. "Is that so? And let me guess. You think she's *really* your friend, don't you, Eva?"

"As a matter of fact, I do, Mrs. Salaam."

My eyes swing to my dad. He shakes his head slightly, advising me not to get involved.

My mom laughs out loud. "You're brainwashed, honey. Do you think for a minute that your white friend sees you as her equal? I bet you're her *only* Black friend."

"Does it matter?" Eva asks.

"Let me ask you something," my mother continues. "How long have you two been friends?"

"For six years now," Eva answers.

"Have you met her family or any of her other friends?"

Eva thinks for a minute. "No."

"Hmmm, has she expressed sympathy or outrage over racial injustice?"

"What do you mean?" Eva asks.

"Just as I thought," my mother says as she shakes her head. "Cops are murdering our Black men on video for the world to see. Black men are being handed long-term prison sentences for charges the average white man gets a pass for. We had a president in office who discriminated against poor people, women, gays, and anybody else who didn't fit his white America criteria. Then he left, and now, we got one who's just as bad. And we're getting criticized for not standing for a flag that was never meant for us in the first place. So, tell me, Eva. Are you and your friend outraged about any of this?"

"Oh, please. None of that is my problem. Maybe if our Black men complied, then cops wouldn't feel threatened. Or, how about this? How about they abide by the law to avoid police interaction altogether? Then they won't have to worry about prison sentences. And our presidents have done the best that they can. I'm guessing you're talking about our past president. You can't believe all the lies you hear in the media. He promised to bring change to America, and that's exactly what he did, Mrs. Salaam. Name another president who made such a drastic change to tax laws for the middle class. And please don't say President Number 44. You probably only voted for him because he's Black."

Fuck! Fuck! Fuck! I rub some of the stress out of my forehead. My mother hates politicians, and so do I. None of them have agendas for the Black community, and because of this, I rarely vote.

"Making change isn't just about changing taxes, girlfriend. There are a shit ton of other issues that need to be addressed. But no, he focused on building a stupid-ass wall, creating enemies instead of allies, and changing laws that benefit the rich. If *that's* your definition of a great country, I feel sorry for you."

"Obviously, you've been misinformed. Maybe if we'd had a wall to begin with, we wouldn't have so many illegal aliens planning terrorist attacks. You talk about creating enemies. America needs to stop being so nice to other countries anyway. It's time we put our foot down and stop thinking that some of these leaders in other countries are our allies. And speaking of the poor, I'm tired of my good, tax-paying dollars being used as welfare, food stamps, and Medicaid handouts. People need to go out and get jobs like the rest of us. I feel sorry for *you*, Mrs. Salaam."

My mouth drops, and so does my father's. We glance at each other briefly, silently asking if we should end this discussion.

"Well, then it's settled," my mother states.

"I guess it is," Eva responds.

"My son has married a coon."

"And you're just a liberal who wants to complain about everything and make everything about Black and poor people," Eva responds.

My dad rises to his feet. "Okay. That's enough."

"No. Let us finish this, honey. It's been a long time coming." My mother shoots up and takes a step toward Eva. "You're a naïve little girl who likes to suck up to crackers. I hope you never end up poor because if you do, you'll need the same handouts you so-called disagree with. Everyone *isn't* lazy, Eva. Some people really *do* need the help."

"If that ever happens to me, I'll be fine. I'm smart with my money and have close friends who would help."

My mother laughs again. "Oh, like your one white friend?"

"Everyone isn't as outspoken about injustice. Just because we don't talk about it doesn't mean she isn't bothered by it."

"You're right. Everyone won't be outspoken about it, but your *friends* should be. But then again, I don't blame her for not speaking about it. Why would she when her Black friend isn't even outraged? You're too busy toting around a Bible, praying to a white Jesus, and hoping your prayers will fix the world."

"Oh, like *your* God is real? Christianity was here way before Islam, and you'll be judged for praying to a false God. You have no right to bash my religion. What are you doing to make a difference besides wearing dreadlocks and dashikis? Your Black Lives Matter antics aren't saving the world either. All it's doing is spewing hate and causing division."

"Stop this right now," I interrupt. "Mom, you crossed the line disrespecting Eva's faith."

"Don't teach my grandbabies that nonsense. Teach them the truth, Sheldon. Allah is the one true God."

"No, that's *your* truth, and I'll teach *my* kids whatever I damn well please!" Eva yells.

I take a step toward my wife. "Let's all calm down. Eva, hand me Junior and wake Kamryn up from her nap so we can go home."

She hands the baby to me and stomps off without a word. I peek inside the blanket and make sure my son is still asleep. "Mom, was that necessary?"

"You know I don't hold my tongue, son, especially in my own home."

"I know that, but Eva is entitled to her religious views the same way we are."

"She isn't right for you, Sheldon. You need a woman who at least has some awareness of what's happening with our people. That girl is just plain clueless."

My dad chimes in. "Khadija, he's right. You can't force your beliefs on anyone, and you shouldn't have insulted Eva that way. She's family."

Eva enters the living room, holding a sleeping Kamryn. She stares at us all for a second before walking away and slamming the front door on her way out. My dad looks at me with pity.

"You're in for a long drive home, son."

I tell my parents goodbye and find that Eva has already placed Kamryn in her car seat. I strap Junior in and climb into the driver's side. Tension fills the air as Eva silently stares out the window. I start the car, but I don't put it in gear. I need to clear the air before we take off. "I'm sorry, Eva. You know how overboard my mom can get."

"You didn't defend me. You watched her belittle me, and not one time did you defend me, Sheldon."

"I did defend you. After you left the room, I told my mom that she was wrong. She was out of line for attacking your religion."

"*After* I left the room?"

"Yeah. What difference does it make?"

"It makes a *big* difference. You should have defended me in front of her."

"She's my mother."

"And I'm your *wife*!" she screams.

Eva may nag at times but rarely does she raise her voice, which means she's angry. *Really* angry. I glance in the rearview mirror to make sure we haven't woken Kamryn and Junior.

"It's funny how you mention that you're my wife when it's convenient for you. You're so quick to say it, yet, you sure as hell don't act like a wife most of the time."

"Why? Because I don't answer to your every beck and call, cater to you like a child like your mother does, or is it because I want to make my own money and not let you control me?"

"It's because you have no idea how to be submissive. I'm the man of the house, Eva. I'm supposed to lead, *not* you. I don't get a word in edgewise when making decisions."

"Submissive? *That's* the kind of wife you want? One that doesn't speak her mind, allows you to control her, and who's lazy and won't work?"

"I want a wife who doesn't put a church before her family, one who can sometimes shut her mouth and allow me to make the decisions. Do you have to argue about every fucking thing?"

"If I don't agree with it . . . yes."

"Well then, I guess we have different views about how our marriage is supposed to be."

"I guess so. I'm not some damsel in distress, Sheldon. I'm an independent woman."

"You're *not* an independent woman. You're a *married* woman. We're in this together, and if you don't learn that real soon, you won't have a husband. Then you can be as independent as you want."

"I don't need you," she says through red eyes and tears.

"Well, why are you married to me then?"

She rolls her eyes, crosses her arms, and faces the passenger's window. I wait for her to answer the question, but when she doesn't, I put the car in gear and drive off.

CHAPTER SIX

EVA

I burst through the church doors, hoping the pastor is still there. As soon as Sheldon pulled into our driveway, I got out of his car, hopped inside mine, and sped off. I needed to get as far away from him as possible. I'm furious right now. So furious that I want to pack the kids' bags and mine and leave him. But that's not what a good wife does.

I see the pastor's door cracked, and I knock. When he sees it's me, he gestures for me to enter. He frowns when he sees I've been crying. He comes around his desk and pulls a chair out for me. I plop down as he grabs a fistful of tissues and hands them to me.

"What's wrong, Sister Eva?"

I wipe my tears and sniffle before answering him. "I've sinned. I'm thinking of divorcing, Sheldon."

He breathes deeply before taking his seat. "What happened?"

"Everything is wrong between us. All we do is argue, and we've fallen out of love with each other."

"That can be common in long marriages. Have you two prayed together?" he asks.

"No. Sheldon isn't the praying type."

"Ah, well, that could be part of the problem."

"My marriage is crumbling, and I don't know what to do."

"Have you two thought of marriage counseling?"

I shake my head. "No. But that's a good idea. Maybe you could counsel us?"

"I don't think that would be a good idea. Your husband came to see me, and he wasn't happy about your donation to the church. I doubt he'll want me counseling you two."

I knew Sheldon was angry with me about the money, but I didn't think he would make good on his threat to come to the church. I blush with embarrassment. "I'm so sorry, Pastor Walker."

He waves me off. "Don't worry about it. Sister Eva, God is the foundation of a marriage. Without him, your marriage is destined to fail."

"But Sheldon isn't religious. He's attended church with me twice and only because I begged him to."

"God is able. Pray for him. Pray for your marriage. Ask God for healing and restoration."

I've done this already, and it hasn't worked so far. It seems the more I pray, the worse it gets between us.

He continues. "Don't let the devil trick you into thinking divorce is the answer. Stay true to your covenant."

I nod. "Thank you."

I rise, and he steps toward me. He takes my hands into his and shuts his eyes. I follow suit. He prays over me. He prays over my marriage. And when he's done, I feel better than when I arrived.

"I'll add your name to the prayer list, Sister Eva."

"Thank you, Pastor Walker."

Sheldon ends his call when I walk into the kitchen. The kids are seated at the table, and Kamryn is eating a snack. He throws an apple into the blender.

"I've been calling you," he says.

"Hi, Mommy," Kam says cheerfully.

"Hi, baby." I turn to Sheldon. "I know. I needed to clear my head."

"I was worried something had happened to you."

"You were?" I ask.

"Of course I was. You shouldn't drive when you're upset like that."

It feels good to know he was worried. That he still cares about me. "I didn't want to argue. I wanted to give us some space."

He glances at the kids to make sure they're still distracted. When he sees that they are, he responds. "I'm sorry about earlier. You were right. I should have intervened."

I sit next to Kam and smile at the picture she's drawing. "Sheldon, I'm tired of fighting. When the kids go to bed, we need to talk."

He nods. "I agree."

He opens the refrigerator to grab the yogurt, and his phone lights up. I hadn't noticed before that it was placed next to Junior. I crane my neck to see who's calling, but I'm unsuccessful. It's on silent, so he has no idea it's ringing. I'm about to slide it toward me. I don't care that he may see me check his phone. But I change my mind. I can't do it right now. Not with the kids here. Instead, I tell him about it. "Your phone is ringing."

By the time he rushes over, it stops. He checks the caller, sends a text, then slides it into his pocket.

"Who was that?" I ask.

He looks taken aback. "Since when do we question each other about our phones?"

I shrug. "I thought it might have been important."

"Well, it wasn't."

I take the opportunity to provide him with the answer to his question now that I have the chance. "Sheldon, you asked me the other night if I would be upset if you were having an affair."

He answers before he tosses in some spinach and starts the blender. "Yeah."

When he stops it, I continue. "Yes. I would be upset. I know we're having problems, but the thought of you being with anyone else hurts."

He slowly blinks before he responds. "You have nothing to worry about."

"So, you're not sleeping with someone else?" I ask.

"No."

I have no way of knowing whether he's telling the truth. But for now, I'm content with his answer.

"I'm going to go read some emails," he continues.

He kisses me on the top of my head before pouring his smoothie into a cup and leaves the kitchen.

I take the kids upstairs for their baths. I'm in a good mood and looking forward to talking with Sheldon tonight. It's been a while since we've done that. Maybe we'll even make love. Pastor Walker is right. I can't let the devil steal my joy. I can't let him fill my head with doubt about my marriage. I made vows, and I intend to honor those vows. I place Junior in his bassinet and give Kam a book to read while I grab their pajamas from the drawer. I look for clean towels and remember I never took them out of the dryer. I look at the kids before heading to the laundry room two doors down.

I swing open the door and step over a pile of clothes lying on the floor. I quickly grab two towels, scoop the clothes off the floor, and place them in the washer. I knock over a pair of Sheldon's pants in the process. Something clinks when they hit the hardwood floor. I look down . . . and my eyes go wide. My heart beats fast, and my breathing slows. Tears fill my eyes as I kneel and pick up the gold key attached to a key ring that reads: The Georgian Hotel. A sticker on the back of the key reads Room 214.

I grab my phone and Google the hotel. It doesn't look fancy, but it doesn't look cheap either. I look at the price per night. It shows $168. Anger slams into me. The amount isn't petty change. And I know my husband. He would not pay that kind of money for a hotel unless he's interested in her. But . . . Maybe *she* paid for it. My mind swirls with a million questions. Who is she? Is she the reason he's been working late? Is she the reason he seems distracted lately? I think about what she looks like. I think about her hands all over my husband, making him feel good in ways I don't. Tears form in my eyes as I wonder about his feelings for her. Does he care for her? Does he love her?

I dial the number to the hotel and a bubbly receptionist answers. "How may I help you?" she asks.

"Yes. I need an itemized stay history for room 214, please."

"For what date?"

"Um, I'm not sure."

"Name?" she asks.

"Sheldon Banks."

"I'm sorry, but we cannot release that information without the guest's permission."

"But he's my husband."

"Is he there to give his consent?"

Yes. But he can't consent because he doesn't know that I know. I end the call and want to scream. I have so many unanswered questions in my head. Questions I know won't get answered because there's no way Sheldon will tell me the truth.

Sheldon Jr.'s cries snap me out of my thoughts. I shove the key back inside the pants, then place them on the dryer. Finally, I gather my composure and rush back into the nursery to bathe the kids.

MARK

I hate Mondays. Always have. It's the fact that I have five long days to get through before the weekend arrives. I thought long and hard on the drive to work. I debated if I wanted to hand in my resignation today and concluded that I'd ask to switch teams instead of resigning. The lights automatically come on when I enter my office. I shut the door and walk over to my window to close the blinds, but I pause when I see my teammates gathered around the coffee machine, probably chatting about the most recent change in management.

They look concerned. Some even look angry. I zero in on Dottie. She shakes her head as she listens to the conversation happening in front of her. She shouldn't be concerned at all. She's over sixty years old and should have retired long ago. The elderly shouldn't be allowed to work. They have difficulty with change, need micromanaging, and have no idea how to use technology. All they do is slow down the team. The fact that she's a woman adds fuel to the fire. Women have no place in the architecture business. They spend way too much time focusing on décor than what's important—the structure.

My eyes swing to Chin. He's from China. Usually, I don't like immigrants, but he's a hard worker and one of the smartest people on the team. But that's to be expected. Chinese people are much more intelligent than Americans. Then Pajel walks in and joins the group. I don't know where he's from and don't plan on asking. He started a month ago, and I have not seen him produce anything worth looking at. So, I stay as far away from him as possible because the minute I catch him speaking in Arabic, his ass is mine. No way am I losing my life because of a terrorist attack.

A knock on my door interrupts my thoughts. It opens, and Andre walks in. "Good morning, Mark."

I grunt in response.

"I was hoping you had a moment to chat." I don't want to *chat*. I want to move to a new team and be managed by a more appropriate boss.

"Sure, you're the boss, right?"

I'm being sarcastic. And honestly, I don't care about the consequences.

He sits in one of my chairs, and I almost lose my cool. He crosses a leg and gestures for me to take a seat. I take a deep breath and sit.

He smiles. "You seem tense."

Of course, I'm tense. "I'm not in the best of moods today."

"Is it something to do with work?" he asks.

"Actually, yes."

"How can I help?"

"I'd like to transfer to another team."

His eyebrows raise with surprise. "May I ask why?"

"I have my reasons."

He rubs his chin before rising to his feet. "Mark, I know this is an adjustment for everyone, but I promise you, I'm not here to ruffle feathers. I'm here to lead this team to the best of my ability."

"Umm-hmm."

"I've seen your work. You're an asset to the team, and that's what I came to speak to you about this morning. I need a department head."

I'm quiet as I digest his statement. I had planned on excelling to a senior designer. A supervisor position wasn't on my radar.

When I don't reply, he continues. "So, what do you think? Is it something you'd consider?"

"What exactly does the role entail?" I ask.

"I've got enough mess to clean up that my predecessor left behind. So, I'll need you to manage the office. You'll be responsible for preliminary design approvals, first-level budget reviews, approving vacation, and stuff like that."

Excitement fills me, but I can't show it. Not to him. I can't have him think that he's doing me a favor. I won't let him reveal his authority to give and take away. "Can I think about it?"

"Sure. You think about it and let me know what you decide," he replies.

"Okay. Thank you."

When he leaves my office, I shut my blinds and let the grin I've been concealing emerge. Department supervisor. This changes the game for me. More money. More benefits. More vacation. Of course, there's the issue of working closer with Andre, but it might work if we stay out of each other's way. Amy will be proud. I reach for my phone to dial her and see that I already have three missed calls from her. I had it on silent when I was talking to Andre.

I quickly dial her, and she answers on the first ring. "Mark."

"Everything okay?" I ask.

"It's your mother."

"Is she all right?"

"No. She collapsed this morning while making breakfast."

"Where is she now?"

"She's at the hospital. I'm here with her."

CHAPTER SEVEN
MARK

The hospital is only a ten-minute drive from my office. So I make it there in record time. I rush down the halls of the ER until I find my family gathered around my wife. She's talking to my father.

"How is she?" I ask.

"Not good."

My father chimes in. "She had a heart attack."

"Heart attack? Mom is completely healthy," I explain.

My father rises slowly. "No, she isn't."

"Dad, what are you saying?"

"Mark, she's had heart disease for over a year now. She made me promise not to say anything. She didn't want anyone worried."

"You mean to tell me Mom has been sick, and you didn't say *anything*?"

"Lower your voice, son."

My brother, Rob, walks over to us. "Keep it down. You two are causing a scene."

I turn to Amy. "Can we see her?"

She shakes her head. "Not right now. We're still waiting on an update from the doctor."

Just then, a doctor approaches us. His expression is solemn. "She's out of surgery. Her heart blockage was extensive."

"Will she be all right?" I ask.

"We're not sure yet, but we're doing everything we can. The cardiologist should be on his way out to speak with you."

Amy replies. "Thank you, Dr. Sheldon."

"When can we see her?" I ask.

"As soon as she's settled in her room."

"Thank you."

I want to scream. My mother is lying there, and there isn't anything we can do to help her. A look passes between Amy and the doctor, and I'm not sure what it means. Finally, when he walks away, I ask, "What was that?"

"What was what?" she asks.

"That look between you and the doctor. Is there something you're not telling me? Please don't tell me you're hiding anything from me, Amy. Mom is going to be okay, isn't she?"

Her shoulders relax, and she releases her breath.

"I can't say for sure, honey. But I know that she has the best team working on her."

Her answer doesn't make me feel any better. I need reassurance right now. I need the doctor to tell me completely and confidently that my mother will pull through because I'm not sure. And the thought of losing my mother is making me sick.

AMY

Sheldon and I had just hooked up in the supply room when we heard the code blue. Imagine my surprise when I saw that it was my mother-in-law they were wheeling in. Panic swept through me as I assisted the emergency room staff with getting her onto a bed. I called her name. I asked if she could hear me. But I got nothing. As the tears started falling, Sheldon asked if I knew the patient. He gently pulled me away when I said yes and told me to let them handle it. As hard as it was for me, I had to. I wanted to get high. I *needed* to get high, but I also needed to think rationally. I shook the thought of getting high out of my mind and checked to see if the family was there. After I located Russell and Mark's brother, I called him to deliver the news, and we waited for him to arrive.

It was awkward when Sheldon came to speak to the family. But we kept it together and remained professional. As I suspected, no one came close to figuring out we were sleeping together. The circumstances had everyone distracted.

I place my hand on my husband's shoulder. "Have a seat. The cardiologist should be coming out soon."

I guide him over to a chair with Russell trailing behind. They both look distraught, and I can tell that Mark is still angry with his father for not telling him that his mother was sick. I try my best to stay calm. I'm also saddened and worried, but one of us must be strong. I place my hand on Mark's knee. "Have you called Russell Jr.?"

Rob answers for him. "I called him. He's on his way."

Mark and his brothers don't get along. Mark is the oldest, and because of this, he feels like he got the brunt of their father's wrath. Rob is the middle child, and Russell Jr. is the youngest. Both Mark and Rob think he's their father's favorite.

The cardiologist finally arrives, and we all stand. I hear him talking, but I'm not paying attention because Sheldon stands beside him. I feel uncomfortable. Guilty and nervous. I snatch my gaze away from him and focus on the cardiologist just as he finishes his sentence.

"There's little we can do at this point."

The family breaks down in tears, including me. This is not the news any of us wanted to hear. Mark takes a step forward.

"Can we see her?" he asks.

The cardiologist shakes his head. "Not right now. But hopefully, soon."

I kiss Mark on the cheek before I step forward. "I'll check on her."

Sheldon looks hesitant but knows there is nothing he can do or say to stop me from seeing Emma. My badge gives me access that family members don't have. He nods before he turns around, and I follow behind him.

When we arrive at the recovery room, his face turns grim. "Are you okay?"

I answer honestly. "No."

He walks behind me and rubs my shoulders, alleviating much of the tension I've had all day. "I've tried to remain as professional as I can. But I hate seeing you hurt."

I place my hand over his, forgetting where we are. I quickly snatch it away and turn around to face him. "This doesn't look good."

He nods. "I know."

He leans in and kisses me gently, not caring if we get caught. And like an idiot, I let him. I'm in the hospital room with my sick mother-in-law, allowing my lover to kiss me in front of her sleeping body. What a horrible thing for me to do. It's downright wrong. But as wrong as it is, it feels right. His comfort is making me vulnerable right now. I move away from him quickly before someone catches us. "Thank you for letting me in here to see her."

"I knew there was no way to stop you." He chuckles lightly before asking his next question. "I'm assuming you'll be taking some time off?"

I nod. "Yes. But I'll call you as soon as I can."

"No need to rush. Be with your family."

He takes one last look at Emma before he leaves the room. I spend some time at her bedside talking to her and letting her know she's not alone. Finally, her nurse walks in and checks her vitals before telling me that now would be a good time to call the family. I text Mark the room number, and Ireland rushes toward me as soon as they arrive.

"Mom, is Grandma okay?"

"She's not doing well, sweetheart," I reply.

Dylan hugs me tightly before he joins Ireland and the rest of the family at Emma's side.

I'm emotionally drained and have a headache, so I decide to grab a cup of coffee. I leave the room and head to the cafeteria to get my favorite. Sheldon's speaking with another doctor, oblivious that she's flirting with him. As I walk by, I shake my head as she twirls her hair and makes googly eyes with him. By the time I reach the elevator, my phone vibrates. It's a message from Sheldon.

I'm not interested in her. I only want you.

When I enter the elevator, a hand stops the door from closing. It's Sheldon. He walks in, pulls me close, and plants his lips against mine.

IRELAND

My feet feel like they are sunken in concrete, and my body doesn't move as a tear slides down my cheek. Then a voice speaks loudly from the hospital intercom, and it causes me to jump. The realization kicks in, and I turn around and walk swiftly down the hall back to my grandmother's room. My father sent me to go with my mother. He said that although she looked like she was doing well, she was probably not, and he didn't want her to be alone. I leave the room shortly after her and see her step inside the elevator. I saw a doctor follow suit and was just about to ask him to hold the door, but I stopped in my tracks when I saw him embrace my mom and kiss her.

I only got a quick view before the door closed, but that was all I needed to see. My mom is having an affair with a doctor that she works with. And not just any doctor. A Black one. This confuses me. My mother hates Black people . . . doesn't she? I mean, she never corrects my father when he talks about them. I take a deep breath before I enter my grandmother's room.

My father looks up. "Did you find your mother?"

"No."

"I'll find her. She shouldn't have left on her own. I know this is a lot for her too."

"No!" I shout quickly.

He squints his eyes with bewilderment.

"I asked one of the nurses to page her. She should be back soon."

I'm lying through my teeth, but I can't risk my dad seeing what I saw. Especially not today when his mother is gravely ill. He seems to buy my lie.

"Okay."

I silently will my mother to return soon to put my father's mind at ease. He thinks she went to get a cup of coffee to calm her nerves. He thinks she's all alone with no one by her side. He's wrong. So wrong. Mom isn't having a nervous breakdown at all. She's having an affair. And she's not alone. She's with her lover, who seemed pretty damn happy consoling her in the elevator. Right now, I need to protect her because if my dad finds out, her mystery lover will end up downstairs in the morgue.

Finally, Mom walks in. Her face is flushed, and her eyes red with tears. She stands next to my dad.

"There you are. I was getting worried. Are you okay?" he asks.

"Yes. I got coffee and some ibuprofen."

She lies so effortlessly. And I suddenly don't feel bad for keeping Austin and my baby a secret. "Be right back. I need to make a phone call," I announce.

I step out of the room and dial Austin. He answers on the first ring. "I got your text. How's your abuela?"

"She's not doing too well."

"I'm sorry, baby."

"I just . . . I needed to hear your voice."

"Let me come to the hospital. I want to be with you."

"That's not a good idea, Austin. Both my father and grandfather are here."

"And?"

"The family doesn't need the drama right now. I told you how they are."

"They're that bad, huh?"

"Yes. They won't accept you. They hate anyone different from us."

"I don't care. I'm used to being discriminated against. I want to be there for you."

I wish it were that easy because I want him by my side right now. He's the love of my life, and his support means the world to me. "Thank you, Austin. But we can't."

I hear him release his breath. "I understand."

I change the subject. "Camilla still hasn't answered any of my text messages."

"She's still upset that we hid this from her. She's not speaking to me either."

"I want to make things right with her. She's my best friend and our baby's aunt."

"Give her some time. She'll come around. I told her about your grandmother, so maybe she'll call you."

"Hopefully, she does."

"If you change your mind and want me to come to the hospital, let me know."

"I will."

"I love you."

"I love you too."

I end the call and hold back the tears.

DYLAN

I hate hospitals. I hate the smell, the uncleanliness, and the sight of sick people. I honestly don't know how my mother can be here day in and day out. Seeing my grandmother clinging to life is heartbreaking and makes me sad again. I kiss her on the cheek before I leave the room. I need to take time to deal with the reality that she may not make it. I walk for what feels like hours and end up at the far end of the emergency room. I stop when I see a familiar face. He's wearing an oxygen mask, and his eyes are closed. His mother turns to face me when I step inside the room.

"Hi, I'm Dylan."

"Hi, are you a friend of Noah's?"

"Yes. Is he okay?" I ask

Her face is stained with tears. "I don't know yet."

"What happened?"

"His brother found him unresponsive. He's been sick before, but I've never seen it this bad."

His father rushes in and yanks his wife into an embrace. They hold each other tightly, tears streaming down both of their faces. I quietly excuse myself to give them some privacy, but my mind is racing. Noah seemed just fine in school today. We were able to sneak away to his car during lunchtime for a quickie.

I want to go in and see him, but I also don't want to intrude on his parents. I pull my cell phone out of my pocket and text my mother. I want her to look into this, but I don't want to ask her in front of everyone because I'm sure my dad, my nosy grandfather, and my uncles will start with the questioning. They've never seen me with friends, and I don't want to raise anyone's suspicions. My system works perfectly right now. My dad has never met Noah. If I mention he's here in the ER, he'll want to meet him and his parents. I'm good at masking my sexuality, but Noah isn't. He's a bit flamboyant and over the top. My dad will immediately know he's gay, and then, all hell will break loose. I send my mother the message.

> **Me:** Mom, I ran into a friend. He's admitted to the ER, and his mom says he's sick. Can you find out what's wrong with him?
>
> **Mom:** I can lose my job, Dylan. Is it really that important? I'm sure he can tell you when he's released.
>
> **Me:** Please, Mom. He's a close friend from school, and I'm worried. I swear I won't mention anything, and can you keep this between us?
>
> **Mom:** Name?
>
> **Me:** Noah Alterman Jr.
>
> **Mom:** Okay.
>
> **Me:** Thanks, Mom.
>
> **Mom:** Of course.

I return to my grandmother's room, but it's now empty. I walk to the nurse's desk to ask about the whereabouts of my family, but I see my mom at one of the computers, so I wait. She types something, stares at the screen for a few minutes, and then exits. Finally, she turns around and walks toward me. "Where is everyone?" I ask.

"Upstairs. Your grandmother's finally been moved to her room. Come with me."

We enter the elevator, and she presses floor number eight. The door closes, and she turns to face me.

"I checked the system for the status of your friend Noah."

"Okay. What's wrong with him?"

"This stays between us. I'm not supposed to discuss confidential patient information, or I could be fired."

"Mom, I won't say anything. Just tell me what's wrong with him."

Her eyes water as she places a hand on my shoulder. "He's HIV-positive."

CHAPTER EIGHT
SHELDON

I wanted to check on Amy one last time before my shift ended, but I didn't want to risk anyone being suspicious. I hate seeing her upset, but as much as I want to be here for her, I know I can't. Not with her husband and kids being there. So, I went home, hoping she would call me when she could.

I enter my home and expect Kamryn to run down the stairs to greet me, but she doesn't. The house is quiet. Eva must have stepped out to run errands with the kids, and I smile at the fact that I may have a few hours of alone time, something I barely get. I climb the steps swiftly. I want to shower and have a beer before they return home. I reach the bedroom, and that's when I see it. There's a note lying on the bed. I drop my duffel bag on the floor and grab it.

Sheldon,

The kids and I are staying at Mom's. I need time to think about if this marriage is worth fighting for.

Eva

I crumble it up and toss it across the room. I plop down on the edge of the bed, and when I stare ahead at the walk-in closet, I notice Eva's side is missing clothes. Anger sweeps through me. Who the hell does she think she is taking my kids away from me? If she wants to leave, fine. But she has no right to remove my children from their home. I call her, but she sends me straight to voicemail. I could call her mother's house, but she'll lie and tell me Eva's not there. Maybe I should drive over there. But not like this. Not when I'm this angry. I need time to cool down.

Suddenly, a thought enters my head. This could be my way out. I've been unhappy for years but could never do anything about it. I'm a man with responsibilities, and I couldn't just up and leave my family. I stayed married to Eva because of the kids and because I couldn't live with the guilt of abandoning my family. But that's precisely what she has done. She's abandoned me. She took my kids and left. Do I want to beg her to come back home? I don't know about the God she worships, but it seems Allah has made a way for me to escape this trap and be happy again. I've prayed nightly to Him for a solution to my misery, and He's finally answered my prayers.

EVA

I watch my mother place food in front of Kamryn and my two nephews.

"Y'all go on and eat now," she says with a smile.

She looks at the kids at the table as they stuff their faces before she sits on the couch across from me.

"Chile, I ain't seen you in a month of Sundays. Let me take a look at you."

"Mom, you saw me at Christmas."

She huffs. "For two seconds. You came in, dropped off my gift, and didn't even stay to see me open it."

She's right. And I suddenly feel guilty. I look up as my sister stomps down the steps.

"That child of yours has some lungs on him. Took me forever to get him to sleep."

"Thanks, Shanice."

She takes a seat next to our mother. "So, what brings you to this neck of the woods? You never visit."

"Shanice, Eva is welcome home any time. Don't you go starting trouble now, ya hear?"

"What? It isn't my fault she thinks she's too good to come around her own damn family." Mom cuts her eyes at Shanice, and she folds her arms. "Sorry, Ma."

I shift in my seat before I respond. "I just wanted to see my mother, that's all."

Shanice looks over at my suitcases before replying. "Oh really? Is that why you have luggage by the door?"

I shake my head. "What is your problem?" I ask.

"My problem is the audacity of you crawling back here. You hardly visit, Eva. You live in that fancy home in the suburbs with your rich husband. Now, suddenly, you want to stay the night in the projects?"

"That's enough!" my mother yells. "Shanice, go check on the kids."

Shanice shoots to her feet and rolls her eyes at me as she walks out. When she's gone, my mother watches me silently.

"What's wrong, baby?" she asks.

My lip trembles, and my chest is tight with anxiety. I'm falling apart, and I don't fall apart. I've always had it together, and this can be no different. I'm the first person in my family to graduate from college. The first person to make good money, not live in the projects, or depend on welfare and food stamps. I waited to have kids until I was married. I did everything right. In my family's eyes, I live a perfect life. A life they could only dream about. I've done everything in my power to keep up with this façade. And if I tell them the truth, it will all come crashing down.

"Eva," my mother calls.

I shake my head. "I'm okay, Mom. I just missed you, is all."

I'm telling the truth in a sense. I have missed her. And with everything going on with Sheldon and me right now, I need my mother. The kids and I could have stayed in a nice hotel, but being around my mother comforts me. I came here for her wisdom. I know that she will tell me exactly what I need to hear. As much as I need her wisdom and comfort, I won't tell her the truth about Sheldon and me. She can't know I'm dying inside, and I definitely can't tell my sister. I won't give her the satisfaction of knowing my perfect life isn't perfect. My mother folds her arms across her chest

"Umm-hmm." She eyes me suspiciously. "Something ain't right, baby girl. But I ain't gonna force you to tell me anything. Just know that if you need to talk, I'm here."

I nod as she stands to her feet.

"Now, come on in this kitchen and get you some of this chili and corn bread," she demands.

"I'll be in there in a second."

She leaves the room, and I stare at the window, wondering how my life has come to this. At one point, I wouldn't be caught dead in this place. Drug dealers stand on every corner. Gunshots ring through the air frequently. The area is unsafe, but you can't convince my mother that it is. She quickly declined when I suggested she come and live with Sheldon and me.

I stand and join her and my sister in the kitchen. I sit next to Kamryn and my youngest nephew, Jameson. I smile at my oldest nephew, Shane, and his friend, Lamar, who sits across from me, playing on their cell phones. Momma places a plate before me, and Shanice shakes her head.

"You always spoiling her when she comes around. She's a grown woman and can make her own plate."

I stand, push my chair back, and slam my fist on the table. "What the hell is your problem?"

Shanice laughs loudly. "Well, well, little Miss Perfect just said a curse word."

"I never said I was perfect. It's not my fault I went to college and have made a good life for myself. Maybe if you had paid more attention to your schoolwork instead of boys, your grades would have been good enough to go to college too."

"You better watch your mouth, bitch."

My mother looks between us but doesn't intervene.

"You've always been jealous of me, Shanice."

"Jealous?" Her mouth parts open, and her eyes widen.

"Yes—jealous. You've never been happy for me. You didn't even come to my wedding. What kind of sister are you?" I'm livid by now. I'm already mad as hell at Sheldon and frustrated with my life at this point. I don't have the time, patience, or energy to deal with Shanice. She takes a step forward and looks me in the eye.

"Do you want to know the *real* reason I didn't come to your wedding?" she asks.

"Shanice, this is going too far now," my mother warns.

"No, Ma, she needs to hear this." She looks me in the eye and smirks. "I didn't come to your wedding because I couldn't stand by your side as your maid of honor, knowing my best friend fucked Sheldon the night before."

"Stop it. Both of you!" my mother yells.

Shanice looks over at her. "It had to be said."

"You're lying," I say with complete confidence.

She shrugs. "Think whatever you want. But ask yourself this. Have you ever looked closely at Lamar? Like *really* looked at him?"

My eyes swing over at him. He's watching the drama unfold. I zero in on him and look closely . . . And I see it. For the first time, I see it. He doesn't look identical to Sheldon but could still be his son. I do the math in my head. Lamar's age aligns with being conceived around the time of my wedding. Shanice is best friends with Lamar's mother, Crystal. She visits a lot, and Shanice constantly babysits Lamar. I even joked that he was like an honorary nephew to me. And all this time, they knew the truth. They knew that my husband could possibly have another child. My eyes swing over to my mother.

"Did *you* know about this?" I ask. The guilt on her face tells me all that I need to know.

"Shanice, go upstairs. I need to speak to Eva."

Shanice chuckles. "Gladly."

Hot tears stream down my face as she walks past me. I grab her arm, and my eyes meet hers. "I'm your sister. And your loyalty lies with your best friend? How could you not tell me this?"

She smirks. "Wasn't my business."

MARK

I watch my mother's chest rise and fall slowly. She looks peaceful, and the attending doctor gave us a glimmer of hope this morning when he announced that her vitals are improving. I knew that Black doctor didn't know what the fuck he was talking about yesterday. Dad and my brothers left with Amy last night and stayed at my house. I chose to stay here with Mom. Someone had to. Her arm jerks, and her fingers move. I jump up from my seat and am at her side quickly. "Mom, can you hear me?" I ask as I grab her hand.

Her eyes flutter open, and she looks at me. She doesn't respond right away. Instead, she slightly squeezes my hand.

"Ma . . . Mark," she coughs as she struggles to say my name.

"Shhh, just relax. Don't try to do too much. I'll call for the doctor."

I try to walk away, but she squeezes my hand tighter. I stop in my tracks, and her fingers let go. It's as if the squeeze has snatched away every ounce of energy she has.

"I ... I have something to tell you," she says in a low, husky voice.

"Mom, I'm sure it can wait."

"No. It can't."

Whatever it is, it seems important. And as much as I want to put my foot down and make her keep quiet until the doctor comes in, I stay put and allow her to struggle as she speaks.

"Okay, Mom. I'm listening, but I'm getting your doctor once you're done."

"You need to go to the house. To the attic," she says slowly but clearly.

"If you're asking me to get your will, I don't need to. You're going to be just fine."

She continues speaking. "Open my safe; the code is 6691."

"Why?"

"Inside, you'll find a black journal. It's for you. It has important information."

"What's so important that it can't wait until you're discharged?"

She coughs and pauses to catch her breath. After a few minutes, she gains enough strength to finish speaking.

"Information about your father."

"You want me to go to the house and get information for Dad? Why can't he get it himself?"

"No, son. Information about your *real* father."

"I think the medicine is making you talk crazy."

"Listen to me," she says as loud as she can. "Russell is not ..." She coughs again. "He's not your father."

My hand releases hers, and I step back. "Mom? What are you saying?"

She doesn't answer me. A tear slides down her cheek, and I feel like time has stopped. I feel like I'm in the Twilight Zone. I no longer hear the beeping of her heart monitor or the sound of the intercom above me. Instead, all I hear are her words replaying in my head.

"I'm sorry," she says in a faint whisper.

"No. No. This can't be true."

I'm in denial and desperately want her to confirm that it's not true. I want her to return to reality and agree that my father is Russell Carson, but she doesn't. She's struggling to breathe as she coughs uncontrollably. "I'll get your doctor. We can finish this discussion afterward."

I watch her for a second. I can see that she wants to fight but is too weak to do so. Her eyes are apologetic, begging me to stay by her side. But I ignore her silent plea. Right now, she needs help. I rush out of the room and grab the first doctor I see. He comes in and examines her while I sit and wait. I'm anxious to continue the conversation once she's strong enough to talk. She's fragile right now and needs rest.

She also needs peace and quiet . . . something I'm not sure I can give her right now. All I can offer at this moment is an overwhelming number of questions about why the fuck she's waited all these years to drop some shit like this on me. I leave the room. I need space to clear my head, and I can't look at her right now. I walk outside the hospital doors to get some fresh air and sunshine. I find a nearby bench and plop down on it. If Russell isn't my father, then who the hell is? Why would she lie to me? Does Russell know? A million questions swirl in my head, and there's not enough room for them. I need answers.

Ten minutes later, I walk back inside and take the stairs until I reach my mother's floor. I reach her room, and when I open the door, I'm met with a swarm of staff surrounding her bed. The doctor is compressing her chest, attempting CPR. My instinct is to run to her. To tell her I need her and to fight through this. But I'm too busy watching the doctor, hoping he can perform a miracle. He stops pushing and looks up at the clock. His gaze meets mine as he speaks to the nurse.

"Time of death 10:36 a.m."

After I called the rest of the family to tell them the news, I decided to head straight to my parents' house. I pull into the driveway and exit my car. As I reach the front porch, memories of growing up in this house flood my mind. I remember my mother rocking in the chair to my left while sipping homemade lemonade. I bury my emotions, unlock the door, and head inside. I go straight to the attic, and once I'm there, I find the safe my mother mentioned. I stare at it for a few minutes. Do I want to know? Do I *really* want to know who my birth father is? Does it even matter? Russell did a great job raising me. No matter who created me biologically, he could never take my father's place.

I press the buttons to the corresponding code my mother gave me, and the door clicks open. I remove the two items inside with my name written on the front. The black journal she mentioned and an envelope. I open the journal, and the tears are already forming. I flip through two pages until I see my mother's handwriting. I read her words.

> *My Dearest Mark,*
>
> *I knew the day would come when I would have to be truthful with you. First, let me start by saying that I love you and am sorry for any pain or anger I've caused you. You deserve to know the truth. Many years ago, I fell in love with a man named Brian Williams. He was my first real love, Mark, and we planned to run off and get married, but my parents moved me away before we got the chance. I was young, and there was little I could do about it then.*

I found out I was pregnant with you shortly afterward. Times were different back then, and I needed you to have a good life. Not one where you would be subject to criticism and bias. So, we agreed that having someone else raise you would be better. I met Russell a month into my pregnancy, and we started our courtship. After a few weeks of dating, I came clean with him and told him I was pregnant and abandoned by the father. He stood by my side, and we told everyone it was his baby.

A few years after you were born, I went to see Brian. I wanted him to meet you. The meeting was brief. He had gotten married and had a baby girl. Yes, you have a sister. That day was the last time we had any contact. In the envelope, you will find the only picture I have of your father, along with his last known address. I ask that you please keep an open mind, Mark. Take the time to find him and meet the other family you never knew. They're your blood regardless of whether you like this situation. I never meant to hurt you, but this is what was best for you to have the life I always intended for you to have. You are my first baby boy, and I love you more than you realize.

Love,
Mom

I wipe away the tears and open the envelope, anxious to see the face of the man who created me. When I see it, I drop to my knees in anguish. I scream as I look at his face. A face that looks almost identical to mine . . . except he's Black.

CHAPTER NINE

AMY

I pop a few pills while patiently waiting for Mark to return home. He left the hospital to gather his mother's important papers. I know this must be hard on him. Mark and Emma were extremely close. He was her first son and somewhat of a momma's boy. She spoiled him rotten, so it never made sense that he opposed me spoiling Dylan. We all said our goodbyes to his mother before her body was taken down to the morgue, and it hurts to know I'll never see or speak to my sweet mother-in-law again.

I hear his pickup truck pull into the driveway and regain some of my composure. His father, brothers, and sisters-in-law are taking this hard, so I need to be strong for everyone. He walks inside the house. His face is flushed, his eyes are bloodshot red, and he looks as if he's in pain. It's to be expected. He just lost his mother. He approaches me and hugs me tightly. His grip is smothering, but I'm guessing he needs it, so I don't oppose it.

"Where is everybody?" he asks as he releases me.

"They're gathered in the family room. Your father wanted to discuss the funeral arrangements with everyone," I respond.

"My father," he repeats.

"Yeah, Russell wants to get it out of the way."

"He has no business rushing things. He just wants to control things as usual."

He's angry. And I've never heard him talk this way about Russell. I always thought he feared his father. But he's grieving, and anger is one of the phases of grief, so I allow him to express it.

"Do you want to join them? I made a pot of coffee," I ask softly.

"No, I don't want to join them!" he yells. "And I don't want to sit around and drink coffee while planning my mother's funeral. It hasn't even been twenty-four hours."

"Mark, I know you're hurting, but—"

"You don't know a goddamn thing, Amy. You can't possibly know how I feel. You were a kid when your parents died."

I don't know if it's the effects of the pills or if I've gotten used to his insensitivity, but his words don't hurt me as they should have. I feel numb. "That doesn't mean I don't know how it is to live without them."

My thoughts shift to my parents. They were killed in a fire. But that doesn't mean I don't think about them every day. I can still smell the scent of my mother's perfume and hear the deep rumble of my father's laugh. It wasn't easy growing up without them. I'm grateful for my grandparents, who raised me. They took me in and raised me like they'd created me. But I still longed for my parents over the years, even though I knew I would never see them again. Mark takes notice of my silence, and his face softens.

"I'm sorry, Amy."

"I know this is hard for you."

"You have no idea," he says as he shakes his head.

"I understand, Mark, and I'm here for you."

He opens his mouth as if he wants to tell me something but doesn't. I want to urge him to speak. To tell me whatever is on his mind, but I don't want to push. He's emotional right now, and the last thing I want to do is aggravate him.

"I'll join everyone," he says before leaving the room.

He exits the room, and I exhale loudly. I cross my fingers that he and his father don't participate in a shouting match over his mother's arrangements. Emotions are running high for both of them, and I'm unsure if either is thinking clearly.

My phone rings, and it's Sheldon. Why the hell is he calling me during a time like this? We have a text-only policy when we're with family. I glance into the other room, and everyone is too occupied looking at funeral home brochures to notice me sneak out the back door.

"Hey," I answer.

"Hey, can you talk?" he asks.

"Not really. This isn't a good time, Sheldon."

"I know, but I had to call you. It was too much to text."

"What's wrong?" I ask.

"Eva's gone. She took the kids and is staying at her mother's."

This is why he's calling me? To tell me that his wife has left him? This changes nothing between us. "Sheldon, this couldn't wait? I'm in the middle of a family crisis right now," I say as I grow frustrated.

"No, it couldn't wait. This is what I've been waiting for, Amy, to break free of this marriage . . . and be with you."

What? Be with me? I thought we had an understanding, but I guess I'm wrong. I almost tell him that he's overstepping. There is no way in hell I'm leaving my family. What is he thinking, even suggesting something like that? Just as I start to speak, the doorbell rings.

"I've gotta go. I'll call you later," I say as I end the call.

I head to the foyer and open the door. Standing in front of me is a teenage boy or a young adult. I can't tell which one. He's got tanned skin, black hair, and a big phoenix tattoo on his left arm.

"May I help you?" I ask.

"Hi, Mrs. Carson. I'm looking for Ireland. Is she home?"

"Yes, and you are?"

His hand is stretched to shake mine, but I don't accept it. I don't know who he is or what he wants with my daughter. All I know is that he looks different than us, and if he doesn't leave before Mark sees him, this won't end well. He pulls his hand back in.

"My name's Austin."

IRELAND

I hear the doorbell ring, but I pay no mind to it. It's probably someone who heard the news about my grandmother and came to visit my parents. My dad is seated beside me. He and my grandfather are going over funeral plans, and they both seem to struggle with it. I hear voices. It sounds as if my mother is talking to someone but has raised her voice slightly. My dad takes notice and rises from his seat. He exits the living room, and I look down at the funeral brochure given to me by my grandfather. Suddenly, I hear someone shouting, someone who sounds like Austin. I quickly go to the foyer and stop once I see the situation before me. Austin is standing in the doorway, and my parents are facing him. It looks like a standoff. My first instinct is to run, but I don't. My father turns around to face me.

"Ireland, who is this?" he asks.

Austin watches me. He's anxious to see if I tell my parents the truth about who he is. He seems to challenge me to do so.

"I said, who is this?" my father yells.

"He's . . . a friend," I answer.

"Boyfriend," Austin corrects me.

"Boyfriend?" Confusion crosses my father's face, then anger.

"Listen here, you lying mutt. My daughter doesn't have a boyfriend and if she did it wouldn't be somebody fresh off the boat like you."

"I'd rather be fresh off the boat than a racist motherfucker like you," Austin responds.

"Austin, please," I beg him.

"No, it's time we stop hiding, Ireland. It's time you stop being scared of your father and tell him the truth. Tell him that we love each other. Tell him we're going to get married and raise our baby together."

"Baby?" my mother repeats.

In the blink of an eye, my dad's hands are wrapped around Austin's throat. He's yelling something, but I don't know what he's saying. I'm too busy watching Austin struggle to breathe and begging him to stop. My grandfather and my uncles rush in, and from the look on their faces, they have no idea what all the commotion is about. Finally, my grandfather pulls my dad off Austin.

"What the fuck is going on here?" my uncle asks.

"Apparently, Ireland has a boyfriend," my father answers.

Austin is out of breath. He is coughing and attempting to breathe as my mother stands in front of him. It's almost as if she's protecting him in a sense. My grandfather gives me a death stare, and so do my uncles. My father steps toward Austin, but my mother stops him.

"You just lost your mother today, Mark."

He listens to my mother and doesn't move any further. I'm crying and shaking uncontrollably. I want to run to Austin's side but know I can't.

"Don't you ever come to my house or contact my daughter again. Now, go back to wherever the fuck you came from," my father says in between breaths.

Austin looks at me, and by now, my shirt is soaked with tears. I mouth the words, "I'm sorry" to him and hang my head low as I realize I'll probably never see him again.

Austin doesn't respond. He quickly leaves the house . . . taking my heart with him.

DYLAN

I stand at the end of the steps and watch the events unfold. I feel sympathy for my sister. I was in my room soaking in sorrow at the news given to me by my mother when I heard yelling and screaming. I quietly walked down the steps and watched the situation go from bad to worse. My father slams the door behind Austin. He turns to face my sister, and in a flash, he backhands her across the face. She falls backward into the wall, and my mother is at her side quickly. I take a few steps toward them but stop. I want to be there for her, but my intuition tells me to stay put.

"You're a liar. After all your mother and I have done for you, *this* is how you choose to repay us? By lying and keeping secrets?" my father yells.

Ireland doesn't respond. She's crying hysterically while her hand covers her bottom lip.

"I thought you raised your kids better than this, Mark," my grandfather states. "Had you raised them the way I told you to, none of this would have happened."

"How could you do this to us, Ireland? Who else knows about this?" My dad continues while ignoring my grandfather.

"Dad, you don't understa—"

"I don't *need* to understand. This is *my* house," my father interrupts. "What you need to understand is that you've failed us.

You've thrown every value I've taught you out the window, and for what?"

"I love him, Dad," Ireland says softly through tears.

"You're a prized possession to him. Ireland, he's using you," my grandfather adds.

"No, he isn't. He's never asked me for anything."

"He doesn't have to," my uncle says from behind my father. "He sees you as an opportunity. He'll make you think he loves you, marry you, and become successful all because he married a white woman. He'll want to use our connections, network with our resources, and help his own kind advance."

"You're wrong," Ireland fires back.

"Stop!" My mother says firmly to everyone.

Ireland struggles to stand to her feet while my mother helps her.

"I know we're all emotional, but let's all just take a minute to calm down, please," my mother announces.

"You expect me to calm down after finding out about *this*?" my dad responds.

"We can talk about this later . . . as a family," my mother reasons.

"All of us are family. So we'll talk about this now and figure out what punishment to give to Ireland."

Silence creeps in as emotions elevate and uncertainty fills everyone's mind. I hurt for my sister. I see the pain in her eyes and the fear on her face.

"How long have you been sneaking around with him, Ireland?" my father asks.

I instantly cross my fingers, hoping she lies about the timing. I'm not sure how long she's been seeing Austin, but I'm sure the longer the time, the more brutal the punishment.

"Not long," she answers.

"If he's telling the truth and you're pregnant, you're getting rid of that thing first thing tomorrow morning," my father adds.

"Mark." My mother shakes her head. "Think about what you're saying." She gently places her hand on Ireland's shoulder. "Ireland, please tell me you're not pregnant."

My sister's expression says it all. Guilt crosses her face at my mother's statement, and I shut my eyes tightly at the realization that my little sister has lost her virginity. I honestly don't care about *whom* she gave it away to. I care that she didn't save herself for marriage, or at least until she's older. I know I'm being a hypocrite. I'm no angel, and I've been sexually active since I was about her age, but she's my little sister. And I can't even imagine some guy with his hands all over her.

"I'm not sticking around for this," Ireland says before flying out the front door.

This is my cue. I head toward the door to follow my sister. She needs me. And since no one else has come to her defense, it's my job as her big brother to take care of her. Unfortunately, just as I reach the door, my father stops me.

"Don't!" he says.

My heart tells me to ignore him and follow her, but my mind tells me not to defy my father right now. I'm already an emotional wreck and in no position to go toe-to-toe with him. So, I do the only thing I can now: turn around and head back to my room to call her.

She doesn't answer. I leave her at least five voicemails and a dozen text messages, hoping she responds soon. Someone knocks at my door, and my mother walks in. I'm angry at her. I'm mad because she did nothing to help Ireland. She stood there while my father berated her in front of the entire family. She even allowed him to hit her.

"Can you call your sister?" she asks.

"No."

"Please. She isn't answering my calls," she continues.

"I don't blame her," I respond.

"Dylan, she's been lying."

"And that justifies you allowing Dad to humiliate her in front of everyone?"

"No, but you know how your father gets. He's upset right now because he just lost his mother."

"That's no excuse. He's *always* like that, even before Grandma died."

"I'm sure Ireland is okay. She's probably just getting some air right now."

"I can't believe you let him hit her. I could kill him for hurting her!" I yell.

"Don't raise your voice at me, Dylan."

"Or what? You'll call Dad to hit me too?" I ask.

She doesn't answer. And right now, I don't want her in my room. I don't want her around me—period.

"I'll let you know if I hear from her, and you do the same," she says before walking out.

I love my mother, but I can't forgive her for not protecting my sister. And I can't forgive myself. I should have stepped in to help her, but I didn't. I stood there and did nothing. I was scared and afraid of my father, grandfather, and uncles. I neglected my sister when she needed me the most, and I hate myself for it. I'm no better than Ireland. As a matter of fact, I'm worse. The only difference is that my dad doesn't know my secrets . . . yet.

IRELAND

I ran as fast as I could from my house and didn't look back. If anyone had followed me, I would have put up one hell of a fight before I allowed them to drag me back there. I hate my father, and I hate my mother for siding with him. She did nothing while my father humiliated me in front of everyone. She, of all people, should know how it feels to love someone you can't be with. I could tell by how she and Mr. Unknown Black Man kissed that day at the hospital. She should have stood up for me.

Austin refused to answer my calls, so I called Camilla instead. She told me he wasn't home and wanted to know why I sounded upset, but I didn't have the strength to explain it to her. I told her I would explain later and made a mental note to call her back once I found Austin. I knew exactly where to look first. I exit the train that stops right in front of the local bookstore and take a deep breath as I head inside. This is Austin's safe place. This is where he comes when he's stressed or bothered about something.

My eyes scan the room once I enter the building. My heart is beating quickly, and I'm extremely nervous I might not find him here. But then I see him speaking to one of the employees on the upper level. His back is facing me, but I know it's him. I can spot him anywhere. I swiftly make my way up the steps and onto the second floor. As I approach, the employee hands him a book, and he sits to open it. He lifts his head as I stop in front of the table he's seated at.

"What the hell are you doing here?" he asks angrily.

His voice rises a bit, and it causes the people around us to stare, but he doesn't seem to care.

"Can we talk?" I ask.

"There's nothing to talk about."

His tone is cold, and his expression is tight, showing no emotion. It hurts me to see this side of him.

"I'm sorry."

"What are you sorry about, Ireland? Are you sorry for how you acted as if you didn't know me? Or are you sorry for allowing your family to attack me? I'm the father of your child."

"I wanted to defend you, Austin, but you don't know my father."

"Oh, I know him all right. I deal with people like him every day. People assume I only speak Spanish the minute they lay eyes on me, or they assume I'm an immigrant. Do you know why none of the big publishers sign me? Because of the color of my skin. They show interest at first, but as soon as I show up for the meeting, all of a sudden, my story doesn't fit the scope of their business. My family has been discriminated against since we came here. The last thing I need is to be discriminated against by the woman I love."

"I don't treat you that way," I respond.

"Yes, you do, by not speaking up for what's right."

"What am I supposed to do?"

"You know your parents' beliefs are wrong. There's nothing wrong with challenging that."

"I can't do that, Austin."

"Not even for me?"

It's a tough question for me to answer. My heart says to forget what my parents think; this is the love of my life. But my mind is saying I can't. It would cause a rift between my family and me. But is he worth it? The tears start to fall, and I try my best not to cry out loud in front of all these people, but it doesn't work. Finally, I break down, and Austin is at my side immediately. He pulls me in tightly, allowing me to soak his shirt with my silent tears. The grip of his arms around me makes me feel safe, his heartbeat makes me feel loved, and his lips softly kissing the top of my head makes me feel protected. I lift my head, and he wipes away my tears. "You're right about everything. I want to be with you, but I don't know what to do."

"Run away with me," he answers.

He waits for me to respond, but his words still swirl around in my head. Run away with him? Where would we go? How would we live? I haven't graduated yet, and he isn't working. But does any of that matter? No. All that matters is that we're together. I'm tired of hiding our relationship, and I'm tired of sneaking around. I want to be with the man I love.

"Okay," I answer before I talk myself out of it.

"Okay, as in . . . yes?"

"Yes, I just want to be with you, Austin."

He leans in and kisses me. "We'll leave tonight."

"So soon?"

"Yes, the sooner, the better."

I nod in agreement. He grabs my hand, and we head toward our new life together, wherever that may be.

CHAPTER TEN
MARK

Tears stream down my face as I watch the casket lower to the ground. The weather today is fitting for a funeral. It's cloudy outside. Gloomy with scattered showers. My father steps forward and tosses his rose on top of her casket. Amy gently loops her arm with mine. I don't recall attending a funeral. And if I have, I don't remember, but today is a day I will never forget. Not only because it's the day we buried my mother but because of how today made me *feel*. I almost didn't make it through. All the crying became unbearable. The sad and low energy was stifling. Grieving on my own is bad enough. Add fifty other people around me crying and weeping, and dealing with my emotions is almost impossible. After the casket hits the ground, the priest says the last prayer, and the crowd makes their way to their cars. I stay behind. "You all go on. I need a minute."

Amy nods, kisses my cheek, and escorts Dylan away from the cemetery with everyone else. My father wipes one last tear from his eyes before he places his hand on my shoulder on his way out.

I'm alone now–just her and me. I look around before speaking to ensure no one can hear me.

"Why would you leave me, especially now when I need you the most?" I stay in silence for a moment before I continue. "Why didn't you tell me sooner, Mom? Why tell me on your deathbed?" I imagine her giving me a reason why she would wait so long to tell me the truth. I imagine her gently placing her hand over mine and telling me everything will be okay. I shake my head. "It won't be okay. What am I supposed to do with this news, huh? How am I supposed to go on living, knowing everything I thought I knew was a lie?" More silence, followed by the sounds of birds chirping. "I don't know if I'm mad at you specifically. Or if I'm just . . . mad."

It takes me a minute to think about what comes next. I am angry. Very angry. But I honestly don't know to whom my anger is directed. Am I mad at Mom for lying to me? "I just wish you would have been honest with me."

All the emotions I've been feeling overpower me, and I drop to my knees on the cold, hard ground. "Mom, please, tell me what you want me to do. Tell me how I'm supposed to deal with this." My tears fall faster, and my body shakes as I sob. "I can't do this alone, Mom. I need you."

I imagine her telling me that she's not gone. I imagine her telling me that she will always be by my side. The wind picks up, and leaves whirl around me. The rain showers now turn to heavy drops. And when I look up, a flicker of lightning brightens the sky. A sense of peace washes over me as I take this as a sign. A sign that my mother hears me. It's a sign that she sees my tears and my pain. I slowly rise to my feet and wipe away the fallen tears. At that moment, the world around me goes still, and I swear I hear two words whistling in the wind. *I'm sorry.*

It almost knocks me off my feet. I look around to see if anyone else heard anything strange, but everyone is talking or pulling out of the parking lot. I take a step forward and peer down at my mother's casket. "I forgive you, Mom."

I wait for another confirmation. I wait for another sign that my mother is speaking to me, but I don't hear it. I chuckle and shake my head. Maybe I imagined it. Maybe my pain is so heavy that I'm hallucinating. "I don't know where I go from here, Mom. But wherever I go, I'm going to need you with me. I love you."

It's been three weeks since we buried my mother and three weeks since Ireland sent us a text telling us she was okay and wouldn't return home. We attempted to get the police involved by issuing a missing person case, but there was nothing else we could do. The case was classified as a runaway. All we could do was hope that she would be found soon. We don't know her best friend or boyfriend's last name because she kept them both hidden. Amy is beyond pissed with me, and Dylan is barely speaking to me either, but I'm too distracted to care. I'm sitting in front of the last known address of my biological father. I try to ignore my mother's words. I try not to think about the fact that she lied to me, but I can't. It consumes my mind, and I have to find out for myself. I need closure. I check the address on the letter again to make sure I'm at the right place before exiting the car.

I stand in front of the building before I take the steps to the fourth floor. I arrive at the front door, but I don't knock immediately. Instead, I contemplate if I should call Amy and tell her where I'm at and why. But as I pull her number up in my cell phone, I decide this conversation is best in person. So, I place the phone back inside my pocket and knock softly on the door. I wait a few more minutes, but no one comes. So, I knock harder.

"I'm coming," a female voice calls out.

The door opens, and a woman appears. She has smooth dark skin and short hair. She's quite pretty for a Black woman.

"Yeah?" she says.

"I'm looking for Brian," I respond.

"What's a man like you looking for Brian for?"

"I—" I stop speaking.

I have no idea how to answer her. Do I tell this woman that he's supposed to be my father? Or do I make up some lie about who I am? She opens the door and moves a little closer to me. Her eyes squint, and she lets out a small gasp.

"Well, praise Jesus. You're him, aren't you?" she asks.

"Who?" I respond.

"You're his son."

She invites me in, and I sit on the couch while she makes some coffee. I look around at the pictures on the walls. The images are the same man in the photo my mother left for me. The resemblance is striking, and there is no denying that my mother was telling me the truth. He seems to be happy in his photos, carefree and lively. I don't like the fact that I'm sitting in a Black person's home, but I push my issues to the side so I can get to the bottom of things. I'm doing this for my mother as well as myself. I want to say that I honored my mother's last wishes. And if what she said is true, I want to make it clear to this man that I want no part of him or his family. She enters the living room with two cups of coffee in her hands. She passes me one.

"We always knew that one day you would look for him," she says.

"I didn't know. I only found out recently when my mother passed."

"I'm sorry to hear that," she says as she sips her coffee.

I take a sip and set my cup down on the coaster in front of me. I don't like to drink after anyone when I don't watch them make my drink, especially when it comes from a Black woman I don't even know.

"Brian, is he here?" I ask.

I don't want to waste time. I want to get this meeting over with so I can say that I met him and go on with my life as if nothing happened. She pauses before placing her cup down.

"Emma didn't tell you?" she asks.

"Tell me what? Wait, how do you know my mother's name?"

"You were a few years old when it happened. I'm guessing Emma didn't know either."

I don't respond. I wonder how she knows about my mother and me when I know nothing about her.

"I'm Belle. Brian's widow. He told me all about Emma and you before we married."

"Exactly what did he tell you?" I ask, trying to remain calm.

If I want to get the information, I have to be polite. I can't say or act as if I'm angry, although I am.

"He loved your mother, and she loved him. But her parents wouldn't accept their relationship. When your mother found out she was pregnant, she was concerned about what kind of upbringing you would have and what her father might do to you. She feared he would take you from her and send you away. So, she and Brian agreed never to contact each other again, and she told her family that she was pregnant by her new boyfriend."

"How do I know that any of this is true? How do I know that he was really my father?"

She stands to her feet. "Give me a minute. I'll be right back."

My plan is shattered. The man I came to see for myself isn't even alive. I didn't come to speak to his widow. She returns with an envelope and gives it to me.

"He wanted you to know the truth if you ever came looking for it."

I open the envelope and pull out a piece of paper. "What's this?" I ask.

"It's a DNA test. Your parents made sure to get one done to prove paternity if they ever needed to."

I read the paper, and it reads 99.9999 percent probable that Brian Williams is the father of Mark Farrow. Farrow is my mother's maiden name, so she must've changed my name once she married Russell. Inside the envelope is a picture of him holding me when I was a toddler with my mother standing next to him.

"I was carrying my own child when this was taken, and you were two years old. It was the last time he saw you."

"Where was this taken?" I ask.

"Your momma snuck you over to see him. She wanted him to meet you and needed a swab of his saliva for the DNA test. Those tests had just been invented back then. After that, they agreed never to contact each other again. It killed your father that he couldn't be there for you."

"Who took the picture?" I ask.

"I did," she answers. "You look surprised," she continues.

"I am," I respond.

"Your mother was a sweet lady, nothing like her parents. She and Brian just wanted what was best for their child, and I supported that. I loved him."

The door opens, and a child comes running in.

"Mom-mom," the little girl squeals.

Another woman walks in carrying a baby. She looks tired and frustrated. She enters the living room, and Belle smiles at her.

"Mark, I want you to meet your sister, Lesa."

I stare at her, taking in her features. She does the same. "Hi," she says.

"Hi."

She has a light complexion with long hair and light brown eyes. The longer I stare at her, the more I realize we look alike. She places her hands on her hips.

"You look just like Daddy."

"Hush, chile. Give the man a minute to take all this in."

I'm suddenly grateful for her understanding because this is a lot. It almost feels like too much. "What was he like?"

I don't know what makes me ask. But I need to know what kind of man he was. Was he a better man than Russell? Would he have been a better man for my mother? A better father to me? She looks at her mother as if waiting for permission to speak. Belle nods, and she looks back at me.

"Daddy was a good man. He worked hard to take care of us. He was funny but stern. Respectful but didn't take no mess. And he talked about you all the time."

"He talked about me?"

"Yes. He came close to breaking the agreement he and your momma had. He wanted to be in your life."

I don't know how to respond. How do I tell this man's family of my upbringing? How do I explain how hard it is to accept this man as my father? How can I possibly explain that I've spent all my life looking down on the race of the very man who created me and even the two of them standing in front of me? They would immediately throw me out of their house if they knew of everything I've ever said and done.

Lesa breaks the silence. "Wanna stay for a spell? Momma's making smothered pork chops and collards."

I plaster a smile and shake my head as I decline. My eyes meet hers, and although we share the same blood running through our veins, I'm not ready to break bread with her yet. I'm not ready to sit around the table sharing stories of our upbringing and differences. I need a little time. "Thank you for the offer, but I'd best be getting home."

She nods. "Right. Well, maybe some other time? After all, we *are* family. So we should get to know each other."

I take a deep breath to calm the anxicty coursing through my body. "Yeah, maybe some other time."

SHELDON

I listened to Eva's voicemail for the third time today. *You have broken my heart for the last time, Sheldon. Of all the women in the world, you had to screw my sister's best friend. How could you? I . . . I just—*

The message ends there. The pain in her voice gives me chills. She left the message last night, and I still haven't responded because I don't know how. I was hoping this day would never catch up to me. I had a bachelor party and one of my friends mentioned it to Crystal. Crystal and Shanice had been best friends since grade school, and Eva considered her a close family friend. Crystal came and threw herself at me the entire night until she got what she wanted.

Sleeping with Crystal was a bad idea. I realized it was a mistake the minute we finished, and she agreed. We felt horrible about betraying Eva. So, we both decided to bury this secret and never speak of it again . . . until now. How did Eva find out after all these years? Did she tell her? Did she paint me as the bad guy? Or was she honest about her role in what happened? It was she who came on to me. It was she who showed up in my hotel room wearing a coat with nothing on underneath. She knew I had been drinking. She knew I would be weak. And she was right. I tried to show restraint. I tried to be the better man and turn her away. But when she dropped to her knees in front of me, I caved. I hated myself afterward for what I did. I almost told Eva the truth but couldn't stand losing her. Not back then, anyway. I was in love with her.

Right now, our marriage is holding on by a thread. We don't share the love we once had or the passion. I can handle the two of us parting ways because it's no longer working for us. I can take us divorcing because we've fallen out of love. But I can't handle being responsible for the pain my wife may never recover from. I'm sure it would hurt her if she ever found out about Amy. She's hurting now, knowing I slept with someone she considered family. I have no idea how to make this right. I'm ashamed and can't even face her. I take a deep breath and gather my composure. I need to deal with this head-on. I need to be mature and man enough to face the consequences of my actions. I grab my phone and call her. She answers, but she doesn't say hello.

"What do you want?"

"Eva, can we talk about this?"

"Is it true? Did you sleep with Crystal?" she asks.

I pause before answering. "I had been drinking—"

"Did you sleep with her or not?"

The purpose of this call was to lay it all bare and come clean. And not just about Crystal, but about my unhappiness and desire to end this marriage. But I have no words as I sit on the phone, listening to Eva breathe.

"Sheldon . . ." Her voice cracks as she says my name, making me panic.

"It's not what you think."

She scuffs. "Not what I think? What else can it be? Sheldon, the least you can do is be honest with me. Please don't make me look like a fool in front of my family."

"Eva . . ."

A minute passes, and she speaks when I don't finish the sentence. "Call me when you're ready to be honest. And by the way, Lamar may be yours."

She ends the call, and my mouth parts open with shock. My brain scans the memories of that night, trying to remember if Crystal and I used a condom. The memories are fuzzy. I was so drunk that night that I can't remember. Could Lamar be my son? I've only seen him a handful of times since Eva and I married, and I never looked closely at him. Fuck! This didn't go as planned. Any chance I had of cordially ending this marriage has just gone out the window.

I have no one to blame but myself. I made this mess, and it's time I stop lying to myself *and* her and take responsibility for my actions. I had the chance to come clean, but I chickened out. It's probably a good thing, though. These kinds of conversations should be done in person, not over the phone. I grab my phone and shoot her a text.

Let's meet soon so we can talk face-to-face. It's time we are honest about the way we feel.

I place the phone down and breathe a sigh of relief, knowing that I can get some things off my chest. I know Eva is just as unhappy as me. We once loved each other. We have kids. There's no reason why we can't separate peacefully and figure out a plan to coparent them. Once we create a solid exit plan, I'll take a DNA test for Lamar. Excitement creeps in at the thought of being free. I can finally see Amy without sneaking around. I can finally go after what I want. And this time, I don't care about what my parents think. I don't care about what society thinks. I'm living life for me, on my terms. I grab my phone and dial Amy, but she doesn't answer. I don't know if she's ducking my calls or if something is wrong. But I need to talk to her soon. Once she finds out I'll be a free man, we can work on a plan for her to leave her husband. And then we can finally be together.

CHAPTER ELEVEN

AMY

Mark has been gone all morning. I have no idea where he went, and I didn't ask. The past few weeks have been tense. Ireland sent me a long text message telling me she loved me and refused to respond when I asked her where she was. It frustrates me. My baby girl is out in the world all by herself, and I'm driving myself sick with worry as I wait for the cops to find her. I contacted the cell phone company and got access to her call log. I dialed every number until I found someone who could tell me something. It turns out that person was Camilla. She told me that it was her brother who had come to our house. She wasn't happy about how he was treated and wasn't afraid to let it be known. But she has a right to be angry. Mark took it too far. Austin is a kid compared to him. Camilla also explained that Ireland and Austin left town to be together, but she wouldn't tell me where they went, just that he was in love with Ireland and would ensure she was taken care of.

I feel at ease that she's with someone who cares about her, but only a little. I know nothing about her boyfriend. What if he's no good for her, but she's too naïve to notice? I've been texting her nonstop, letting her know I understand what she's going through and to come home so we can talk this out, but she hasn't answered.

The doorbell rings, and I wipe my tears before heading to the foyer. I open the door and stumble back at the sight of the person standing before me.

"Wha . . . What are you doing here?" I stutter.

Sheldon forces his way into my house. "You've been ignoring me."

I angrily slam the door behind him. "How did you find out where I live?"

"I'm highly respected at work, Amy. It was easy."

"That's a breach of my privacy."

"Are you serious?" he asks.

"I haven't been ignoring you. I was going to call you back. But, unfortunately, things have been crazy since my mother-in-law died and my daughter ran away."

He closes the gap between us. "Why didn't you tell me? I told you I'm here for you, Amy."

"Sheldon, this is a family issue. It's not your place to be there for me."

"Really? So, what *is* my place then?"

I change the subject. "You know I care about you."

"You care about me? Amy, I'm divorcing my wife for you, and all you can say is that you care about me?"

He's laying it on thick, and I must get him out of here before Mark comes home. "Can we talk someplace else? Mark could walk in any minute now."

"I tried. But you wouldn't answer your phone, so here I am."

"Sheldon, I'm sorry. But I'm not leaving my husband and kids."

"I have kids too—a baby at that. But I'm not happy, and neither are you. We deserve to be happy. Together."

"Sheldon . . ." Shit! I never anticipated this would happen. Isn't it usually the woman who catches feelings? "I thought we were just having sex."

"So, all this time, all you cared about was the sex?"

"No. I mean, we're friends too. And we work together. But—"

"Well, I'll be damned. So, you *used* me?"

"We used each other, didn't we?"

"I never used you, Amy, and especially not for sex. I can get that from any woman I want."

"What do you want from me, Sheldon?"

"I want you to admit how you feel about me. I know I'm not crazy. I can feel it."

"You're right. I have feelings for you, and I've thought about a life with you. But it's a fantasy. We can never be together."

"Yes, we can."

He leans in and kisses me. I kiss him back and almost forget I'm in my own home. I'm turned on, and I want his hands all over me. But not under the roof I share with my husband. I pull away. "I need some time, Sheldon. I have a lot on my plate now, but I promise we can talk more about this."

"Okay. Can you meet me tonight after my shift?"

"Where?" I ask.

"At the hotel."

"All right. Just text me when you get there."

He kisses me once more on the lips before he opens the front door and leaves.

About thirty minutes later, Mark walks through the door. He looks angry and upset. Did he happen to see Sheldon leaving? Did any of the neighbors see him go? I'm paranoid, but I decide to play it cool.

"I was just about to call you to see what you wanted for dinner."

"I'm not hungry," he answers.

"Are you okay? You look upset."

"No, I'm *not* okay," he responds.

He heads upstairs without saying another word, and I let him have his space. He's been touchy lately, and I don't want to do anything to make matters worse. Mark isn't a communicator, and I've learned over the years to let him be when something bothers him. I'm his wife, and I want to support and be there for him, but how can I support him when he hardly expresses how he feels?

I decide to see if Dylan wants any dinner. He's been quiet these past few weeks, and I've neglected to spend time with him to see if he's okay. I see him briefly when he gets home from school, but then he's in his room for the rest of the night. I head upstairs to check on him. I knock on the door, but he doesn't answer. I knock again, and still no answer. Finally, I open the door, walk in . . . and scream at the top of my lungs.

I rush over to Dylan, hanging from his ceiling fan with a rope tied around his neck. By now, Mark has joined me in my efforts to free him. Somehow, one of us manages to remove the rope, and he drops to the floor. I immediately begin CPR.

"Call 911," I shout to Mark.

He's already beaten me to it. I can hear him providing our address to the operator as I'm trying my best to resuscitate my son.

"Come on, Dylan. Breathe, baby, please," I say to him repeatedly.

I'm not getting a pulse, he's not moving, and I fear we've lost him. Mark stands beside me with a frightened look. I compress Dylan's chest repeatedly—one, two, three—before exhaling air into his mouth. I do this repeatedly until the paramedics arrive and force me to step back while they attempt to revive him.

My shoes create a permanent path in the carpet of the family room floor while we wait for the doctor to fill us in on Dylan's condition. Since I'm an employee of the hospital, no one would let me anywhere near him, and none of the nurses would tell me what was happening. The door opens, and the doctor finally walks in.

"We got a heartbeat," the doctor says.

"Oh, thank God," I say with a sigh of relief.

"He's still in critical condition, but we're doing everything we can to make sure he pulls through."

"Thank you, doctor," Mark replies.

"The paramedic found this on his bed. It seems he left a note for you two."

Mark grabs the note. "Thank you. We didn't even notice," he says.

"You did good, Amy. He might not have made it if you had not found him when you did."

"Thank you," I answer. I'm not familiar with this doctor. He usually doesn't work my shift, but word spreads quickly around the ER. It isn't surprising that he knows I'm a nurse here.

"I'll be back when you two can see him."

He leaves the room, and Mark opens the letter and reads it out loud.

> *Mom and Dad,*
>
>   *I'm sorry, but I can't live like this any longer. I'm tired of hiding who I really am, and I'd rather leave this earth than continue living a lie. I'm gay, and I've been attracted to boys ever since I can remember. I never told you because I knew you wouldn't understand. I met someone I really liked, but he's sick. He's HIV-positive. I'll answer the question you're both asking in your heads. Yes, I slept with him unprotected, so there is a possibility*

that I too can be HIV-positive. So, instead of shaming the family and dealing with a death sentence, I decided to end my own life.

Mom, please don't be too sad, and please forgive me, but this is best. I know you would have accepted me regardless and continued to love me, but I couldn't make your marriage to Dad miserable because of my choices. You know he wouldn't have accepted me. Thank you for always supporting me, and I love you. Dad, you were right. I was a faggot, and I'm nothing like you. But that's okay. I love you anyway. Please don't be sad. This is what is best. Please tell Ireland I'm sorry for not having her back and that I love her so much.

Dylan

EVA

So much has happened this past week. I found evidence that my husband may be cheating on me, and I found out he slept with someone else the night before our wedding. I haven't slept in days. I haven't eaten and can barely keep it together for the kids. I sat down with my mother, and she admitted that Shanice had confided in her about Sheldon and Crystal. Yet, neither of them thought it was necessary to tell me about it. Instead, both allowed me to walk down the aisle with a liar and a cheater. Words can't explain how painful the sting of this betrayal is. Then there's the other matter . . . the hotel key card I found in Sheldon's pocket. Is it possible that he and my sister's friend have continued to sleep together over the years? If so, does Shanice know about it? We don't have the best relationship, and she loves nothing more than to see me unhappy.

Sheldon wouldn't answer my question, but I could tell he was guilty. His unwillingness to explain . . . How quiet he got when I asked him to tell me the truth. All I wanted was for him to come clean. But he didn't. He chose to keep me wondering. He decided to keep me up at night, anxious about our next conversation. How cruel of him to play games with my mind. How selfish of him not to offer me the respect and decency I needed.

I look over at my children, napping on the bed. I couldn't stand to stay another night in the house with my mother and Shanice. So, the kids and I checked into a nice hotel until I was calm enough to go home and figure out things with Sheldon. But do I really want to? I'm not the one sneaking around. He is. He's committing adultery, and if he had a relationship with God, he would know what that means for his soul.

I take a seat on the king-size bed and crack open my Bible. I go straight to Ephesians 5:25: *Husbands, love your wives, as Christ loved the church and gave himself up for her.* I then skip over to Matthew 19:9: *And I say to you: whoever divorces his wife, except for sexual immorality, and marries another, commits adultery.*

This verse confirms what I already knew. I slam the book shut and think about the state of our marriage. I've been fighting for it. I've been trying to get him to see reason, but none of it is working. It's clear he doesn't want me or this marriage anymore, and it's becoming exhausting trying to change his mind. Maybe I should just give up and let it happen. I could always remarry. But would I? Would I have anything left to give after this? Probably not. Sheldon is all I know, and the thought of getting too close to another man scares me. I could end up living the rest of my life alone, and it's not fair. *He's* the one who's cheating on me. *He's* the one so unhappy he wants out of the marriage. And I'm suffering in the process. My eyes burn with tears, and I shake my head. I look up at the ceiling and speak to Him.

"What do you want from me? I've done everything you asked. I've prayed. I've honored my husband. I've served you. And *this* is what you do?"

The tears spill over, but I try not to cry loudly out of fear of waking the children. The Bible drops out of my lap and onto the floor while I cradle my face and sob. "Why didn't you save my marriage, God?" I release more tears. "Can't you see that I'm hurting? Can't you see that I need you?"

I cry for what seems like hours, allowing myself to release all the emotions I'm feeling. And when I'm finished, I'm no longer sad. I'm angry. I'm numb. I rise to my feet, slowly stretching my body. I pick up the Bible lying on the floor and take a good, hard look at it. This book has been my life's guide. It's what molded me into the woman that I am. With this book and God, I've lived a Christian life . . . and it's gotten me nowhere. Where was God when my husband was out here screwing some woman who wasn't his wife? Where was God when he was lying to my face? Where was He when Sheldon and I were barely speaking to each other?

"I prayed to you every night, and you haven't listened!" I scream out loud.

Maybe Sheldon's mom was right. Maybe I've been brainwashed into believing that God loves me. Maybe I am naïve for believing there's truth to what's in this book I'm holding. Not anymore. If this is what living a life of Christ looks like, then I don't want it anymore. I prayed for my husband. Hell, Sheldon and I even went to premarital counseling. I did all of *that* to receive *this*? I walk over to the nightstand and open the top drawer. As I suspected, there's already a Bible in there. I take one more look at mine before I place it on top and close the drawer. Then I walk away from it, symbolizing me walking away from the church and away from God. No more praying. No more Sunday services and Bible study. No more believing. From here on out, I'm seeing life for what it is. I won't sit around and wait for miracles to happen. Suddenly, my phone buzzes with a text message from one of the ushers at the church.

> **Her:** I'm not feeling well. Think you can cover for me at Bible study?

> **Me:** No. I'm not returning to church. Feel better.

SHELDON

My shift started fifteen minutes ago. I would've been on time if I hadn't been arguing with Eva over the phone in my car. I haven't seen my kids since she left, and I won't allow her to use them as a pawn. I was so angry that I told her that if she didn't meet me halfway with this coparenting thing, I'd take her to court and sue her for full custody. She finally relented and agreed to let me see them this weekend. But I don't want to wait until then. So, I asked her to bring them to the ER to see me today.

I rush inside, apologize to the chief physician for being late, and grab my first chart. I look around for Amy, but I don't see her. I know she has family issues, but I'll be glad when she's back at work. She gives me something to look forward to. I took a gamble by going to her house; her husband could have been home. But I didn't care. I had to show her that I won't be ignored. I know she loves me, even if she won't admit it. It's time for her to be happy, and I can make her happy.

I grab the chart for my patient and smile excitedly about seeing my kids before I meet Amy at the hotel. My name is paged over the intercom, and I go to the front desk. Eva rolls her eyes as I approach her and the kids, but I ignore her.

"Daddy," Kamryn squeals as she runs toward me.

I pick her up and spin her around, causing her to giggle. She holds onto me tightly, and it kills me that I haven't been able to see her in weeks.

"I missed you," she says.

"I missed you too, sweetheart."

"I don't understand why you insisted on me bringing the kids here instead of to the house," Eva says as she pops a pacifier in Sheldon Jr.'s mouth.

"I already told you I have plans after my shift," I reply.

"Plans that are more important than your children?" she asks.

"Of course not, but I'm the one who's been begging you to see them, so don't try to make me out to be a bad father because you finally agreed on a day that I made plans."

"Sheldon, I didn't want to bring them until we discussed things."

I place Kamryn down and look around me. Everyone seems to be working or occupied, but I know better. The ER is filled with women, nosy women. They're probably all listening while pretending to work.

"Come on, let's go to the conference room for some privacy."

Eva and Kamryn walk quietly in front of me down the hall. I can see her eyeballing every single nurse we pass, wondering if I'm having an affair with them. She hates my job. She hates that I work closely with these women. She's never trusted that my relationships with the ER nurses are strictly professional. It may be hard to believe, but I kept it professional until I met Amy. She's the only nurse I ever crossed the line with. So, while she thinks I've slept with every nurse here, she's wrong.

As we walk down the hall, Amy steps out of one of the exam rooms. I'm taken aback because I didn't expect to see her here today. She's not expected back at work until next week. She doesn't see me, and I'm hoping we can stroll past her without her noticing. Her back is turned to us as she dials a number on her cell phone.

This is good. Eva and I will keep walking while Amy makes a call. After Eva leaves with the kids, I'll check in with Amy to make sure she's okay. Then my plan fails.

RING!!!

My phone rings loudly, and Eva stops in her tracks. She turns around and looks at me. Then she looks at Amy. Amy's eyes widen when she realizes what's happening and ends the call.

"Dr. Sheldon. I've been trying to reach you," Amy says nervously.

"I thought you weren't coming back until next week," I respond.

Eva walks back toward us, and when she reaches us, she repositions her hold on Sheldon Jr. Her eyes bore into Amy's, and it's only a matter of time before she starts asking questions. I'm nervous and sweating bullets under my clothes. My hands are clammy, and I'm trying my hardest to be calm and act normal. I turn to Eva.

"Amy, this is my wife, Eva. That little guy she's holding is Sheldon Jr., and this . . ." I gently yank one of Kamryn's pigtails. "This is our daughter, Kamryn."

Amy smiles genuinely and extends her hand to Eva. "It's such a pleasure to meet you."

Eva looks down at her hand before she replies. "Can't you see I'm holding our son?" Her tone is curt, and she's going out of her way to be rude.

"You're right. My apologies," Amy responds. "Dr. Sheldon, I was calling to inform you I'll take some days off. My son was just admitted."

Eva takes a step closer. "Tell me something. Do you have access to all the doctors' personal numbers? Or just my husband's?"

"Eva!" I warn.

"It's okay," Amy replies. "I tried to reach him on his work number, but he didn't answer, and given the seriousness of my son's situation, it was important for me to reach him to let him know that I need an extended absence. I meant no harm."

"Umm-hmm," Eva replies.

"Eva, take the kids to the conference room, and I'll join you in a few minutes," I demand.

She chuckles. "Yeah, that's not gonna happen," she responds.

"Excuse us, Amy." I gently tug Eva's arm and pull her to the side. "What are you doing, Eva? This is my coworker and my place of work. You're acting crazy."

"Don't you dare call me crazy. I've never known you to give your personal number to any of your coworkers. You said only your boss has the number. What makes Amy so special, Sheldon?"

"You're overreacting. Her son is in the hospital, and she needed to get in touch with me; that's it," I argue.

"Are you her boss?" she asks.

"No."

"Then why is she calling you?"

Fuck! She got me, and my mind isn't clear enough to think of a quick comeback that makes sense. "Eva, I don't have to explain how things work around here, especially since you've decided to walk out on our marriage. Please, take my kids to the conference room, and I'll be there in a minute."

I'm not in the mood to argue, especially in front of Amy. I can't look weak in front of her. I can't let her see the dynamics of Eva's and my relationship, or she'll start thinking she can treat me the same way. I have to be firm and show that I'm the man of my household. Eva cocks her head to the side and narrows her eyes.

"Who the hell do you think you're talking to, Sheldon?"

I lean in and speak firmly. "Calm. The. Hell. Down."

Her eyes narrow, and she raises a brow. "I knew this was a bad idea." She grabs my daughter's hand. "Come on, Kamryn."

She walks away, and I jog after her, attempting to stop her, hoping she sees reason. "Eva, stop. Let's talk about this."

She walks faster away from me. "No. There's nothing to talk about. You can see your kids when you can make time for them."

I hear my daughter whining as they disappear around the corner and out of my vision, and it breaks my heart. This isn't what I had planned when I asked to see my children. Is this how things will be when we divorce? I can feel Amy approach me from behind.

"I'm sorry. I didn't mean to cause any trouble," she says.

I shake my head. "It's not your fault."

"Yes, it *is* my fault. Had I not called, this wouldn't have happened, and you would have been able to see your kids. I only wanted to tell you what had happened with Dylan."

I spin around to face her. "What happened? Is he okay?" I ask.

Tears stream down her face. "No. He hung himself, and, Sheldon . . . I don't know if he's going to make it."

"I'm so sorry, Amy."

I want to pull her in and squeeze her tight. I want to console her and tell her everything will be all right. But I can't. Too many people are around.

"Where's your husband?" I ask.

She points behind me. "He's in the room with Dylan. Room number three."

"Anything I can do to help?"

"Actually, there is."

"Anything."

"Dylan is gay."

It doesn't shock me. Not in today's society, where more people can live their truth. Surely, Amy doesn't need my help with this, as there's nothing that I can do about Dylan being gay. I remain silent, processing what she just said. She takes a deep breath and continues.

"One of his partners has tested positive for HIV," she continues.

"Has he been tested yet?" I ask.

"They've taken his blood and are running tests, but I'm sure that isn't one of them. I need you to test him and get me the results."

"Why not ask the attending?"

"I don't trust anyone but you, Sheldon. If word of this got out, it would destroy my family and reputation."

"Amy, what are you asking me to do?"

"I'm asking you to order an HIV test discreetly and get me the results. If they're positive, I need you to delete any record of it from the system."

"If they're positive, he'll need treatment. He could die," I reply.

"I'll make sure he gets it, but not here. Not at this hospital where everyone will know and judge me."

I'm quiet as her request weighs on me. I watch her curiously, wondering how she could ask me such a thing, knowing what's at risk.

"Amy, I could lose my license. I could be prosecuted."

"I know. But I need you, Sheldon. Please," she begs.

My mind plays tug-of-war between right and wrong. My moral compass uncontrollably spins as I contemplate her request. I worked my ass off to get where I am today. If I do this and get caught, everything I've worked for is gone. Every obstacle I've ever overcome would be for nothing. My instinct is telling me to say no. But my heart is telling me that the woman I'm in love with needs me. I slightly touch her hand and answer her.

"Okay. I'll do it."

CHAPTER TWELVE
IRELAND

I stare at the text message received from my mother and cross my fingers that my brother will be okay. I want to be there. I really do. But I can't stand to look at either of them right now. I'm still angry and don't want anything to do with my parents.

Austin squeezes my hand lightly. "We can go back if you want. I know you want to be there for your brother."

"No. Nothing is more important than this," I reply.

We're at the hospital for an emergency visit because I woke up this morning with some mild cramping and spotting. I'm scared shitless. I don't know much about being pregnant yet, but from what I've read, I understand that any form of bleeding is a cause for concern. My heart beats fast with anticipation of what the doctor will tell us. My leg shakes as I silently pray that my baby is healthy. Finally, my name is called, and Austin and I stand. We follow the nurse to a room, and after she takes my vitals, she informs us that the doctor will be in soon. I turn to Austin.

"I'm scared."

"Everything is going to be okay. I'm right here with you, baby."

The doctor walks in and greets us. "I understand you're having some cramping and bleeding?" he asks.

I nod. "Yes."

"Have you lifted anything heavy, fell, anything like that?"

I shake my head. "No."

"How's your stress level?" he asks.

Austin's eyes meet mine. My life has been a whirlwind. After we decided to run away together, we stopped at his house to pack a few things. His parents weren't home, but Camilla was. And for the first time since Austin and I met, I was honest with her. I told her how much I loved her brother and how much I loved her as my best friend. She understood. She apologized for being mad at me and hugged us both goodbye. After that, Austin withdrew some money from the bank, and we caught a flight. We landed in Baltimore, Maryland. Austin has a friend who owns a house where he's not living. He's chasing his dream as an actor in California and agreed to rent the house to us.

I respond to the doctor. "It's been a stressful few weeks."

The doctor smiles at us. "I see."

He calls in his nurse. He takes a peek at my cervix, and then they perform an ultrasound. After he's done, the nurse turns the lights back on, and he stands.

"Everything looks good." Austin and I both smile and exhale with relief. "But . . ." Our smiles quickly fade. "Your cervix is opening."

"Is that bad?" I ask.

"Yes. It can be," he replies. "You need to stay off your feet as much as possible, so I'm placing you on bed rest."

"For how long?" Austin asks.

"For the remainder of her pregnancy."

My mouth parts open, and I glance over at Austin, who takes my hand in his.

"So, I can't go out of the house?" I ask.

The doctor shakes his head. "I prefer that you don't. I want you in the bed unless you're taking a shower or using the bathroom."

Disappointment fills me, but Austin rubs my hand to calm me. "I'll make sure she rests, Doc. Can you tell me if there are any more restrictions?"

"No heavy lifting, baths, climbing stairs, prolonged walking or standing, and exercising. Those are the main things for now."

"What about sex?" Austin questions.

I blush with embarrassment at his question, and the doctor chuckles. "Sex is fine, but give it a few weeks. And be gentle. I'd discourage rough sex for now."

Jesus, kill me now. I'm mortified and ready to get out of here. "Thank you, Doctor," I add, hoping he gets the point that I'm willing to wrap things up.

"You're welcome. I'll have the nurse draft your discharge papers and get you on your way."

We return to the house, and Austin is in nurse mode. He has me in the bed with my feet propped on a pillow. The nightstand is crowded with water, books, snacks, and a remote control.

He plops down beside me. "Are you okay?"

"Yes," I reply.

"Well, it's a good thing we didn't go back to Georgia. It wouldn't have been safe in your condition."

"It wouldn't have been a good idea anyway. I'm sure my parents have the police looking for me. Had we showed up at the hospital, you'd be arrested."

"They can't arrest me if you agree to come with me," he responds.

"Yes, they can. Even though I ran away with you, I'm a minor. Trust me. My dad would do everything possible to make sure you're thrown under the jail."

"Maybe, but it would most likely get thrown out of court once the judge sees what an asshole of a father you have."

I laugh at his joke. "Thank you for taking care of me."

"Ireland, you're my life. I wouldn't have it any other way."

"I can't believe we are finally together. It's all I ever wanted."

"Me too. Are you hungry?" he asks.

"I'm starving."

"Okay. I'll order takeout."

"Wait. Shouldn't we be saving our money?" I ask.

"Saving our money for what?"

"Austin, you just took a large amount of money from the bank. You think it's a good idea to spend it all? Until you start working, we need to save whatever we have to get us by."

He gives me a weird look, then chuckles.

"What's so funny?" I ask.

"The fact that you think I would run away with you and be unable to provide for us."

"But you don't have a job," I respond.

"Ireland, I earn money. I don't have a traditional job."

"I'm confused."

"I own a small publishing company with some pretty talented authors. And I do professional editing on the side."

"But you withdrew $5,000. You said that was all that you had."

"In *that* account. I wanted us to use cash until this whole running away thing blows over. I don't need anyone trying to track locations where I'm swiping my card. But I have money in other accounts."

"But Camilla—"

"Doesn't know jack shit." He laughs. "I'm sure my sister filled your head with crazy stuff."

On the one hand, I'm thrilled to know that he's not flat broke. It was part of what was stressing me out. But on the other hand, I'm pissed that he never shared this with me.

"Why didn't I know about this?" I ask.

He waves me off. "It's nothing, really. I don't share much information regarding my writing because folks don't understand it. They think I'm chasing an unreachable dream."

"But I'm not *folks*."

"I know. And I'm sorry. It's enough income for us to live off until I write my bestseller. Then I can give you the life you deserve."

Dread sets in at the thought of him working so hard alone. "I feel horrible that I can't work. As your partner, I should be able to contribute."

He shakes his head. "As long as you're with me, you don't have to work unless you want to. You can stay at home with the kids."

"Kids?" I ask.

"Yeah. I want at least two more."

I laugh. "One step at a time, Romeo."

He leans in and kisses me on the lips. After pulling away, he stands. "I'll go order that takeout."

I grab his hand and stop him. "All this time, I thought you were flat broke."

He smiles at me. "And you loved me anyway."

"Yes. Always and forever."

"Rest, baby. You have nothing to worry about. I got us."

He leaves the room, and I place my hand over my belly and smile. This is happening. I'm creating a life with the man of my dreams. I'll rest comfortably through this pregnancy. And when I have this baby, I'll be a stay-at-home mom for the first year if we can still afford it. I'll finish an online GED program, and after my baby turns a year old, I'll enroll in college and obtain a business degree. I've always been interested in the business world. And I got straight A's in my college prep business classes. Besides, Austin will need someone to manage his career and money once he becomes famous. I want to be that for him. I wish I could pick up the phone and call my brother. I'd love to share this news with him, but I can't because I'm quickly reminded that he's in the hospital. I shake away the thought of him lying helpless in a hospital bed. The doctor says I need to stay as stress-free as possible.

My thoughts shift back to Austin and our life together. This is only the beginning of that life. We're going to be successful spouses and parents. I can feel it. Life isn't easy, and I know we'll have our fair share of highs and lows. But as long as we have each other, I know there isn't anything we can't do together.

DYLAN

The familiar scent of a hospital causes my eyes to flutter open. I look around me, and my suspicions are confirmed. I'm in a hospital room because my suicide attempt failed. Part of me is relieved. I mean, who *really* wants to die? But the other part of me is disappointed. Me dying would have been much better than the wrath I'll receive from my father. A nurse I've seen before walks in and smiles at me. Great. I'm at the hospital my mother works in.

"Dylan, you gave us quite a scare. Do you remember what happened?"

I nod. "Are my parents here?" I ask.

"Yes. They're in the cafeteria getting coffee. Neither of them slept a wink since you've been here."

I feel guilty about the pain my mother is feeling. She's probably worried sick and doing everything she can to make sure I'm being properly treated. But Dad is different. Dad hasn't slept a wink because he's probably thinking of all the ways he can kill me without getting caught. He won't care about how I'm feeling. He won't care about the pain I feel every day, knowing that I'm living a lie. It doesn't matter to him that the weight is too much to bear at times.

"We got your vitals stable, and you're gonna be just fine," the nurse continues.

The door opens, and my parents walk in, each carrying a cup of coffee. Mom rushes toward me.

"Dylan!" She places the coffee cup on the tray beside me and leans in to hug me. "Your father and I were so worried."

I glance over at my father, and I know she's lying. He doesn't look worried at all. He looks disgusted. Angry. His eyes bore into mine for two seconds before he drags them away. It's like he can't even face me right now. The nurse rechecks my blood pressure before leaving the room. When she's out of sight, my father steps toward the bed.

"So, you like men, huh?" he asks.

"Mark, please. Let's not do this right now," my mother pleads.

The time has come. This is it. This is where I finally live my truth and be honest with the people around me. I'm tired of lying. I'm tired of trying to make my father love and accept me as I am. I. Am. Gay. It's who I am. It's who I'll always be.

"Yes." My answer is firm. Strong and without hesitation.

"Mark, please," Mom pleads.

My father looks over at her. "This is between father and son, Amy."

"But he's just waking up and doesn't need to be stressed."

"Stop defending him!" my father yells. "He isn't normal. None of this is fucking normal."

I cock my head to the side as my blood boils with anger. I'm tired of this. I'm tired of him. All the years of my father treating me differently rise to the surface. All the years of hearing his discrimination and offensive rants come full circle. I sit higher in my bed.

"Just because I'm not like you doesn't mean I'm not normal."

He looks at me with surprise as if he can't believe I just said what I did.

"This has nothing to do with being like me, Dylan. This has *everything* to do with the fact that you're seventeen and should be upside down in pussy at this age. But instead, you choose to live your life as a goddamn punk."

"Mark, stop," my mother says firmly.

"I said stay out of this, Amy."

I'd punch him if I didn't feel so weak right now. Each blow would be for my mother. For Ireland. For myself. But instead, I keep firing back. Today, he will learn I'm done allowing him to talk to me however he pleases. I deserve the same respect he demands.

"You're the sissy, Dad. You're scared of anyone who doesn't look or act like we do. At least I don't judge people."

He takes two strides until he's at my bedside. He points a finger in my face. "You better watch your mouth, boy."

The room grows quiet, and my mother watches on with fear. But I won't back down. "Dad, I'm tired of pretending. For once, I want to be happy."

"You think living as a faggot in America will make you happy? You better wake the hell up, Dylan. You think *I'm* bad. Wait until you're publicly holding hands with another man, and you'll see just how bad the world is. You were better off dead than choosing to be a punk, especially a punk that could be HIV-positive."

My mother gasps. Her hand covers her mouth, then rises and slaps my father so hard across the cheek that it echoes in the room. I shift in the bed, watching my father grab his face. She now points *her* finger at him.

"You will *not* speak to my son that way. It's bad enough I let you run our daughter away. I'm not losing another child, Mark."

My father's face is red, and his eyes are wide with shock at the fact that my mother hit him.

"Excuse me," a voice speaks from the doorway.

We all turn to face the woman. She's tall and slender with gray hair.

"I'm Dr. Tess. I'll be in charge of Dylan's psychiatric treatment."

She enters the room, and we all attempt to get our shit together and act normally, but it's too late. I can already tell she's witnessed enough by the concern in her eyes. Finally, my mother extends her hand. "I'm Mrs. Carson, Dylan's mother."

"It's nice to meet you, Mrs. Carson, and you must be Mr. Carson?" she asks my father.

My father doesn't respond. Instead, he looks at my mother, then back at me.

"I was just leaving."

What just happened was one of the most profound moments of my life. Standing up to my father was long overdue, and I felt a sense of relief at being able to speak my truth. A rush of emotions swept through me, and I was on a high as I gave him a piece of my mind. Unfortunately, that high quickly lowered when the counselor entered my room. Reality sets in that my actions may have labeled me mentally unstable. I nervously shift as Dr. Tess writes something in her notebook. When she's done, she looks up at me.

"How are you feeling, Dylan?"

I don't answer right away because it could be a trick question. If I answer incorrectly, I could be sent to a mental institution. "Um, okay, I guess."

She smiles. "Dylan, I want you to know that it's okay to be completely honest when you speak to me."

"Okay." Never. I will *never* be completely honest because no one gets me.

"What you say to me is strictly confidential."

This piques my interest. "So, no matter what I tell you, you can never tell anyone else?"

"Right. Unless you tell me you will harm yourself or others."

"Okay."

"I'm here to help you."

I nod this time. I mean, she seems genuine. She looks like she wants to help me. But how do I know if I can really trust her? "I'm going to ask you that question again. How are you feeling right now?"

"Anxious. Sad most times."

The words blurt out without a thought. Maybe it's because no one ever asks me how I'm doing. Or maybe it's because I'm tired of wearing a mask.

"Were you feeling this way before or after the incident?"

She's careful with her words, but I want her to know it's okay to say it. "You mean when I tried to kill myself?"

"Yes."

"Both."

"Do you want to tell me why?" she asks.

This is where it gets tricky. I feel like it's too much to unpack, especially since I just met her. Where do I even begin? I feel like

I've lived in a state of anxiety most of my life, so I wouldn't even know where to start.

"I honestly don't know. I've always been anxious. I've always had this unsettling feeling about myself."

"When did you first realize you were attracted to the same sex?"

I think about her question and conclude that I've always liked boys. "For as long as I can remember."

"And you've kept this a secret until recently?"

"Yes. And after seeing what you just saw, I'm sure you can see why."

She writes something else in her book, and I cross my legs, wondering what she's writing. She places her pen down and folds her hands when she's done.

"Dylan, your father was furious. Is he always that way?"

Uh-oh. Now I see what's going on. Now I see the *real* reason I'm here. I'm a minor. And my parents' actions back there were borderline abusive. Fuck! Why didn't I catch on before? One word about how horrible of a man my father is, and Child Protective Services will investigate us.

"No. We were all just emotional, considering the circumstances."

"Hmmm." She writes something else down, and I rise from the bed.

"I don't want to talk anymore."

"Dylan, please have a seat."

I shake my head. "No. I don't want to talk anymore. I see what you're doing."

"Dylan, I'm only trying to help you."

"You don't want to help me. You want information so that you can call social services. My mom is a nurse. I know how this works."

Confusion crosses her face, making me angrier that she's pretending to care. "Dylan—"

"No. Let me out of here!"

I become frantic. I suddenly feel claustrophobic and need fresh air. I run to the door, but it's locked. I grab the knob and try to open it while yelling at Dr. Tess. "Let me out of here."

She grabs her phone and dials a number. By the time she places the phone down, the door behind her opens, and two security guards enter with another doctor. He's holding a needle. I become aggressive at that point. I don't know what's in the needle he's holding, and I don't want to know.

"No. Stop. Please!" I yell. "Somebody help me!"

They all crowd around me, trying their best to calm me down. But I don't see them as allies. I see them as enemies. I need my parents.

"Mom!" I cry out. But she doesn't answer me. One of the security guards manages to pin me down, and the doctor pulls the cap off the needle. I'm restrained and hysterical. "Don't. Please."

"Dylan. This is just something that will help calm you down," the doctor says.

His eyes meet mine just as he inserts the needle into my arm. It hits me instantly, causing me to lose all strength and my body to go limp. I release my grip on the security guard and slump to the floor, but not before I see my mother rush in.

CHAPTER THIRTEEN
MARK

I had to leave quickly. I almost slapped Amy back, which is not something I want to do. Never in a million years would I think about hitting my wife. But my anger got the best of me. How dare she defend Dylan, let alone in front of me? We agreed when the kids were born that we would be a unit. We wouldn't let them come between us. And she broke that agreement when she chose Dylan's side over mine. I rub my hand at the base of my neck to ease some tension. How did this happen? How did my son end up this way? I knew early on that something was off with him. He'd rather play with dolls than trucks for Christmas. He'd rather play dress up than football. As he got older, he didn't seem interested in girls. I wanted to accept it. He's my son, and I love him. But I just couldn't. How would I explain it to my father and my brothers? When they questioned his behavior over the years, I brushed it off and defended him. And *this* is how he chooses to repay me?

I won't stand for this. I won't have a faggot living under my roof, even if it is my son. He can choose to leave, just like Ireland did. Five minutes in the world as a gay man will be enough to teach him a lesson. I'm willing to bet it'll make him run back home as a straight one.

I leave the hospital. I need some fresh air and time to think. I decide to drive to my parents' house. With everything going on, I haven't had time to speak to my dad since the funeral. I need to let him know what's going on with his grandson. He won't be happy about it, but he'll know exactly what to do. I've also been trying to find the right time to tell him about the letter Mom left for me. And now is as good of a time as any.

I arrive at my father's house, and grief sets in immediately, knowing my mother won't be here. I miss her, and the fact that she lied to me all these years doesn't change that. My father sits on the porch, smoking a cigar. He yells out to me as I approach the porch.

"What are you doing here? Did you find Ireland?" he asks.

"No."

"Oh, well, I'm sure she'll turn up soon. Have a seat. Take a cigar."

He pulls one out of his shirt pocket and hands it to me. I take it from him, grab the single-blade guillotine on the table next to me, and cut it. I place that down, grab the lighter, and light it. I relax as I inhale the smoke. I put the lighter down and dread the words I'm about to say.

"Dad, it's Dylan."

He takes a few puffs before answering me. "What's wrong with Dylan?"

This isn't as easy as I thought it would be. A small piece of me wants to back down and tell him never mind. But it's too late. I've already piqued his curiosity.

"He's in the hospital."

"What happened?" he asks with concern.

"A suicide attempt."

He yanks the cigar out of his mouth. "Why in the hell would Dylan try to kill himself?"

I hesitate before answering. "He's gay."

My father stands to his feet slowly. He watches me before he dips the end of the lit cigar in a glass of water.

"Did I just hear you say that my grandson is queer?"

"There's more," I announce with my head down.

"Don't tell me he has AIDS too."

I don't know how he suspected it, but he does. So I don't answer him. He shakes his head in disgust.

"Not AIDS. But he may be HIV-positive."

"AIDS. HIV. It's all the same, and all the faggots have it. How the fuck could you let this happen, Mark?"

"It isn't my fault. I had no idea he was gay."

"That's bullshit. How could you not see it? The rest of us saw it a mile away."

I put my cigar out as well and rise to my feet. "I guess I didn't wanna see it. He's my only son."

My dad shoves his hands into his pants pockets. "We can't have this in the family."

"How am I supposed to fix this?" I ask.

For the first time in my life, I feel defeated. I feel confused, and it doesn't sit well with me that I don't have a handle on the situation. My wife and kids are an extension of myself. They're supposed to represent me and the family name with dignity, class, and grace. But instead, I have a wife who doesn't support my parenting style, a daughter who's run away, and a son who likes sucking dick.

"There's only one way to handle this," he answers.

"How?"

"Give him a choice to change. If he doesn't, you have to get rid of him."

Did I hear him correctly? Did my father just suggest that I *get rid* of my son? No, he couldn't have. I must have misunderstood him.

"Get rid of him?" I repeat.

"I didn't stutter, boy," he answers.

"Get rid of him. How?"

"Send him away. Boarding school. A mental institution. Anywhere, as long as it's far from here."

"He's my son."

"And he's gay. Is *that* how you want the Carson legacy to carry on?"

"No."

"Then you know what you need to do."

"That won't fix him, Dad. All that will do is make him hate his mother and me. I've already got one child gone. I can't have another. That may be the straw that breaks the camel's back, and Amy will leave me."

"You're weak, Mark. And I don't know why because I didn't raise you that way."

"I can handle this. I can find a way to fix Dylan while he's under my roof."

"You're being naïve."

"And you're sick for suggesting that I send him away. If Mom were alive, she'd be devastated to hear you say something like that."

"If your mother were alive, she would agree with me. And she would hate this just as much as I do."

"Mom wasn't like you. She didn't have a hateful bone in her body."

"She was *exactly* like me, although she didn't show it as much as I did."

He's lying. And it's making me angrier by the second. My mother isn't here to defend herself.

"I'm not listening to you. I'm leaving."

"I'm disappointed in you, Mark. I can't even call you my son if you allow this to go on."

I stop in my tracks. It was a mistake coming here. It was a mistake to think that maybe, just for once, my father could help me find a solution without criticizing me and my family. He's done nothing to help. All he's done is attack my character, put me down, and make me feel incompetent. My fists are balled at my sides. I look him square in the eye.

"You don't have to call me your son because you're not my real father anyway."

This is not how I imagined myself telling him about the letter that Mom left for me. It's a delicate situation that requires delicate handling. But at this moment right now, standing here knowing my father is doing his best to hurt me on purpose makes me want to return the favor. I want to hurt him like he's hurting me. I want to teach him a lesson. I stare at him, expecting confusion. Expecting surprise. But instead, he smiles. It's a sinister smile.

"So, you know?" he asks.

I have no idea what's happening right now or why my father seems happy about what I've just told him.

"Yes."

"I knew from the moment you were born. But by then, I was already in love with Emma."

This can't be real. So, not only did my mother lie to me, but my father did too. Suddenly, my mind flashes back to the picture of my biological father. There's no way in hell my father would have accepted me had he known.

"Did you also know—"

He interrupts me. "That you're part nigger?"

His words sting me like a colony of bees.

"Yeah, I did."

"But how could you raise me knowing this?" I ask.

"I wasn't going to at first. But then I thought about it. What could be better than raising a Black man to hate his own people? Talk about sweet revenge."

"So, everything you taught me was a lie? My entire upbringing was all about you and your vendetta?"

"Yes. I fell in love with Emma when she was pregnant. At the time, she said the father had abandoned her, but she failed to say he was Black. It only took me a few seconds after you were born to figure it out."

"And she told you the truth?"

"She had no other choice. Your skin color showed the truth, boy. There was no way she could hide it."

"So . . . Mom doesn't have Italian roots? That was a lie?"

"No, none that I'm aware of. We needed to tell you something to justify why you're darker than the rest of us."

I have no words right now. No word in the dictionary can describe how I'm feeling. I can't make sense of any of this. My father continues speaking.

"I felt betrayed when you were born. Emma knew how I felt about the Blacks, yet she hid the truth about who your father was. But I insisted on knowing who he was."

"And she told you?"

"No. But I found a picture of him she thought she had hidden away, with his name on the back. I was so angry that me and the fellas went looking for him. I couldn't stand the thought of his hands ever being on my Emma."

"Did you find him?"

"Yes. And we killed him."

"You . . . You were the person who murdered him?" I ask.

"Yes," he answers proudly. "I killed him. Then I raised his Black son to live as a white man and hate his own race."

Emotions ambush me. I feel humiliated. I feel used. "All these years, all this hate I've carried for anyone who doesn't look like me . . ."

He laughs loudly. "Genius, wasn't it?"

CHAPTER FOURTEEN
AMY

I can't take it anymore. I feel like I'm dying inside and need something to calm me down. Viki went on some expedition in the Arctic, and I need something more potent than the pills she provides. She's the only person I know who can tell me where to get something. I'm on the wrong side of the tracks, cruising the streets, hoping to get what I need. I see a group of men standing in front of a gas station, so I pull over. I'm nervous, but I need this. I get out of my car, and as I suspect, they all stop talking and stare at me. One of them speaks.

"You're on the wrong side of town, ain't you, sweetheart?"

"I—" I stop for a second to gather my thoughts because how do I ask for drugs from a stranger? "I'm meeting someone."

"Oh yeah?" he asks.

"Yeah. He has something for me."

I hope that this gives them a hint and keeps me safe. Then they won't try to rob me if they think I'm meeting someone. They continue to talk and laugh, and I stand there quietly. I look around as if I'm waiting for someone. Fifteen minutes pass. Then one of the men approaches me.

"Doesn't look like your boyfriend is showing up."

"I'm not waiting on a boyfriend," I reply.

"Then who are you waiting for?"

"A friend. He has something for me . . . if you know what I mean."

I try to give him the eye, but I make a weird face, and then he laughs.

"Yeah, I know what you mean. But how do I know you're not a cop?"

I pull my hospital badge out of my pocket. "I'm not. I'm a nurse."

He nods. "All right, what are you looking for?"

"Something to calm my nerves yet keep me normal. Nothing that has me so wasted people notice."

"How much you got?" he asks.

"Whatever it costs."

He looks around before he slides his hands into his pants pocket. He pulls out a small bag with a white powder—most likely cocaine. I've never used coke, but of course, I know its effects. It can make a person energetic or tired. Talkative or quiet. And the best part about it is that the effects can disappear anywhere from a few minutes after snorting it to a few hours. I could get high for short periods.

"Just give me a little bit for now," I demand.

"Okay. That little bit is one hundred dollars."

I take two fifty-dollar bills from my purse and hand them to him. He pushes them into his pocket and smiles.

"Come back and see me if you need any more. I'm usually here."

He walks away, and I call after him. "Hey, what's your name?"

He smirks. "They call me Smoke."

If I didn't have to be back at the hospital, I would have snorted a line of coke to calm my nerves right away. But I can't attend my meeting with the chief high. Especially considering I don't know how it will make me react yet. I have it hidden in one of the pockets of my purse until I'm able to try it. And I hope that it takes away this constant dance of emotions. I'm sad one minute and angry the next. Sometimes, I feel helpless, and other times, I feel overwhelmed. Seeing Dylan hanging in that room made me so grief-stricken that I couldn't bear it. It made me want to bottle all my emotions and place a lid on it so tightly that it can never be opened. The pain is indescribable. The moment I thought he was dead, something snapped in me. I changed. I felt like my life was on autopilot, and I was just going through the motions. I don't get to be vulnerable and sad. Mothers never do. No matter what happens, we have to keep it together for the sake of our family. Someone has to be the strong one, and it's almost always us. I'm hurting right now. I'm hanging on by a thread. But I can't let Mark or Dylan know this. This is the reason for the drugs.

Drugs numb your pain. They make you forget all about your problems and bring you a little bit of happiness. When I'm high, I don't feel sad. I don't feel helpless. I feel excited. I feel energetic. I feel unstoppable, like I can take on the world. And, boy, is it a good feeling. I know that drugs can be dangerous. I treat addicts daily. But this is different. I'm not an addict. I'm not homeless in the streets, begging to get high all day. I use drugs now and then when I need to calm my nerves. I still go to work and take care of my family. One might say that I'm in denial. Hell, I've said this to patients myself. But I've been doing this long enough to recognize a drug addict, and I don't fit the description. I'm just taking something to help me through a tough time. As soon as everything is back to normal, I'll stop. Maybe switch to wine or something to take the edge off. Suddenly, a text comes through. It's Viki.

Her: Did you find what you needed?

Me: Yes.

Her: Be careful, Sis. I don't like this at all, and once I'm back, you and I will have a long talk about why you feel you need this.

She won't understand. She'll never understand. Because while she's out living her carefree life, I'm stuck in a boring, loveless marriage.

As I sit in the conference room waiting for the chief of medicine to arrive, I debate if I should go to the bathroom and use the cocaine now. I sure could use something before I dive into this conversation with her.

Images of Dylan flood my brain. It was torture watching the doctors struggle to get him stabilized. I demanded to speak to the chief of medicine about how they handled things. My son isn't crazy and doesn't deserve to be treated as such. They were too rough with him. They treated him like an animal, and I won't allow it.

I take a second to send Sheldon a text message. We have plans to meet at the hotel, but I need to handle this first. The door swings open, and I stand.

"Amy, hi."

"Hi, Doctor Ni."

She gestures for me to take a seat, and I do. "I hear you are concerned about how your son was treated."

"Yes. Whatever the therapist said upset him, and instead of allowing him to speak his mind, she probed further. He became upset, and they held him down and drugged him."

"I was told that your son was asked to take a seat several times and refused," she responds.

"It was his right to leave."

"Amy, you've worked at this hospital long enough to know that our procedures differ with mental health patients."

I instantly become angry and no longer care that I'm speaking to the chief of medicine.

"My son is not a mental health patient," I say through gritted teeth.

"Amy, Dylan experienced a mental breakdown. Everything he's bottled up inside came to the surface, and his mind couldn't handle it."

"Yes. Well, he's been having a tough time lately. Most kids do at this age."

She glances down at his chart. "He was admitted due to a suicide attempt. Dylan's mental health declined so low that he wanted to take his own life to escape how he felt. So that's something to be concerned about."

"No. I mean, yes, I understand. But he doesn't have mental health issues. He tried to commit suicide because—"

I stop speaking, and the many reasons Dylan wanted to kill himself enter my brain. They don't understand. None of them do. Dylan didn't try to kill himself because he has a mental disorder like depression or is bipolar. He tried to kill himself because he was tired of living a lie. He tried to kill himself because he was tired of his father looking at him with disgust. He wanted a way out—a way to be free. My eyes swell with tears as I think about the weight he must have been carrying for him to go as far as trying to harm himself. Is it possible he was depressed? Most people who suffer from depression don't show it. Shit! I missed the signs. They were all there, and I should have known better.

"Amy."

Her voice interrupts my thoughts. "Yes. I'm sorry."

She smiles at me with genuine concern. "Listen, I'm sure this is hard for you and your family. But I want you to know that no one in this hospital would ever put your son in harm's way. We are all here to help him."

"You're right, Doctor Ni. Dylan was suffering, and I didn't see it."

"It's not your fault. But he needs help."

I wipe a tear away. "I agree."

"Support him through this. Let us help him, knowing he's in good hands."

I nod because she's right. Part of the reason I work for this hospital is that they are superb at treating patients. They treat every patient like family and have skilled and caring staff. But when I saw my son being restrained and a needle shoved in his arm, none of that crossed my mind. She hands me a tissue.

"We're not sending Dylan to the psych ward."

"Oh, thank God," I reply.

"We know that his situation is more circumstantial than anything relating to a chemical imbalance."

"So, what happens now?" I ask.

"Now, we keep him for observation. We would like for him to open up more to the therapist. Maybe you can help us get through to him."

"Yes. Whatever you guys need."

"Good. Once she's done an evaluation, we'll set him up for outpatient treatment before releasing him in your care."

Relief travels through my body. "Okay."

I'm about to stand when she continues speaking. "What about you, Amy? Are *you* okay?"

"Yeah. Why wouldn't I be?" I ask.

"You just lost your mother-in-law. Your son tried to commit suicide, and the therapist said she walked in on a pretty nasty argument between you and your husband."

I shake my head. "I'm fine. Every family has its issues."

She nods. "As you know, we care about our employees. So, if you need to use our therapy resources, let me know. And don't hesitate to take some extra time off."

"Thank you."

I stand, and she does the same. "Don't worry about Dylan. We'll take great care of him."

"Thank you. I'll be back to see him later."

—⁓—

I feel much better after speaking to Doctor Ni, but I'm still stressed about Ireland. I have no idea where she is, and she's still not answering my calls. I texted her, letting her know her brother had been admitted to the hospital, but she never responded. I thought this would bring her home. She and Dylan are close. I know she's worried about him. Why did I let her run away? Why didn't I try to stop her? I should never have allowed Mark and his family to overreact and treat her like they do. She did nothing wrong. She's the typical teenage girl who's in love with her boyfriend. And if Mark weren't such an asshole, maybe she wouldn't have hidden the fact that she had a boyfriend from us. This is all his fault. He's a jerk. And because of him, my daughter is gone, and Dylan almost took his life.

Watching him kick Dylan when he was down was the last straw. I refuse to put up with it any longer. I don't know what made him act so mean and cruel to our son when he's lying in a hospital bed from a suicide attempt, but you know what? I don't care. The bullying has to stop. Dylan is my son, gay or not gay. And I know this must be very hard on Mark, but that doesn't mean our son deserves to die. The fact that he could say something so evil has me questioning everything I ever thought I knew about him. I've got a lot of thinking to do and some decisions to make. If it comes down to my children and Mark . . . Well, let's just say that *he* can be the one to leave. He better get his shit together quickly before I have his bags packed and placed on his father's porch.

———

I arrive at the hotel, park the car, and breathe deeply. This is just what I need right now—a distraction. I need to blow off some steam, and hopefully, Sheldon can deliver. I don't want to discuss our future, marriages, or kids. Instead, I want to do one thing . . . Fuck! I want a toe-curling orgasm that will make me scream at the top of my lungs. I knock on the hotel door a few times before Sheldon answers.

"It's about time you answered," I say as I walk inside.

"I was in the shower," he responds.

He's wearing only a towel, and his skin is still slightly moist with tiny water beads. He smiles at the fact that I'm lusting over him. It's evident, as I make no point in hiding it. I'm sure he sees how hard my nipples are through my shirt. I know he can see how my breathing changed when I walked inside the hotel room. My eyes sweep him from head to toe. I watch him like prey, eager for the moment his hands are all over me.

"Looks like I arrived right on time," I reply.

I approach him, but he stops me. "I did what you asked."

"I don't wanna talk about that, at least not right now anyway."

I attempt to place my hand on his chest, but he stops me. "Wait, Amy. We need to talk."

I drop my hand, and my entire body deflates as I sit at the edge of the bed.

"I didn't come here to talk, Sheldon."

"But we need to."

"Okay, about what?" I ask.

He sits right beside me. "About us," he answers.

I should've seen it coming. He's been begging me to talk for a while now.

"Okay."

"I did what you asked about Dylan. He's HIV-negative, but I suggest he continue getting tested over the next six months."

"Oh, thank God," I say with a huge sigh of relief.

"Had he tested positive, I would have done what you asked and switched the results."

"Sheldon, I—"

"No, let me finish," he interrupts. "I was willing to put my career at risk for you, and I'm not even sure where this is going."

"I'm sorry. I didn't mean to drag you into my family mess, but I couldn't ask anyone else. You are the only one I trust."

"That's the thing. I didn't mind helping you. I want to be there for you. I want to support you. But I can't if you won't let me. Do you *really* not see a future with me?"

This is not how I imagined this evening to be. I'm supposed to be on my back right now with Sheldon between my legs. But instead, we're wasting time discussing a future we'll never have.

"Sheldon . . ." I pause for a minute before continuing to speak. "Of course, I would love to be with you, but I can't put my own needs above my family's. That would be selfish of me."

"Do you love me, Amy?"

"I care for you."

He's about to respond, but suddenly, someone knocks at the door.

"I ordered room service. I'm sure you haven't eaten," he says as he rises.

"You gonna answer the door like that?" I ask.

"Yeah," he answers.

"In a towel? No. You stay put, and I'll get the door."

I walk to the door with a sigh of disappointment. I am hungry, but not for food. I'm hungry for him, but it doesn't look like I'll be getting what I came for now. I open the door . . . and I'm hit with a force so strong I can hear a bone crack. I stumble back, wipe the blood flowing out of my nose, and come face-to-face with the person who punched me—Sheldon's wife.

SHELDON

I blink to make sure I'm seeing this correctly, and as the focus sets in, it confirms that I am. How the fuck did Eva know I was here? I'm immediately between the two of them.

"*This* is what you've been doing when you say you're working late?" she yells.

"Eva, stop," I say as I prevent her from jumping on Amy again.

Amy holds her nose, which is probably broken, and Eva tries her hardest to bypass me and get to her.

"I catch you having an affair, and you tell *me* to stop?"

"That's not what was happening," I explain.

"Sheldon, you're wearing a towel. Do you honestly think I'm *that* stupid?" she asks.

I'm holding onto Eva, and my grip is tight. She's out of control right now, and I need to calm her down to get Amy out of here.

"Eva, honey, let's talk about this."

"*Now* you want to talk?" she asks.

"Yes, I can explain everything."

She stops moving. She looks at me with red, swollen eyes and nods.

"Okay then. Talk, and you better tell me everything. I want the truth, Sheldon," she demands.

"I will. I promise." I continue to hold her tightly as I turn to face Amy. "I need to talk to my wife," I tell her.

She nods with understanding. She grabs a nearby towel to hold against her nose and heads for the door. She stops just as she opens it and removes the towel from her bloodstained face.

"I'm sorry," she says before walking out.

The door closes, but I give it about five minutes before I let go of Eva. I don't trust that she won't run after Amy. "Eva, what are you doing here?" I ask.

"I knew something was off between you two. So I dropped the kids off, returned to the hospital, and waited. When I saw her leave, I followed her. Not that any of that matters. How I found you shouldn't be your concern right now."

"Yes. You're right."

I grab my boxers and slide them on. Then I step into the pair of jeans lying nearby.

"I knew you were seeing someone."

"I—" I don't know how to answer her. I've been caught red-handed and can do little to convince her otherwise. A tear drops from her face, and it kills me. She looks distraught, and I feel like shit that I'm the cause of her tears. She wipes them away.

"Tell me the truth, Sheldon. Did you sleep with Crystal the night before our wedding?"

I nod. "Yes. She came to my room. One thing led to another, and . . . I was wasted, Eva."

By now, the tears are flowing heavily. Things haven't been good with Eva lately, but that doesn't mean I want to hurt her. The pain in her eyes almost causes me to cry along with her. She sniffles before replying.

"Is that supposed to be an excuse?"

"No. I don't have an excuse. I was wrong, Eva. Dead wrong. But it happened before we were married, and I felt horrible about it. Every time she came around with Shanice, I felt guilty."

"I can't believe you would do something like that. I thought you loved me."

"I do love you."

It's true. I do love my wife. Just not the way that I used to.

"Did you know there was a chance that her son could be yours?" she asks.

"No. I think I used protection. I just . . . I was so drunk I don't remember for sure."

"Jesus, Sheldon."

"Eva, let's sit down and talk, okay?"

She sits on the bed but then immediately shoots to her feet. She looks down at the messy bed.

"Did you two—"

"No. I told you that's not what we were doing."

She sits back down. "How long have you been seeing her?"

"About seven months."

"Do you love her?" she asks.

I think carefully before I answer her question. She's hurting, and I don't want to hurt her more. But I also want to be honest. I'm no longer happy in this marriage, and I can tell that she isn't either. So, we need to agree if we will split and amicably coparent. The only way to do that is to be completely honest with her.

"Yes. I love her."

She recoils at my answer. It's as if my response has pulled the very life out of her body. "Do you want to leave me and be with her?"

"Eva, you left me."

"No. I was giving us some space, Sheldon. I thought it would make you come to your senses."

"By taking my kids and disappearing for weeks?"

"I was gonna come back, but I had to show you I'm strong. I had to show you that I don't need you."

"That's the problem, Eva. You find the need to display your independence every other second. I'm your husband. Did it ever occur to you that I want you to need *me* occasionally?" She's quiet as I continue to talk. "You don't allow yourself to be vulnerable with me. Everything turns into a fight with you, and you complain about every little thing."

"I've been a good wife to you. I've never cheated on you."

"Fidelity is important. But there's so much more to being a wife than being faithful. When was the last time we had sex?"

"I tried."

"Yeah, after you 'scheduled' it. You don't enjoy it when I make love to you. You make it seem like it's dirty or something. We used to have chemistry. That all changed when you started going to church."

"My body is a temple of God. I don't have to enjoy it. Sex is for making babies. It's for you to enjoy, not me."

I place my hand over the top of hers. It's the most genuine display of affection we've had in months.

"Yes, Eva, you do. Because the more you enjoy it, the more I enjoy it. I want to know that I'm pleasing my wife. When you lie there motionless, I feel like I'm hurting you."

"So, is that why you're having an affair?" she asks.

"That's why it started, but then it grew into something more."

Her eyes flinch with pain. "You're in love with her."

"I don't know. But I do love her."

"What about us? What about our children?"

"I love all of you too."

We both grow quiet at our revelations. It's the most we've talked in months. Shit, it's probably the most we've talked in years. Had we done this sooner, maybe things would be different between us. Now, we're too far gone to turn back.

"Why didn't you come to me instead of having an affair? We could have worked this out," she asks.

"You're stubborn, Eva. You wouldn't have listened. You would have gotten offended, and it would have turned into an unnecessary argument."

"So, what do we do now?"

"We're not happy. And now that you know that I've been unfaithful, the trust is gone. There's also the betrayal of my sleeping with Crystal. Eva, those things are hard to bounce back from. Do you honestly think we could work this out?"

She thinks long and hard. "I do. If we get counseling and work on ourselves, we can do it."

I shake my head. "It's not going to work, Eva."

She watches me for a second before she shoots to her feet again. "Wait, you don't *want* to work this out, do you?"

"Eva—"

"No. You want to leave me. For her."

"I didn't say that."

"You don't have to say it. We have kids, Sheldon. And you're willing to throw away our family like a piece of trash because you fell in love with your mistress?"

I rise to my feet quickly. "Amy is not the reason I suggest we split."

She smiles at me. "Okay. I'll give you what you want. I'm not about to sit around and beg for you to work on a marriage you clearly don't want."

"Eva, you know this is what's best."

"No. It's what's best for *you*. I'll give you your divorce but know that I don't want my kids anywhere near that whore, or you'll regret it."

She gives me a last look of disgust and walks out of the room, slamming the door behind her.

CHAPTER FIFTEEN
EVA

I end the call with satisfaction. I just got off the phone with Sheldon's parents, telling them about his affair and his choice to leave me for another woman—a white woman at that. Take *that*, Mrs. Pro-Black. It gave me pleasure to tell the very woman who hates white people that her son is sleeping with one, but the satisfaction only lasts a second before the pain sets back in. The nerve of him, trying to pin this whole thing on me. We both contributed to the failure of our marriage, but for him to try to blame his cheating on the lack of intimacy is ridiculous. Sex hasn't been great for me either, but I'm not out here sleeping with other men. I look over at the children. They're sleeping without a care in the world. They have no idea that their lives are about to be turned upside down when they have to split their time between two homes. My heart breaks for them.

Leaving Sheldon was only supposed to be a wake-up call. It was supposed to show him what life would look like without me and the kids. He was supposed to miss us. He was supposed to grovel at my feet and ask me to take him back, but my plan backfired. The pain grows heavier, and I almost drop to my knees and pray. But then I remember I've denounced the church and my faith. I've been a devout Christian all my life. Once I got married, my relationship with God grew stronger, and the church became my second home. Now, I don't know who to turn to. I don't know where to start. First things first. I need to file for divorce, which means I'll need to hire a lawyer. And lawyers are expensive. Suddenly, a thought crosses my mind. I grab my phone and dial the number.

"Sister Eva, I was just thinking about you."

"Hi, Sister Clarice."

"How ya doing, baby?"

"I'm hanging in there."

"Good."

"Sister Clarice, isn't your son a lawyer?"

"Yes, he is. And one of the best too. My Terrance has always been smart."

"Do you think you could give me his number?"

"Sure. Is everything okay?"

I can't get into it with her right now. It'll end with me being a mess and her spreading my business around the church for gossip.

"Yes. Everything is fine."

"Okay. Sure, I'll give you his number."

Terrance and I decided to meet at a nearby restaurant. He had just finished meeting another client there and thought it would be easier for him to stay put instead of driving across town to his office. I rush into the restaurant in a hurry and quickly close my umbrella. It's rainy and dreary outside, a symbol of how I feel on the inside. I look around until my eyes land on a man sitting by himself. I walk toward the table, and as I get closer, I realize he looks familiar. He looks up and smiles when he sees me.

"Eva Matthews."

I laugh at the irony. "Terrance Stanley."

I feel his rock-hard chest when he pulls me in and hugs me. My mind wonders what his chest would feel like with his shirt off.

"You're Mrs. Clarice's son?"

"Yeah."

I shake away the thought. This isn't like me, and I don't like having such impure thoughts about him. He helps me remove my coat before I slide into the booth.

"Wow, you did exactly what you said you would do. You became a lawyer."

"I sure did. And what about you? What are you doing these days? Wait, let me guess. You're the CEO of some big company."

I shake my head. "No. I wish. As of right now, I'm a wife and mom. Well, soon to be ex wife."

I'm embarrassed as I say it because I think I've disappointed him. Terrance and I were top scholars in college. We took many of the same classes and were both voted most likely to succeed. I always had a crush on him, and we dated briefly, but it didn't last because he was a ladies' man. And I've never been the type of girl to share.

His smile disappears. "That's why you needed a lawyer?"

"Yeah."

"Eva, I'm so sorry."

I brush him off. "Don't worry about it."

I slightly blush as I sit across from Terrance. He looks the same, yet better: smooth brown skin, a neat, thick beard, light brown eyes, and full lips. I'm so attracted to him that I can hardly contain myself, and I'm not just attracted to him physically.

Terrance is one of the smartest men I've ever met, and it's such a turn-on.

"You know, I thought about you often over the years."

"You have?" I ask.

"Of course. I mean, with the connection we had in college. How could I not?"

"Yeah, we did have a strong friendship," I reply.

"Friendship? That's what you called it?" he asks.

I honestly don't know what to call it. Terrance and I had a triple connection. Mental, emotional, and physical. We would have been great together, a real power couple. But as strong as our connection was, it wasn't strong enough to make him take us seriously.

"Yes, that's what I called it. What else should I call it?"

"I had feelings for you," he responds.

"And I had feelings for you. But let's face it, Terrance. You weren't a one-woman man back then."

Guilt flashes in his eyes, and he nods. "You're right. I was an idiot back then. Always chasing the next best thing when it was right there in front of me all along." He searches my eyes once more before he moves on. "So, tell me what happened with your husband."

"He had an affair."

He's quiet as he takes it in. "Do you have proof of this?"

"Yes."

"And who asked for the divorce? You or him?"

"Neither of us has officially asked for a divorce. But he declined when I suggested we see a therapist and work on our marriage. He said it's better that we part ways, so I know he's considering it."

"Okay, so basically him. How many kids?" he asks.

I clear my throat. "Two."

"Wow, you always wanted kids. I bet they're beautiful, just like you."

"Thank you, Terrance."

"How old are they?"

"Five and three months."

"Okay. You'll make out well with young kids. Child support is usually higher."

"Okay."

"Do you know how long he's been having an affair?" he asks.

"Yes, seven months. But there's something else I found out."

"Tell me."

"I recently found out he slept with a family friend the night before our wedding. As a result, her son may be his."

He shakes his head. "Holy shit!"

I blush and lower my eyes. "I know. I don't know why I even considered giving him another chance."

He takes a deep breath. "I know why. You love him."

Tears form. "Yeah. Unfortunately for me, I do."

He nods. "Well. This is an easy case. Husband cheats. Leaves wife. Wife gets everything."

"So, you'll represent me?"

He sits back in his chair and watches me before he responds. "I don't know yet."

"Why not?" I ask.

"Because if I take you on as a client, there are rules."

"What kind of rules?"

"Rules like, I can't be biased. But that would be hard for me because of our history."

Confusion sets in. "I'm sorry. I don't understand."

He leans in. "I think you do."

It suddenly clicks, and I blush again. "Are you flirting with me, Terrance?"

He smirks. "I'm sitting across the table with the one who got away, and she's still sexy as hell. So, yeah, I'm flirting with you."

His statement gives me butterflies, something I haven't felt in a long time. "We dated for like two months. And . . . You shouldn't have let me get away, then."

Am I flirting back? He chuckles before he replies to me.

"Long enough to leave a lasting impression. And . . . I was young and stupid."

"And now?" I ask.

"And now. I'm a grown-ass man who knows *exactly* how to treat a woman."

Something ignites in my core. Something I haven't felt in years. Heat. Tingling. Pulsing. I squeeze my thighs together tightly, trying my best to get rid of this feeling. Terrance isn't my husband, and lusting over him is a sin. But then, I remember it doesn't matter because God has forgotten about me anyway. I relax my thighs, reveling in this newfound feeling.

"Well, I'm still a married woman."

He smirks again. "Well, how about we take things one step at a time? I'm willing to wait as long as I have to."

"That's sweet of you, Terrance. But I have so much happening in my life right now, and I can't risk the distraction. Besides, I'm not my husband. He's the cheater, not me."

He nods. "You've always had morals, Eva. That's what made you special. It's not my intention to make your life complicated. But you look like you need a friend right now. I can be that for you."

I nod. "I'd like that."

"Good. How about we meet later for drinks and just talk?"

"Sure. But I have something I need to do first. It should only take me an hour, less than that, probably," I reply.

As much as I'd like to stay here with Terrance, there's no way in the world I'm going to miss out on the chance to blow up Amy's world. I've been planning this for a whole day now, and it's time I act on it.

"Okay. You take care of your business, and I'll stay here and wait for you."

"All right."

He jots down some notes and explains the process to me. I listen, but I also envision what my life would be like without Sheldon. Will it be easier? Harder? Will I miss him? Whatever my life will be like, I know I can handle it. I'm strong. I was good to him, but he couldn't see it. He thinks the grass will be greener on the other side, but I'll show him. I'll show them both. By the time I'm finished, they'll both wish they had never met.

MARK

I'm back at the hospital. I need to talk to my wife and finally tell her everything that's happened. I also need to apologize for being an ass earlier. Actually, I owe her and Dylan an apology. I walk inside Dylan's room, and no one is there. I go to the nurse's station and ask about his whereabouts. They tell me that he's in session with his therapist. I walk back inside his room, sit down, and wait for his return. There is a lot we need to discuss. I've spent all my life hating others, all because that's how I was raised to be. I wanted to be just like my father. I wanted him to be proud of me. But now that I've learned the truth and how I was used as a pawn, I want nothing else to do with him or his ideals. But it will be hard. How do you change your perception of people over thirty years later?

The door opens, and Amy walks in. She's been crying, and her face looks swollen. I quickly stand. "Amy, what happened? Are you okay?"

She doesn't answer me. Instead, she cries and tells me she's sorry.

"No. I'm the one that's sorry, Amy. I shouldn't have said those things to Dylan."

"Mark—"

"No, listen to me. There is something I need to tell you. It's important."

Suddenly, the door opens, and in walks a petite Black woman. I don't recognize her, but she's screaming at Amy at the top of her lungs. She's threatening to have her fired for sleeping with her husband. She moves closer, and I step in front of my wife to protect her.

"What's this all about?" I ask.

"Move out of my way." She glances between Amy and me. I don't budge, and she repeats herself. "I *said* move out of my way."

Amy takes a step forward. "Eva, please, not here. My son's been admitted, and this is his room. This isn't a good time."

"Do you honestly think I give a shit?" she responds.

"What in the hell is going on here?" I ask. "Amy, you know this woman?"

The woman places her hands on her hips and laughs. "Yeah, she knows me all right. She's sleeping with my husband."

Amy places her hand on my arm. "Mark—"

"Is she telling the truth? Are you having an affair?" I ask.

"I . . ."

I wait for her to answer, but she doesn't. Instead, she watches me with frightful eyes and panic. She doesn't have to utter a word because I already know the answer. The guilt is written all over her face. I look back at the Black woman with her head cocked to the side, daring Amy to lie. Then I turn my attention back to my wife.

"Amy, I said, is this true?" I ask.

"Yes," she answers.

I see red. I grab her by her shirt and slam her back against the wall.

"I know my wife of almost twenty years didn't just tell me she's been fucking someone else."

"I'm sorry, Mark."

"Sorry? That's all you have to say to me right now?" I release my grip on her. My anger is out of control at the moment, and I don't trust that I won't seriously hurt her. She cries, but her tears mean nothing to me. I step back from her.

"How long?" I ask.

"Seven months," the woman answers from behind me. "And now it's time that you know. She ruined my family, and I'm here to return the favor."

I ignore her and speak to my wife. "Seven months, Amy?"

She nods her head, agreeing in silence.

"But how? You're always at home when you're not working."

"Oh, you're gonna love this," the woman answers. "My husband, Sheldon, is one of the doctors here."

The name sounds familiar. Sheldon . . . Then it hits me. I step closer to Amy until we're face-to-face.

"Sheldon. The same doctor who attended to Mom?"

"That was a coincidence, Mark," she explains.

"Are you fucking kidding me? You pranced him around and had him in my face knowing you two were screwing each other?"

The door opens again, and I turn to see who walked in. It's *him*. In a split second, my mind goes blank, and then I lunge at him.

CHAPTER SIXTEEN
MARK

My head leans against the cold wall of my jail cell. I've been here for hours, waiting for my arraignment, and for some strange reason, it doesn't bother me one bit. The change of scenery and people is refreshing, even though it's from behind bars. I'm not at home with Amy, where I'm reminded of her infidelity and my children's transgressions. I'm not accessible to my father, who has pretty much ruined my life. And I'm not at work where I'll have to battle the decision of quitting or staying. Being here, behind bars, takes me away from my life right now. It puts me in a position of solitude, and I'm welcoming it for now. My name is called, and I stand up. The officer displays his handcuffs, and I turn around willingly and allow him to place them on me. I follow him silently down the hall. When we arrive at a door, he speaks to me. "Hey, if I caught my wife cheating, I would have kicked the man's ass too."

He chuckles, but I don't find it funny. This is my *life* we're talking about. I don't know what will happen once I stand before this judge to face my charge of assault and battery. What happens if I'm convicted? Will I lose my job? I'm still on grief leave, so missing days isn't an issue, but what happens if this goes on my record? Could I be fired? Would it prevent me from finding another job? Suddenly, I regret my actions.

I'm led inside, and the courtroom is empty except for the public defender, the officer, the bailiff, and the judge. The public defender asks me how I would like to plead, and I say not guilty. My reasoning for this is simple. I haven't had time to consult an attorney to see what my options are. I explain my situation, and although the judge is sympathetic, he isn't happy about me attacking someone. He releases me on my own recognizance, and the handcuffs are unlocked from my wrists. I walk out of the courtroom a free man . . . for now. I have to return when I receive a notice for my hearing.

I walk to the processing area, sign for my things, and exit the precinct. I stand still and exhale when the air hits me. I take a few minutes to think about my next steps. Do I go home? Do I let Amy know that I'm out of jail? The answer is no. I don't want to go home. But I have nowhere else to go. I refuse to stay with one of my brothers. I refuse to go to my father's home. And I refuse to spend money on a hotel room. I want to sleep in my bed, under the roof where I pay the mortgage. Before I can call an Uber, Amy's car pulls up in front of me. She puts it in park and exits the driver's side. Our eyes meet, and I grow angrier. She bites her lip, and tears fall from her face. She walks toward me, and when she reaches me, she tries to hug me, but I stop her.

"Can we go home and talk?" she asks.

"Yeah, we can go home. But I'm not riding with you."

SHELDON

I've avoided getting arrested for over thirty years, and now that streak has ended. I hang my head low in my hands as I think about how my life has taken a drastic turn. I didn't graduate top of my class, become one of the best doctors in the state, and build a stellar reputation to have it all come crashing down to this. I lift my head and look around at the men I share a cell with. One looks homeless, like the cops picked him up from the dirty streets. Another one looks like he's asking for trouble; his pants hang low. So low that you can see his boxers. He's wearing a cut-off shirt and has locs past his ass. He looks grimy. I shoot to my feet and place my hands around the bars, hoping one of the guards will walk past. As soon as I see one, I yell for him.

"Excuse me."

He ignores me. He continues talking to the guard next to him. "Excuse me," I say louder. This time, he turns around. "I'd like my phone call, please."

He looks over at the other guard, and they laugh loudly together. Then he takes a few steps toward the cell I'm standing in.

"Maybe you didn't get the memo, but you don't dictate when you get a phone call."

"I have rights. Give me my phone call so I can call my lawyer."

He laughs again. "Give me my phone call so I can call my lawyer," he mimics.

Seeing him mock me makes my anger build stronger. I want to reach through the little bit of space I have between us and choke him. But I'm in unfamiliar territory, and I need to be careful. When he's done laughing, he places his hands on his holster.

"The phones are all occupied right now. When one frees up, I'll come get you, pretty boy."

He walks away, and I grit my teeth and shake the bars I hold as if they'll give way.

"First time?"

I spin around to the guy speaking behind me. It's the one with his pants hanging low. "No."

I've seen movies about what happens when you admit to never being incarcerated. I know what happens when people think you're soft. They fuck with you. They make your time here a living hell. This guy looks like he's from the streets. He looks like he's got a rap sheet five miles long and is one charge away from the three-strikes law. He's a thug. He smirks at my comment.

"Listen, they're just fucking with you. They know they have to give you your one call." He sticks his hand out. "I'm Dax."

Even his name sounds tough and gritty. "I'm Sheldon."

He looks me up and down. "How the hell did you end up in here wearing scrubs? You a doctor or something?"

I nod. "Yeah."

"Oh shit, for real? I thought about being a doctor once."

I don't know what his motive is or why he's being nice to me, but I'll take it. I'm not interested in making enemies or rubbing anyone the wrong way.

"Well, why didn't you?"

He shrugs. "Teacher said I wasn't college material, so I didn't bother. Dropped out in ninth grade."

I can't fathom dropping out of school at such a young age. "Your parents let you drop out of school?"

He laughs. "Parents? I didn't have parents, man. My mom was a dope fiend, and my father, well . . . never met the guy."

"Oh."

He brushes it off. "But hey, it's all right. I turned out pretty good."

I nod. "Yeah."

The guard approaches the bars. "Dax. It's time."

He stands to his feet. "It's been twenty-four hours already?"

"Yeah. Now get the hell out of here."

"Okay. But listen, give my man his phone call, or I go public with how this precinct treated him."

Confusion sets in at his statement. I glance back and forth between the guard and him, wondering what in the hell he's talking about. The guard shakes his head.

"You're a piece of work. You know that?"

He unlocks the door, and Dax walks out. He turns around to face me when the guard locks the door again.

"Whatever it is you did, make sure you never return here. I was that guy, and something tells me you're *not* that guy."

I nod. I am still confused about what just happened. He's led away, and another guard approaches.

"Come on, pretty boy. Time for your phone call."

He lets me out of the cell, but I can't help but wonder about Dax. "Do you know the guy they just let out? Dax?" I ask.

"Who doesn't know Dax?"

"I don't," I admit.

He chuckles. "You don't know the highest-paid actor in Hollywood?"

I don't watch many movies. It stemmed from med school. I kept my head in the books with little to no distractions, and I guess it stuck with me. I'm out of the loop regarding celebrities because neither Dax's name nor his face rings a bell.

The guard continues talking. "He was here preparing for a role. He dressed the part and spent the last twenty-four hours remembering what it's like to spend a night in jail. The kid had a rough start in life but cleaned himself up and became a multimillionaire."

By the time I reach the payphone, I'm at a loss for words, and I feel stupid. Stupid for judging a man based on how he's dressed and how he wears his hair. I did the same thing my parents warned white people would do to me. And I did it with my own race. It's because of Dax that I got my phone call, and now I won't get the chance to thank him because I didn't know he was a man who would be far out of reach. There's no way I could get in touch with him if I tried. The guard checks his watch.

"You've got two minutes."

I pick up the phone and dial my lawyer as fast as possible.

CHAPTER SEVENTEEN
MARK

Amy left the precinct alone, and so did I. I called for an Uber to drop me off at the hospital parking lot so I could pick up my car. I was grateful to find that it hadn't been towed, probably because of Amy. When I hopped inside, I didn't go straight home. I drove around for a while to clear my head. I needed space to think, and driving always helped with that. When I pull into my driveway, my heart sinks. When I walk inside my home, my chest tightens. When I walk inside the kitchen to find Amy sitting at the table waiting for me, my head starts to hurt. Just the sight of her disgusts me right now. I walk past her to the refrigerator to grab a water bottle.

"I don't feel like talking, Amy."

"Mark, please."

I turn around to face her. "What is it you want to say, huh? Because there isn't shit you can tell me that will make this right."

"I'm sorry."

Is she really sorry? Does she think that saying she's sorry will make things right?

"Is that it?" I ask.

"No. I didn't mean for any of this to happen."

"So, tell me. What did you *want* to happen, Amy? I'm out here busting my ass to take care of our family. I'm the best man I can be for you, and you're out fucking some nig—"

I don't say the word because, at this moment, I realize I'm half of the word I was about to say. This adds fuel to my anger, along with the confusion surrounding an identity I can't relate to. She wipes away her tears.

"What I did was wrong, Mark. And I'm sorry. Please tell me what I need to do to make this right."

I turn around and open the refrigerator, grabbing my water bottle. When I turn back to face her, I answer her question.

"There's nothing you can do."

AMY

I'm completely devastated. I always wondered what would happen if I ever got caught. Now that I have, it's much worse than I imagined. Watching Mark walk out on me just now was the equivalent of him walking out on our marriage. I know he probably needs time. I know he probably needs space, but seeing that he feels betrayed by me hurts. I'm anxious to make it right. I want him to talk to me. Yell at me. Throw something! Whatever it takes for him to release even a tiny bit of his anger. He looked at me differently just now. Like he doesn't recognize me. Like he doesn't . . . love me.

I should be at the hospital with Dylan right now. He's being kept there for observation, and I promised him I wouldn't leave his side. But right now, my marriage needs me more. My phone rings. It's Sheldon, of all people. I'm instantly annoyed. Doesn't he have common sense? Obviously, I won't be able to answer his calls after what happened at the hospital. I think back to the encounter. Mark pounced on him like a lion does his prey. Fists were thrown. Bodies were swung. There was blood. The horror I felt at watching my husband attack him was unimaginable. The nurses called security, who then called the police. Both Mark and Sheldon were arrested. I tried to bail Mark out, but he hadn't seen a judge yet for bail to be set. I called every fifteen minutes until the receptionist told me he was being released. I rushed down there in a hurry—only to be turned away. My phone rings again. It's Sheldon. Before, I didn't have a problem stepping away to answer his call. The idea of sneaking around with him excited me, but now, it feels wrong. I place my phone on silent and ignore the incoming calls. Tomorrow, when I see Dylan, I'll call Sheldon and break things off for good. And if he doesn't listen, I'll get a restraining order against him.

I wish my grandparents were alive right now. They'd know what to do. But instead, I'm in this alone. I have no one to turn to for help. My conscience suddenly reminds me that I made this mess by myself, so it's only right that I fix it myself. So many thoughts run through my head. Will Mark divorce me? Will the kids hate me for cheating on their father? I suddenly panic at the thought. I've been with Mark since I was nineteen. I don't know anything else or how to begin living without him. Yes, he has flaws. All of us do. But I promised to stand by his side for better or for worse. And right now, we're at our worst. I walk up the stairs to bed but pause, wondering if it's a good idea. Mark won't want to lie next to me if he can barely stand the sight of me.

I decide to sleep in Ireland's room tonight. It's nicer and much cleaner than Dylan's. I enter her room and fall back on her bed. I'm drained. So drained that I don't want to get high. I want to shower but can't muster enough energy to walk to the bathroom. I feel like life has been sucked out of me. My entire world has collapsed, leaving me bruised and broken. My heart feels tight, my pulse is pounding, and my mind is racing. Anxiety sweeps through me, yet I don't feel the energy from it. I feel weak. Worn out and run-down. I shut my eyes, giving way to the weight and stress of the day. It doesn't take me long to drift off. I fall into a deep slumber, hoping this all is a dream when I awake.

I was up early this morning. I cleaned the house, except for our bedroom, because I didn't want to wake Mark. I also cooked breakfast for him. I know this won't make things right, and I know that I have a lot to make up for. But it's been a while since I've cooked a spread like this. Besides, I'm sure he's hungry after being locked up for hours. I step back and look at my work. I made sausage gravy over biscuits, applewood bacon, cheesy grits, fluffy pancakes, and eggs over easy, just how he likes it. I also made a pot of coffee, a small fruit salad, and squeezed some fresh orange juice.

I look at the time, and it's after nine. Mark rarely sleeps this late. My phone rings. It's Sheldon again. I debate answering it, but if I don't, he'll continue calling, and I don't want to risk him calling when Mark comes downstairs. So I answer.

"Sheldon."

"Amy, we need to talk."

"There isn't anything we need to talk about."

"The hell there isn't."

I speak firmly and low into the phone. "It's over, Sheldon. Please don't call me anymore."

"You're ending things. Just like that?" he asks.

"Yes. This was a mistake. Look at the mess we've made. Do you know how embarrassing it is for your spouse to be arrested in front of your coworkers?"

"At least he was escorted out properly, Amy. I was aggressively taken into custody and thrown into the back of the cop car. Not to mention, the cops somehow 'accidentally' slammed me to the ground in the process. At least that's what they told the judge."

I don't reply and allow him to continue.

"Your husband is still alive and breathing without a scratch. He didn't have to worry about being killed like I did. Yet, *he* is your concern. What about me?"

I don't have the mental space to unpack what he's getting at, nor do I care at this point. Sheldon and I have run our course, and now . . . It's time to let go.

"Goodbye, Sheldon."

I end the call. A small piece of me is saddened that I've ended things, but it quickly passes. I climb the steps toward my bedroom. I'm taking a risk by waking Mark, but it's a risk I'm willing to take. I knock but get no answer. So I open the door . . . and find the bed empty. He's gone. I rush to the closet in a panic and check for his clothes. I exhale a sigh of relief when I see they're all there. I plop down on the bed as tears slide down my cheeks. Is he that disgusted that he can't stand to be around me? I grab my phone and call him. I'll mask it as if I'm checking to make sure he got to his destination safely. Short and sweet. I dial his number, and it goes straight to voicemail. I'm disappointed. I was hoping we could talk this morning, but it seems Mark doesn't want to talk. And if I'm not careful, he may not want me anymore.

SHELDON

Humiliated. Used. That's how I feel right now after speaking with Amy. She ended things between us before we even got the chance to be together. This is not how this was supposed to go. I'm supposed to tell her that Eva and I are divorcing. She's supposed to leave her husband. And we're supposed to be together. But that's not what happened. Amy tossed me to the side the minute things got rough. I risked my job for her. I lost my family because of her—all for nothing. I would be lying if I said my pride didn't take a hit because it did. The fact that she ended things punched me in the gut much harder than that officer did before throwing me in the back of his car.

My mind suddenly shifts to the events that happened. I was yanked off Mark, slammed against the wall, and handcuffed before I could even give them my name. I was slammed on the ground once, shoved twice, and punched several times before I reached the station. Fear can't even describe how I felt, thinking I'd never see my children again. I just knew that officer would take a detour down a hidden path, pull me out of the car, and kill me. My phone vibrates with an incoming message. It's Eva.

Her: I saw a divorce attorney. You'll be served soon.

Fuck! She's seen an attorney already. I know she told me that she would, but it didn't bother me at the time. I was kind of happy about it, to be honest. But now . . . Now, I'm not so sure. Suddenly, the thought of losing my family bothers me. I fucked up. Big time. For the first time since I started seeing Amy, I feel bad about what I did. I go into survival mode. I need to do damage control. Eva mentioned counseling. She said she was willing to work things out. Maybe it's something she'll still consider. I pick up the phone and dial her.

"Yes."

She sounds cold.

"I don't want a divorce." I blurt it out because it's the first thing I want her to hear. I don't want to give her a chance to hang up. She's silent. "Eva?"

"Yeah."

"I said I don't want a divorce."

"I know. I heard you."

"Well, do you have anything to say about it?" I ask.

She takes a deep breath. "I can't talk right now."

The line goes dead, and my pride and ego have been bruised for the second time this morning.

———

"Affairs are hard to come back from, son."

I watch as my father grabs the remote and pauses the television.

"I don't know what I was thinking."

"You weren't thinking," my mom chimes in. "Eva and I don't see eye to eye, but I'm a woman first, and I don't condone cheating. Especially with other races. Sheldon, a *white* woman? What the hell were you thinking?"

"Mom, does it matter at this point?"

"Yes, it does," she replies. "After everything we taught you, *this* is what you do? Have an affair with the enemy?"

I shake my head at her ridiculous comment. "Mom, please. White people are *not* our enemies. Yeah, some are racist, but not all."

She turns to my father. "This is *your* doing. *You* are the one who wanted to send him to that boogie-ass school with all those white people. We should have sent him to Morehouse like I suggested."

My father scuffs. "You wanted him to pass up the opportunity to go to Harvard?"

"Yes. Harvard isn't all that. It's only *prestigious* because white folk *say* it is."

I'm frustrated. I didn't come here to be lectured by my parents about social and racial issues. I came to get marital advice.

"Mom, Dad. Please, I need your help. I want my family back."

My mom sits beside me on the couch. "Have you told her that?"

"Yeah."

"And what did she say?"

"She said nothing. She hung up on me."

My mom recoils. "Oh, it's worse than what I thought. Sheldon, honey, Eva sounded distraught when she called here. She barely kept it together when she told your father and me what you had done. Hurt like that can take a long time to bounce back from."

"So, what do I do?" I ask.

She places her hand on my shoulder. "You give her time."

My dad chooses this time to chime in on the conversation.

"Son, I've been with your mother for over thirty years. I've never once thought about stepping out on her. It would be best if you thought long and hard about what made you cheat in the first place. A man's job is to protect his woman. Make her feel safe. It's a possibility Eva may never feel safe with you again. And if that happens, you need to be prepared for it."

My mother nods in agreement, and they share a tender look. My father's words sink in, and I realize I took my wife for granted. Yes, I was unhappy about some things, but we could've worked through them. At the end of the day, Eva was a good wife and mother. She always had my back. She supported me. She encouraged me. She kept a clean home and always had dinner on the table for me before the kids came. She may not have been as sexual and intimate as I wanted her to be, but she was grounded in her morals and faith. She was loyal and a woman of high standards. And I broke her heart. I tore our family apart. I wish I could go back in time. I would do things differently. I would help her around the house more. I would help her with the kids more. I would be more romantic and show her that she and the kids are the most important people in my life. But I can't go back in time because time marches on. Years. Months. Weeks. Days. Hours. Minutes. Seconds. They all move forward, forcing me to move with it despite the pain.

CHAPTER EIGHTEEN
EVA

I stare at the body next to me and tightly pull the blanket up and around me. Terrance rolls over and smiles at me.

"Good morning."

I smile back, but it doesn't reach my eyes. "Good morning."

His eyes narrow as concern crosses his face. "Are you okay?"

Am I okay? Am I okay with what I've done? Flashbacks of last night cross my mind. When I returned from the hospital, Terrance was right there waiting for me. We briefly discussed my case, then we ordered food . . . and drinks. I'm not a drinker, but lately, I've been so stressed that I thought a glass of wine could help calm my nerves. The next thing I know, we're at his house, and he's undressing me, roaming his hands all over my body, and using his tongue to do things to me that I'm too embarrassed even to think about right now. I didn't want to sleep with Sheldon later in our marriage. Once I got saved, I learned there were so many other ways to be a good wife, and sex for me was no longer a big deal. But last night changed me. Having sex with Terrance felt . . .

good. I felt things I hadn't felt in a long time. I released in a way I desperately needed. I've had orgasms with my husband before, but none lately because I just wasn't into it.

"Yeah, I'm fine."

He inches closer. "Eva, I don't want you to feel bad about this."

It's sweet of him to say, but I can't help but feel bad. I had sex with someone other than my husband, which makes me just as wrong as him. I texted him right before Terrance led me to his bedroom. I don't know why I did it. Maybe I thought it would lessen the guilt. I didn't expect him to reply, let alone call me back. Terrance and I had just finished when he called. So, imagine my surprise when he said he changed his mind about getting a divorce. He blindsided me. I had no idea how to respond, especially with Terrance in the bathroom a few feet away.

"I don't feel bad about this," I respond.

"Yes, you do. I can tell."

I exhale. "Is it that obvious?"

He chuckles. "Yeah. But you're a good woman, Eva. So, it doesn't surprise me that you feel bad about sleeping with another man while you're still married."

I turn slightly to face him. "I've never been with anyone except for him."

He nods. "I remember. You wanted to wait until God sent your husband, which I quickly knew wasn't me since you wouldn't give up the goods."

I giggle and playfully punch him in the arm. "I saved myself for him. I never thought that we'd be here."

I can feel the pain about to crash down on me. I can feel the sea of tears struggling to break free. But I keep it all at bay because this is not the time or place for that. He rests his hand on my shoulder.

"Hey, I understand, and it's okay." He places a finger under my chin and lifts it slightly. "He's a fool for letting you go."

"He called me this morning."

"When?" he asks.

"When you were in the bathroom. He said he doesn't want to get divorced anymore."

"How do you feel about that? Do you want to take him back?"

I don't need to think about it because I already know the answer. Too much has happened between Sheldon and me even to *consider* reconciling.

"No. It's time I move on," I reply.

"Eva, you deserve so much more than what he gave you. That son of a bitch has no idea just how lucky he was. You're a diamond in the rough. Always have been."

"Thank you, Terrance."

"And I'm not just saying that because you finally let me make love to you."

I chuckle, and he continues. "But seriously, let me take you on a proper date."

"I don't know if I'm ready for that," I respond.

"We can go as slow as you want."

"Okay. No harm in going out, I guess."

His eyes search mine before he leans in and kisses me. "You know what this means, though, don't you?"

"No. What?" I ask.

"I can't represent you anymore."

"Why not?"

"Because I want to court you properly. Which is hard to do when it's against the rules to date your client."

"I see."

"But I have a colleague in mind who is just as good. So I'll set something up for you two to meet."

"Okay. Thank you."

I met with the attorney that Terrance recommended, which made this surreal. He was thorough and attentive, and I walked away content that he would properly handle my case. Now, I park the car and walk up the stairs to my mother's house. When I open the door, Kamryn greets me. I scoop her up and squeeze her tightly.

"I missed you, buttercup."

She giggles and runs into the kitchen when I place her down. My mother walks out, wiping her hands on a dish towel.

"She's eating a snack. And I just put the baby down for a nap."

"Thanks for watching them, Mom."

"Um-hmm. Where were you all night?" she asks.

"I had some things to take care of."

She watches me closely. "Who you think you fooling, gal?"

"I don't know what you mean."

"I wasn't born yesterday, honey. You're blushing. And you got a certain sass to you that you didn't have before."

It's crazy how a mother can tell things about you without you confessing them. She continues to speak.

"Well, I know you weren't with your husband because he called here looking for you."

Before I can respond, my phone rings. It's Terrance. "Mom, I have to take this." I step into the bathroom and answer the call. "Hey."

"Hey. Did you make it in safely?" he asks.

"Yeah, I did."

"When can I see you again."

I take a deep breath. "Terrance ..."

"Uh-oh, I see where this is going."

"I made a mistake."

He's silent before he responds. "I understand."

I grip the phone tightly. "I'm sorry, but I can't see you again."

"I respect that. If you ever change my mind. You know how to reach me."

"Thank you."

I end the call and return to the room where my mother scrutinizes me. "If Sheldon calls back, please tell him I'm not here. I don't want to talk to him."

"You don't want to talk to your husband, but you're okay talking to another man? I heard you in there."

"How is any of this my fault? Sheldon is the one who made it clear he doesn't want me or this marriage."

"And you wasted no time sleeping with someone else."

"Are you judging me?" I become angry, and my voice escalates. "*He's* the one who cheated. He's the one who left me for his mistress. He's the one leaving me, Momma, not the other way around. What am I supposed to do?"

"You're not free until the ink is dry on that paper, sweetheart. And even then, you're still married in God's eyes."

"I don't have time for this today."

"You *need* to make time. Talk to your husband, Eva. He realizes that he's made a mistake."

"Are you defending him?"

"No. I—"

"No. You are. Just like you always defend Shanice. When are you ever going to have *my* side, Mom, huh? Why is it that every time someone hurts me, you never have my back?"

She doesn't reply right away. Instead, she only stares at me with concern etched on her face.

"It was wrong of me not to tell you about Crystal and Sheldon, and I apologize for that. But, Eva, I'm your mother. And I love you. But I'm not going to defend you if you're wrong."

She doesn't get it. And she never will. My mom is one of the most stubborn people on the planet. It's why we don't see eye to eye. It's why I don't come around so much. And it's why I don't share much of my personal business with her. She always tries to tell me what I'm doing wrong. She always tries to lecture me. But for once, I want her to be my mother. For once, I want her to listen to me and let me cry on her shoulder while she strokes my hair. I want her to be there for me, even if I'm the one who made a mistake.

"Mom, I'm going through a lot."

Her eyes turn glassy. "I know, baby."

She walks over and pulls me in for a hug. As she holds me tightly, the tears rapidly fall.

"It hurts so bad," I say in between my sobs.

"Honey, God can take away your pain. Just lean on him."

I gently pull away from her. "I need you too, Mom. I always have."

She searches my eyes before a tear slides down her face.

"I know I was hard on you and your sister. But I always wanted what was best for you girls. I wanted you two to have opportunities that I didn't have. You exceeded my expectations, Eva. You went on and made a life for yourself that I could only have dreamt of. I am so proud of you, baby."

"You're proud of me?"

"Yes, I am. I always have been."

"Thank you, Mom."

She nods. "You will get through this. And I will be here, supporting you every step of the way. I love you."

"I love you too, Mom."

I smile, and a sense of peace washes over me. For the first time in my life, my mother told me she's proud of me. That she loves me. She's not affectionate, yet she hugged and kissed me. We've made a breakthrough in our relationship, and it feels good.

"I'm tired. Is it okay if the kids and I crash here tonight?" I ask.

"Of course. You and the kids can stay as long as you need."

"Thank you."

I turn around, and she calls my name. "Eva."

"Yes, Mom."

"That house belongs to you just as much as it belongs to Sheldon. If anyone is going to be crashing on people's couches and sleeping in hotels, it's him. After all, he's the one who messed up. You make sure your lawyer fights to get you everything you deserve."

I nod and smile. "I will. Thank you, Mom."

MARK

I wanted to leave early this morning before Amy awoke. She wanted to talk, and I wasn't sure I was ready to face her yet. I didn't know if I wanted to sort things out and fix our problems. But I can't avoid her forever. I need to fix things with her as well as everything else I'm dealing with.

When I opened my eyes this morning, I had an epiphany. My life is chaotic right now, and only I can change that. I can't and won't live like this any longer. The anger I feel for my dad is draining. The hurt caused by my wife cripples me. And the disappointment I have for my kids saddens me. It's too much. If I don't get help soon, I'll crash and burn.

The first decision I made this morning was simple. I'll never speak to my father again. I just can't. I know if my mother were here, she wouldn't like it, but I have to do what's best for me. And what's best for me is to remove him from my life. The second decision I made was to save my marriage. Amy and I sat down and had a long talk. We were able to air out unresolved feelings.

Although it wasn't easy, it was necessary. As hard as it was, I had to take accountability for my role in the destruction of our marriage. Lastly, I've decided to educate myself, for my marriage and for me. I disadvantaged myself by allowing my father to teach me everything I know. After learning of his deceit, I no longer know what's right and wrong. So, I have to take matters into my own hands.

I stop when I enter the building. This is a big step for me, and I'm scared shitless to go through with it. But if I don't go through with it, I rob myself of the opportunity to learn. So, I walk down the hall until I reach suite number one hundred. I pause and look inside through the glass. There's a group of people sitting around in a circle. I turn the knob and slowly walk in. A few people glance my way, but the room is filled with chatter as people mingle. I grab a bottle of water and take a seat. A few minutes pass before two men stand at the front of the room and introduce themselves as the group leaders. One is white, and one is Black. The room quiets, and then the white man speaks.

"Let's get started. I want to thank you all for coming tonight. If you're an existing member, welcome back. If you're a new member, welcome to the BWRCT group. Now, that's a long acronym, so if you don't know what that means, it stands for the Black and White Racial/Cultural Trauma group."

A woman raises their hand, and the Black man steps forward. "Yes."

"How does the group work?" she asks.

He smiles before answering. "Well, it's like Narcotics Anonymous. It works if you work it. This group is for anyone who has experienced racial or cultural trauma due to being Black or white. We talk things out here. We talk about our experiences and are very open with our biases in hopes of shedding stereotypes and ending hate on both sides."

Happy with his answer, she nods.

"Any more questions?" he asks. When no one responds, he continues. "Okay. Who would like to go first?"

A man next to me stands on his feet. "Hi, I'm David, and I'm biased."

"Hi, David," the group says in one voice.

"I grew up in a predominately white neighborhood in suburban Idaho. I was one of two Black kids that went to my school. When he graduated, I was the only one left. After graduating, my parents thought Howard University would be a good choice for me. They had an excellent prelaw program and produced some of the best lawyers. I got in. Full ride. But I wasn't prepared for life at a historically Black school. I couldn't relate to my peers. I didn't talk like them. I didn't dress like them. We didn't share the same interest in music or movies. I often got picked on for the way I spoke. They said I talked like a white boy. For four years, I had no friends. No girlfriend. I had no social life whatsoever, and because of the way I was treated, I gained a dislike for my race."

My head whips around. Did he say that he gained a dislike for his race? I don't see how that is even possible, which baffles me. He sits, and the group speaks again.

"Thanks for sharing," they say in unison.

The Black man steps forward and speaks. "There's a misconception in the Black community that if a person doesn't use slang and speaks proper English, they talk like a white person. And if a white person uses slang, they are often viewed as trying to talk Black. Of course, none of this is true. The English language doesn't depend on color. It's all one language that has been chopped and screwed repeatedly to create various abbreviations, slang, etc. What you experienced is very common and a direct result of biases," he continues.

"Now, with that being said, you *did* conform to the white culture. You were more immersed in their culture because you attended a white school. Your peers were white, so it's only natural that you have more in common with those you associate yourself with. And when you left an all-white school and attended an all-Black one, it was a culture shock for you. What you're struggling with is an identity issue. But if you keep coming back and doing the work, we'll help you work through it."

A young girl across from me stands to her feet. "Hi, I'm Laura, and I'm biased."

The group speaks. "Hi, Laura."

She takes a deep breath before speaking. "I got robbed last year. The criminal was Black. I never got over it. Now, I deeply fear Black men. They all look scary to me. And I hate being anywhere near them."

The white group leader speaks this time. "Let me ask you a question if you don't mind."

She nods, giving him the green light. "If the criminal had been a white man, would you be scared of all white men?"

She shakes her head. "No."

"Why not?" he asks.

"Because I don't feel threatened by them."

"So, before you were robbed, you already felt threatened by Black men?"

"Well, yes. They're tall and big. And they carry guns and stuff. Most of them have been in jail for doing bad things."

The white group leader nods. "I see. It's not the robbery incident that's making you fear Black men. When it happened, you already had a preconceived stereotype in your head that amplified it. Keep coming back. We'll work on and get to the root cause of your bias."

I listen as a few more people speak. They all have different stories and backgrounds to share. I don't have the urge to share. Not right now, anyway. I have too much to sort through before I can put it all out there on the table. But this was the first step for me. The meeting wraps up, and I stand, anxious to leave the room before someone notices I'm new. I make it to the door and leave the building in a hurry. When I reach my car, I take a deep breath. Can people *really* change? Can a person shed all the stereotypes they've formed over the years? It seems impossible. It seems unrealistic. But somehow, the leaders of this group think that a person can be different with work. This was my first time attending, so I don't know for sure if this group is the real deal. I have no idea if the group has made anyone better. I don't know the group's effect on anyone, but I also don't care because regardless of whether they've changed doesn't matter. The only thing that matters is the group's effect on me.

CHAPTER NINETEEN
SHELDON

Eva still isn't answering my calls. I'm convinced she's never coming home, and I'm fearful I'll never see my kids again. I'm their father and have rights, but I would never take her to court to enforce those rights. I've hurt her enough. I took some time off work. I've been a mess without my family. All I want to do is sit in the house with the blinds closed and play sad love songs. It's Sunday morning, and I'm up early doing something I never thought I'd do. I'm going to church.

It's funny, really. All these years, I was angry at Eva for devoting so much of her time to the church, and now, I'm about to spend time in one. After the conversation with my parents, I came home and thought about what they said. I felt lost. When Eva wouldn't answer my calls, I called her mother, but I couldn't reach her there either. I miss her so much. I wanted to feel close to her. So, I grabbed her study Bible off her nightstand. She has several of them, but this is the one she took to church with her often. I open. And I read the first book. The next thing I know, I'm knee-deep in it and can't put it down. I've never read the Bible. As I mentioned, my parents forbade me. For the first time in a long time, I feel different about Christianity. And I realize my parents' teachings are wrong. The Bible teaches us to love one another, regardless of race. My parents' hatred for white people is wrong on so many levels.

As I read each book, I learned about love. I learned about forgiveness and that everything I was taught growing up was a lie. God doesn't want us to hate someone because of their race. God doesn't want us to worship any other God because there is only one of Him. My parents say that Christianity is false. They say that it's the white man's religion, one that was forced on us as slaves. But I no longer believe them. They grew up in a different time . . . a time when the world was reeling from segregation, Jim Crow, and other racial injustices. It caused them to think that all white people are alike.

There are some bad apples, but that's true for every race. I've been wrong all this time . . . about everything. I should have listened to my wife. She tried to tell me. She tried to get me to see reason, but I was too stubborn and let my ego get the best of me. I kept telling myself she was difficult to be with. That she didn't appreciate me when, in reality, it was the opposite. It was me who was difficult to be with. *I* was the one who didn't appreciate what I had. This pain I'm feeling is inexplicable. God is the only person I can turn to now. He's the only person who knows what I'm going through. He's the only one who can help me through this. I've spent every night praying for forgiveness. I am praying that He brings my family back to me. I only hope that He's gracious enough to answer.

___

I sit in the back of the pew, waiting for the service to start. I couldn't show my face at Eva's church, not with the way I left things with the pastor there. I Googled some churches in the area and chose one with a five-star rating. It's a little bigger than Eva's church, but

I don't mind. All I care about is learning the truth. I've done some reading and research, but I still have much to learn. I'm still new to it all and have so many questions, questions I'm hoping the pastor can help me with. The service starts with praise and worship. After that, the pastor steps forward and prepares to speak to the congregation. He asks us to turn to Proverbs 6:32. He reads it aloud.

But the man who commits adultery is an utter fool, for he destroys himself.

He goes on to speak about the topic of infidelity, and I cringe at every word he says because I feel as though he's talking to me. While doing my reading, I came across verses relating to infidelity. And it doesn't take a rocket scientist to know that infidelity is a sin in almost every religion. But hearing the pastor put it all in context somehow affects me differently. It somehow amplifies the seriousness of my mistake. By the time he's finished, I feel shackled down with guilt. I feel covered in a sinful cloak of lust and filth. The choir sings a song, and I break. I raise my hands and cry out to God. I hear the pastor say something, but I can't decipher what he's saying. But I do hear four words. *Come to the altar.* And I do just that. I walk to the altar, and when I reach it, I drop to my knees . . . and I release it all. The pain. The anger. My arrogance, pride, and my lustful spirit. At that moment, I leave it all there.

I feel the pastor's hands on my head, and a group of ushers surround me with their arms outstretched, hovering over me. They all pray for me, and one of them speaks in tongues. I can feel the weight of sin being lifted from me. I can feel the power of their prayer. I call out to God. I ask Him to restore my marriage. I ask Him to bring Eva and the kids home to me. I make a promise to be a renewed man.

When it's all said and done, I stand while the congregation screams out to God. My display of repentance and faith has caused many of them to be filled with the Holy Spirit. They stomp, dance, and shout. Some even fall to the floor. A sense of peace washes over me as I take long strides toward the pew. I lower myself to my seat and let this new feeling wash over me. My life will be different now because I know what I need to do.

First, I need to forgive Amy. I've been so angry with her rejecting me that harboring it causes me to feel bitter toward her. Then, I need to make things right with my wife. And the first step is asking for her forgiveness. We'll go to counseling. I'll do whatever I need to do to make things right. And lastly, I need to be baptized. If I'm going to be a new man, I must do it correctly. Maybe Eva and I can be baptized together. I smile at the thought. Yes, that's it. We'll be baptized together, and not only will we become renewed with Christ but also in our marriage.

DYLAN

My outlook on life has changed. It's funny how it took a near-death experience for me to finally see reason. When I stepped on the chair in my room to hang myself, I didn't want to live anymore. I felt helpless. I felt my life had no purpose and no one would love me for who I am. Dying was an easy way out for me. I needed peace in my life, and at that moment, that was the only thing I knew for sure could bring it to me.

But I immediately wanted to live as I felt my life sway between the afterlife and the present. I suddenly didn't care what people thought about me, including my father. I decided that it was time for me to live in my truth. I made a promise that if my life were spared, I would never take it for granted again. I am who I am, and nothing will ever change that. I've come to grips with the fact that my father may never accept me, and you know what? I'm okay with it. I wish my mother could escape from under him and his controlling ways.

I was so scared when the therapist asked about my home life. I've heard about parents being investigated by social services, and I just knew that's what would've happened to my mother if I'd said the wrong thing. But it turns out I was wrong. The therapist walked in on my parents having a nasty fight, but it wasn't enough for them to be reported. Once the therapist explained this, I opened up more. I found she was easy to talk to. I also found that being open and honest with her made me feel free. She understood me. She understood what I'd been dealing with all my life, and it felt good. I'd never thought of seeking therapy before. My father doesn't believe in it. He says no one should pay anyone to help them with issues they can resolve themselves. But he's wrong because had I had therapy sooner, I would've never tried to hang myself. And if he had gotten treatment at some point in his life, maybe he wouldn't be the kind of man he is today. Suddenly, my phone rings. It's Ireland.

"Hey."

"Thank God you're okay."

"Yeah. I'm okay," I reply.

She breathes a sigh of relief. "Mom and Dad aren't around, are they?"

I watch my mom carry a bag into the house. "No."

"Dylan, why on earth would you do something like that?"

"I was in a bad space, Sis."

"You should have called me. You could have come and stayed with us."

"Where are you?"

"We're in Baltimore."

"How the hell did you wind up way up there?"

"Long story. But please, don't tell anyone."

"I won't," I assure her.

"Are you okay now?"

"I will be. I'm getting help."

"I shouldn't have left you. I'm sorry."

"No, Ireland. Dad was an asshole, and I should have protected you. *I'm* sorry."

"How's Mom?"

"She's okay. She's worried about you, though."

"I'm not ready to talk to her yet."

"I understand." A few seconds of silence pass. "Ireland?"

"Yeah?"

"I'm glad you got away. But whatever you do, don't come back. Mom and I will visit you when the time is right."

"Okay."

"I gotta go, but I'll call you later, and we can catch up."

"Okay. I love you, Dylan."

"I love you too."

I end the call and take a second to gather my emotions. I miss the hell out of my sister. She sounds happy, but I'm still worried about her. She's just a kid, and Austin is young himself. How the hell will they make it with a baby? However, my concern quickly turns into pride. My baby sister traveled all the way to another state to raise her baby in peace. She knew what would happen if she stayed here and refused to let it happen to her child. I couldn't be prouder of her. Moving away from family with no money or job takes a lot of guts, and as much as Mom and I worry, I have a feeling Ireland will be just fine.

Thoughts of moving away creep into my brain. I think about how different life would be if I moved from Georgia. I think about how things will be if I move to one of the big cities like Manhattan or Los Angeles. I'm sure those places have way more diversity than this tiny town of Georgia. People wouldn't bat an eye if they knew I was gay. I could get a higher-paying job, start fresh, and never look back. Those thoughts are ambushed as thoughts of Mom creep in. I would be leaving her alone with him. She wouldn't have either of her children with her, and it would break her heart. She does a good job of hiding it, but I can see the toll it's taking on her that Ireland left. I can see the pain in her eyes when Ireland won't return her calls. If I were to go too, it would destroy her. Take that with my dad's quick temper and controlling ways, and she might need a shrink.

I grab another bag and walk inside my home. Mom places the last box on the living room floor and shuts the door behind her. Then she takes a deep breath.

"Well, that's everything."

"Thanks, Mom."

She steps in front of me. "You know you can stay home. You don't have to do this."

Anxiety and panic set in as soon as she says it. The thought of being anywhere near my father right now makes my head hurt. I shake my head.

"Mom, I can't go back there."

She knows it, and I know it. Now that I've discovered my sexuality, Dad will never let me live it down. Instead, he'll spend every moment trying to convince me that something is wrong with me and that being gay isn't normal. And I refuse to live like that.

"Give him time, Dylan. He's trying. He's even started classes to get help."

She's still defending him. She still tries to make him seem like a loving father. But he's not. And I'm no longer the six-year-old kid who thought his father would one day come around and love him. I'm old enough to see the reason now. I'm old enough to accept it for what it is.

"It's too late. I gave him enough time, and now, it's time for me to live my life."

She nods, and her eyes turn glassy. I hate knowing she's hurting. But it needed to be said. I can no longer pretend that the way we've been living is okay. I can no longer pretend that my father isn't the cause of my emotions being so fucked up. She quickly pulls herself together.

"So, what else do you need?" she asks.

"I'm good. You've done enough by signing the lease for me."

"Well, you're not an adult yet. You have to be eighteen to sign a lease on your own."

I can tell that this bothers her, and I hurt knowing she's hurting, but I can no longer stay under the same roof as my father. Not after the awful things he said to me. Some things can't be forgiven. Even if we apologize and try to be cordial, we'll never be the same. "I know this hurts you, Mom."

She shakes her head. "No. I understand, Dylan."

Her understanding warms me, and I realize that I will miss her as much as she's going to miss me, even though I'm only seven miles from her home. I pull her into a tight hug, and we hold each other. My mother has always been supportive of me. She's been my confidante, my protector, and my best friend. I love her with all my heart and hate what she's been through. I'm not mad at her for having an affair because I understand it. If I were married to a man like my dad, I'd cheat on him too. Hearing about the events in my hospital room that day was horrifying. But it was also rewarding to imagine the pain in my father's eyes as he discovered that my mother was having an affair. I've recognized that same look of pain in my sister's eyes, my mother's eyes, and my eyes when I look in the mirror. And the pain was always caused by him. So, knowing he's in pain, knowing he's angry and hurt, gives me a sort of satisfaction that, for once, he can finally see what it feels like. My mom releases me, and I ask the question I've always wanted the answer to. "Mom, why do you stay with him?"

"Your father and I are working through our issues, Dylan. You should try to do the same."

"No. And I honestly don't know why you would ever speak to him again after what he did."

Shock crosses her face. "Dylan, you wouldn't understand."

"Try me."

She's quiet for a second, but then she responds. "He wasn't always like this. Your father was a good man once. He was fun. Caring. And he swept me off my feet." She smiles as she reflects on the past. "Sometimes things change you, son. And well . . . Some things happened over time that changed the course of your father's life. He became a different person. You can't unlove someone because they change. Not when you're in love. And not when you're married with kids. One day, when you're married, you'll understand."

I want to tell her that she's wrong. I want to tell her that although you may not "unlove" someone, you can leave someone bad for you. I want my mom to be free from my father's grip. I want her to be happy and carefree, not anxious and walking around on eggshells. But I don't say this. I'm still young and will be the first to admit that I don't know anything about true love yet. Clearly, she loves my father, and she's honoring her commitment to him and their marriage. And who am I to judge that? I nod and then kiss her cheek.

"Now, there are some rules," she says, changing the subject.

"Okay."

"I'm aware you may have . . ." she clears her throat, "company. And if you do, please, Dylan. Use protection."

She doesn't have to stress this because, after my HIV scare, I will never have unprotected sex again. Hell, I'm not sure if I'll ever have sex again. "I will, Mom."

"Remember, you have to get tested again in six months."

"Yes, I've already made the appointment."

A moment of silence passes between us. "Have you heard from your sister?"

I have heard from Ireland. But I don't want to hurt my mother's feelings. Ireland isn't ready to speak to Mom or Dad. I've tried to explain to her that it's Dad she should be mad at, but she's still angry that Mom didn't defend her when she needed her the most. "No. Not recently."

"Well, if you do, tell her to please answer my calls and texts. I worry."

"I will, Mom."

"Thank you."

She turns around and opens a box, but I know it's to prevent herself from crying. So, I turn around and do the same to stop myself from crying with her. I'm going to miss being under the same roof as her. But this is a new start for me. I'm graduating this year, and after that, I'll head to college—hopefully New York University. I'll graduate with honors, get a great job as a chemist, and make lots of money. I'll show him. I'll show him that despite his ridicule and mockery, I was able to make something of myself. He'll wish he would've been a better father when he sees my success.

AMY

I glance down at the paper I'm holding, and the words leap out like a 3D picture. *Drugs Anonymous, Inc.* I fidget with it as I look up and around, attempting to see all the other *addicts* in the room. People are still flowing in, and fear shoots through me at the thought of seeing someone I know. I've officially been labeled an addict and wouldn't say I like it. I don't deserve to be here with people addicted to heroin or crack. My desire to pop a few pills here and there is nothing compared to their addictions.

When Mark and I sat down to talk, I told him about my taking the pills. And as horrible as it sounds, I don't regret it. It was the only way I could deal with him at times. When I told him, he made me sign up for these meetings. I agreed since we both wanted to do the work and fight for our marriage.

I won't lie. I do feel a little ashamed. I feel some embarrassment. Each time one of these people looks at me, they know that I'm here because I get high. They're probably judging me as we speak. A woman about my age sits next to me.

"Is this seat taken?"

I shake my head. "No."

She opens the pamphlet and starts reading before she lets out a chuckle.

"What's so funny?" I ask.

"I find it funny that the person running this meeting is an ex-boyfriend of mine."

I look across the room and spot the man she's referencing. He's too busy talking to someone to notice the woman beside me. "Does he know you're here?" I ask.

"No. And I didn't know he was hosting this meeting until I saw his name."

"Are you going to stay?"

"Why wouldn't I?" she asks.

Because there's no way in the world I could sit through a meeting like this if my ex-boyfriend was hosting. As a matter of fact, I wouldn't sit through this meeting if anyone I *knew* was hosting.

She extends her hand out to me. "I'm Danielle."

I place my hand in hers. "I'm Amy."

"To answer your question, yes, I'm staying."

I nod, but I don't respond to her. Instead, I look back at the pamphlet I'm holding. I read about the twelve steps, which are supposed to help get me through the program.

Danielle inches closer. "So, what's your drug of choice?"

I shake my head. "Oh no, you must be mistaken. I don't use drugs."

She looks at me with shock. "Oh, I'm sorry, I assumed. Are you here with someone then?"

"No. I'm here alone. My husband suggested I come after he learned I take pills."

She crosses her arms. "Oh, you're one of them?"

"One of what?" I ask.

"You're one of those people who think you're not an addict because your drug of choice can be picked up at a pharmacy. Listen, doll, I've been sober for two years, and I always seem to meet someone who thinks they don't need help because their drug of choice is weed or pills." She speaks with conviction, like she's been through some things.

"That's . . . That's not what I meant."

"Okay then, what *did* you mean?" she asks.

"Taking pills helps me cope. It's not like it interferes with my job or my ability to care for my family."

She nods. "Umm-hmmm. Just like I thought. One of the first signs of addiction is denial. But I'll spare you the lecture. By the time this meeting ends, you'll realize you *are* an addict."

She stands to her feet and goes to mingle with the other guests. I suddenly feel uncomfortable, and I no longer wish to be here. Mark wants me to complete this program in order for us to work on our marriage. He said we wouldn't be able to do it if I'm taking things that alter my mind, but it's not true. I'm sick of him, Danielle, and anyone else who seems to think I'm this drug-addicted person. Everyone is overreacting, and it makes me want to scream.

Danielle sits back down beside me. "You're thinking of leaving, aren't you?"

"Yes. I think all of this is unnecessary," I reply.

She smiles. "I used to be you. I had a good life. I was college-educated, had an amazing career, and an amazing fiancé who loved me." She takes a minute to think to herself before she continues. "But that all changed when the pressures of work became too much. I started smoking marijuana and was just like you in my thinking. It was just weed. It's from the earth. I thought I could stop anytime but realized I couldn't."

"What happened?"

I'm getting ahead of myself by inserting myself in her personal business. She may be in a support group, but it doesn't necessarily mean she'll openly share. But I'm curious. She wastes no time answering my question.

"I was so addicted it took over my life. I couldn't eat, sleep, or function without it. It made me moody. It altered my thinking, and it made me make bad decisions. For example, that amazing fiancé I just mentioned, I cheated on him with . . . him."

Her head jerks in the direction of the ex-boyfriend, and my eyes go wide as saucers.

"Him?"

"Yup. He was my supplier. I hooked up with him, and my fiancé found out. He left me, and I became depressed, which led to me fucking up at work. Eventually, I lost my job. Eventually, I lost everything."

Her story resonates with me. Never in a million years would I think a person could lose it all just by smoking marijuana. I mean, it's a plant. It's from the earth and has many medicinal benefits. "Wow, I'm sorry."

"Don't be. It was my life. My decisions. But if I can help someone else, I'm going to."

I suddenly feel differently. Mark was right. This meeting is a good idea. I was able to meet someone who has a story similar to mine. I haven't lost it all yet. I still have my husband and children, but if I continue on my path, all that could change.

"Thank you for sharing your story with me."

She smiles at me. "You're welcome." She leans and speaks in a low voice. "I'm no therapist, but I'm here if you ever need anyone to talk to. Most of my friends can't relate, and it would be nice to speak to someone who knows exactly how I may be feeling."

"Okay."

"And don't worry about what people think. You are here for yourself. Everyone in this room needs help. That's why they're here. They're not judging you. They're not here to gossip about your personal business. Every person in this room decided that they wanted to stop using drugs and decided that this program may help them. But unless you take this program seriously, it won't work. You'll walk right back out that door and take your pills again."

I laugh a little. "You seem passionate about this group."

"I am. Because without it, I wouldn't be where I am today. And . . . There's something about you, Miss Amy. I was moved to come and speak to you, and I'm glad I did."

"I'm glad you did too."

We're interrupted by the speaker, and I take a second to think about what she said. At this moment, I realize I never told Mark I was unhappy. I never sat him down and told him how his actions affected me and our children. I hid my thoughts and feelings. For the most part, I kept my opinions to myself to avoid an argument. When I couldn't take it anymore, I sought comfort elsewhere. Shit! I was wrong—I am wrong. A person can't change or do better if they don't know that they're wrong in the first place. It turns out Danielle is right. Not only have I been in denial about the effects of using pills, but I've also been in denial about the state of my marriage. If I had been brave enough to tell Mark I was unhappy, maybe we could have gotten on the right track long ago. I should've been vocal about what I wanted and needed.

I see why Mark feels betrayed. It's more apparent to me now. I walked around with a smile on my face. I acted as if I were a happy wife who didn't have a care in the world. But deep down, I was miserable. And instead of me being honest with him, I took the easy way out.

I shift in my seat and pay attention to the speaker. Like, *really* pay attention to him because, for the first time since I got here, I feel like I need this program. And not just for the sake of saving my marriage but for the sake of my own well-being.

CHAPTER TWENTY
SHELDON
THREE MONTHS LATER

Kamryn runs into the bedroom, excited. "Daddy, can I color?"

"Yes, but quiet down. Your brother is sleeping."

I look at Sheldon Jr. to make sure Kamryn hasn't woken him up. Then I grab the coloring book and the box of crayons and set them on the tiny dining room table. Kamryn jumps into the seat in front of them, opens the box, and grabs a purple crayon. I smile as I watch her color. She's growing. Each day, she's getting taller. Smarter. And I'm grateful to be spending more time with her. Suddenly, the doorbell rings.

"I'll be right back, sweet pea."

I swing open the door and am surprised to see Eva. I check my watch. "You're early."

"I know. I have somewhere to be."

I open the door wide and allow her to walk in. When I close the door behind me, I take her in. She looks good. Very good. She cut her hair in layers and dyed it a brownish color. She's also shed some weight, not that her weight was ever an issue. But she's slimmer now, yet still filled out in the right places. I shake away that thought, remembering that she's no longer my wife, and I shouldn't lust after her as I am. I could argue that she will always be my wife in a biblical sense, but I'm too distracted by her outfit to think about a scripture right now. She's wearing a form-fitting dress and boots that come over her thighs. My mouth opens with shock that she would wear something like that outside. I had gotten used to the conservative look. But right now, she's dressed like one of those video vixens. I snap out of my thoughts.

"You know my work schedule makes it hard for me to get as much time with the kids as I'd like. Do you have to take them so soon?" I ask.

"Yes. I have plans. I'm meeting someone."

"Is it important?"

"It's a date," she replies.

Her answer hits me like a ton of bricks. Our divorce is still fresh, and I have no desire to date anyone right now. In fact, some small part of me still thinks that I can win my wife back. So, hearing that she's dating breaks my heart into two.

"A date? Don't you think it's a little too soon, Eva?"

She scuffs. "Too soon? For whom, you or me?"

"I—"

She interrupts me. "Oh, I get it. I'm supposed to sit around and cry, right? I'm supposed to be a boring stay-at-home mom with no social life because my focus is my family. Well, that woman is gone, Sheldon. She left when her husband had an affair, and guess what? She's *never* coming back."

I take a step closer. "I didn't want a divorce."

"Yes, you did. You made it clear we wouldn't work, remember?"

"I was wrong, Eva. I hate what I did to you. I'm ashamed. But I'm different now. I'm not the same man that I was during that time. I want you back. I want our family back. I pray about it every night."

This seems to make her angry. "Oh, you pray now? Please! Don't bring God into this. How many nights did I pray that He would save my marriage? How often did I pray and ask Him to take away the pain? To make you love me? And guess what? He abandoned me."

"God would never abandon you, Eva."

She tosses her head back with a hearty laugh. "Let's not act like you're some saint now, okay? Sheldon, did you forget I know the word of God like the back of my hand? Stop it. Now. Before I embarrass you."

She sounds cold. Heartless. Just like she did in the courtroom during our divorce proceedings. She's too far gone for me to reason with her, and I don't want this to escalate in front of the kids. "Okay. Let me get them ready. But, Eva, I don't want my kids around some strange guy."

"You can't tell me what to do. You have no say in who gets to be in our lives."

I close the gap between us. "Eva, please, don't do this to spite me. Think about the kids."

She crosses her arms. "Just get them ready, please."

I walk away and gather the kids' things. I place them neatly in their overnight bags. I kiss them both goodbye and hand them over to Eva. Kamryn turns to me with sadness.

"Bye, Daddy."

"I'll see you soon, sweet pea."

Eva opens the door, and I call after her. "Eva." She turns around slowly. "I love you. I doubt I'll ever stop loving you. And I know that deep down, you still love me. Isn't that love worth fighting for? Isn't our family worth it?"

Her eyes fill with sadness and tears. Her face softens, and it's the first time she's shown any vulnerability since the divorce started.

"Sheldon, at one time, I did think it was worth it. I would have done anything to have you and our family back."

My heart anxiously pounds in my chest as I wait for her following sentence, hoping she's had a change of heart. But when her face turns back to stone, I know she's not about to deliver the words I want to hear.

"But not anymore."

She walks away with the kids in tow. Then I shut the door. I walk into the kitchen and grab a glass of iced tea, wishing it were whiskey. The divorce was one of the most challenging things I've ever gone through. Eva filed on the grounds of infidelity, and it didn't take long for the judge to rule in her favor. She got the house, the cars, spousal, and child support. I moved into a tiny apartment and have been picking up additional shifts at the hospital for extra money. Thank goodness, the charges were dropped against me, and I could keep my job. Otherwise, I'd be homeless right now. I lost everything. And I deeply regret my actions. But I must move on. Eva has made it clear time and time again that she wants nothing to do with me. As she said, the woman I knew as my wife is gone and never returning. And it's about time I listen.

EVA

Seeing Sheldon every other weekend is an adjustment for me. The court granted me full custody of the kids in the divorce settlement. They also awarded me spousal and child support, totaling $5,000 monthly. I felt a little guilty at first, leaving Sheldon with nothing. But then I thought about his cheating ways and realized he deserved it. This may teach him a lesson down the line.

It still angers me knowing that he shared himself with someone else. It still hurts to know his feelings were so strong for her that he was willing to leave his family. Today was one of those days. It was a day when I couldn't stop thinking about his betrayal. So, I decided to be petty. I did my hair. I purchased a sexy outfit and pretended I was going on a date. I wanted him to see that I could still be sexy . . . for another man. If Sheldon knew me as well as he thought he did, he would have figured out it was all for show. He would've called me out and knew I was lying about dating, but he failed the test.

I have no desire to date or have sex with anyone, not after what happened between Terrance and me. I felt horrible about it. And as good as he made me feel, I couldn't share myself with him again or anyone else any time soon. As pleasurable as it was, it was also painful. It made me miss Sheldon.

I'm not dating right now, and I don't want to. But it doesn't mean I want Sheldon back because I don't. I'll never forgive him. I feel hatred when I look at him. Ephesians 4:31 says, *Get rid of bitterness, rage, and anger, brawling and slander, along with every form of malice.* If I were still a godly woman, I'd ask for forgiveness and try to remove the anger and bitterness I feel. But I'm not. That part of my life is over, so I can be as bitter and angry as I want.

Once I've healed and am over Sheldon, I might start dating. But for now, I want to focus on myself and live my life to the best of my ability. Being a divorced mother of two isn't easy, but this is my life now, and I must get used to it.

Deep down inside, I miss him. I miss our family and the life that we built. But I won't look like a fool. I won't embarrass myself by taking back a liar and a cheater. Instead, I'll move on and have peace of mind instead of wondering what he's doing and who he's with every second of the day.

I place Kamryn and Sheldon Jr. in their car seats and slide into the driver's seat. I look at the apartment building, specifically building number twenty-one. My eyes fill with tears as I think of Sheldon living inside that tiny space. I wonder if he's eating well. He was never a good cook, and I'm sure he can't afford to eat out every night. I wonder if he's sleeping well. He used to have nightmares about the patients he lost, causing him to toss and turn for hours. For a quick second, I think about jumping out of the car, running up the stairs, and banging on the door, demanding he come home. The urge to have him hold me tightly intensifies with every second I stare at his door. The tears fall, and I sniffle as weakness takes over my body. Images of Sheldon kissing me flash in my mind. I remember him hugging me. I remember us laughing together and playing with the kids.

But then, those images mix with the images of seeing him and Amy together, and the tears dry. I snatch my eyes away from the building and start the car. I look at my children through the rearview mirror. They're in their own worlds, playing and looking out the window. I put the car in drive and head toward our home—a home where my children and I can have a fresh start.

AMY

It's been three months since Mark discovered my affair, and I must admit I didn't think we'd make it. I for sure thought he would divorce me, but he didn't. We started going to marriage counseling. In addition to marriage counseling, we also attend individual counseling. This doesn't mean that things are back to normal. This doesn't mean that we don't have bad days. It just means that we're trying. It means that we made a commitment and decided to honor that commitment.

I take the pecan pie out of the oven, which looks identical to Emma's. I hope it tastes the same.

"That smells good," Mark says as he enters the kitchen.

I smile as he takes a seat at the table. This time, it's a genuine smile. Mark and I have been given a second chance, which makes me happy.

"I followed your mother's recipe to a tee."

His phone vibrates. As he reads a message, concern crosses his face.

"Is everything okay?" I ask.

He nods. "They want me to speak at tonight's meeting."

Words can't express how proud I am of Mark. He's striving to become a better husband, father, man, and overall person. He's been attending his BWRCT meetings frequently and actively participating to be a reformed racist. I've even attended a few with him for support.

"I think that's a great idea."

He shakes his head. "I don't know, Amy. Sharing with the counselors is one thing. But I'm not ready to share my story with the group yet."

I cross over to the kitchen table and place my hand on his shoulder. "Mark, I think it's time. You've been doing so well. Your story could help someone else."

"I don't know."

"What's your hesitation?" I ask.

"I know it sounds weird, but . . . I'm actually embarrassed."

"About what?"

"About all of it. My way of thinking. The names I called people. The things I taught my children. I was a horrible person, Amy. And yes, I'm trying to change, but the shit is hard. Sometimes I find myself backsliding."

His transparency warms my heart. It was something the therapist suggested we work on to strengthen our union. She said that for it to work, we must always be honest with each other about everything . . . always. Secrets have no room in this house anymore.

"That's all the more reason to share. You're probably not the only one struggling to reform, Mark."

"Yeah, I guess you have a point."

I walk back to the counter, hoping the pie has cooled by now. When I see it has, I take a knife and slice a small piece. I grab the nearby plate and place the piece of pie on it. Then I put it in front of Mark and hand him a fork. I anxiously watch as he takes a bite. He doesn't react immediately, but he turns to me once he swallows and smiles.

"Tastes just like Mom's."

Mark misses his mother terribly. And the fact that he and Russell are estranged makes him miss her more. I could kill Russell for what he did to Mark. I never liked him. I always thought he was just plain evil, but I also second-guessed myself. How can a man so evil be married to a woman so sweet and kind? Mark not only lost his mother. He lost his father as well. Even his brothers stopped speaking to him when they learned the truth. All he has is us.

"Is Dylan still coming over for dinner?" he asks.

"Yeah, and remember, he's bringing a date. Honey, be nice."

He nods. "It doesn't bother me like it used to, honey. If my son is happy, that makes me happy."

I wasn't sure if Dylan and Mark would ever speak again. And I was prepared to live two separate lives—one as a mother and one as a wife. Dylan was turning eighteen, and as much as I wanted to demand that he come home and work things out with his father, I knew I couldn't. I had to allow him to decide on his own. Mark takes a sip of his freshly squeezed lemonade.

"Have you heard from Ireland?" he asks.

Joy shoots through my heart. "Yes. And she's supposed to call me today."

I miss my daughter terribly. I've tried to arrange a day for me to visit her and Austin, but she is still a little hesitant about it. I will be a grandmother soon and want to have a relationship with my grandchild. But I have to give Ireland her space right now. I can't force things, or it'll push her further away.

"Have you decided if you're going back to work?"

I clear my throat as I think about his question. It's a sore topic for us. I quit my job because I couldn't stand the embarrassment of working at the hospital where my husband and Sheldon got into a fight. All my coworkers witnessed it, and I know my scandal was the gossip topic for weeks.

"No. I want to take some time off work if you don't mind. So I can focus on myself. And focus on us."

He nods. "If you want to do that, I support you."

MARK

My life has been one hell of a ride. If someone had told me I would be an ambassador to help end racism, I would have laughed in their faces. I would have called them a liar and sent them on their way. Learning that I was biracial was one of the hardest things I've had to deal with in my life. There are so many habits I have to break and false teachings that I have to unlearn. I haven't had a chance to speak to my children about what I learned. I asked Amy not to mention the fact that Russell isn't my biological father to them. I've caused too much damage to bring more drama into their lives. My priority is to rebuild my relationship with them first. Once I do, then I can tell them the truth about everything.

They don't know it, but I'm proud of them. As I think back over the years, my kids didn't share my views. No matter how much I tried to drill it in them, they had their own minds and knew I was wrong. They didn't share a hatred for other people like I did. They didn't discriminate as I did. They stayed true to what was right, and I'm grateful they did. As a result, my kids won't have the issue of unlearning things. They won't have to worry about changing who they are because, on the inside, they've always been exactly who they should be.

Amy ends the call with Ireland and turns to face me.

"She's having a boy."

I'm filled with pride . . . and sadness—satisfaction because I'm going to have a grandson but sadness because she's still not speaking to me. I miss my baby girl. I tried to reach out to her, but she still hasn't responded to my calls and messages. And I'm not sure if she ever will. I will spend the rest of my life begging for her forgiveness, even if she refuses to accept me. I was not a good father.

"Wow, we're having a grandson," I reply.

"Can you believe it? Our baby is having a baby," she says.

"Seems like yesterday she learned to walk."

The room grows silent as remorse creeps in, and Amy places her hand over mine.

"She'll come around, Mark."

"She may not. And I have to be prepared for that because I blame only myself."

"I know. There's something else."

"What?" I ask.

"They're getting married."

On the one hand, I'm happy for them. Her boyfriend is making an honest woman out of her, which makes me happy. But then I think about how young she is.

"Is she really ready to be a wife, Amy?"

"We can't judge him. People sometimes fall in love when they shouldn't be together."

She's hinting around about my mother and my biological father.

"You're right," I respond.

Boy, has life kicked me in the ass. I revisited my dad's widow and spent the day talking about him and looking at more pictures. I wanted to know what he was like and if I had any similarities. Surprisingly, I do. He was very crafty with his hands and could fix anything in sight. He was also left-handed like me. I promised to stay in touch with my sister, but only after Amy and I worked out our issues. I had to fix my own family before I could embrace another.

I took a leave of absence from the firm, but not because my manager is Black. I left because I no longer had the right mind-set to do my job effectively. Losing my mother, finding out the truth about my biological dad, disowning the man who raised me, and finding out Amy had an affair were enough to have me locked in a padded room with a straitjacket on. I needed time to heal, so I took some much-needed time off. It was hard to disown the man who raised me. But I had to. He was my role model, and I wanted to be just like him. But now it makes me sick to even think about being like him. Everything I ever thought about a person's race, age, or sexuality has now been questioned. But I'm actively seeking answers. It will take some time, but I know I'll get there. And if I can try to live the rest of my life filled with peace, understanding, and love . . . I'll have to get there.

EPILOGUE

TWO YEARS LATER

EVA

I look up at the sky before I walk into the church. "Okay. Let's try this again."

It's been two years since I stepped inside a sanctuary. Once I denounced Christianity, I never opened my Bible or prayed again. My heart was hardened, and I was too angry to talk to God. But I'm a different woman now. I went to therapy. I got the help I needed to let go of the anger and bitterness I felt after Sheldon and I divorced. I also went back to work and got my dream job. I'm in such a happy and grateful headspace right now, and I know it's only possible because of one person . . . God.

I've never been to this church before. My coworker suggested it, and she keeps raving about this new up-and-coming pastor. Besides, my life has been about change and fresh starts lately, so returning to my old church was not an option. I walk inside, and I'm immediately greeted by the ushers who lead me to the front of the church. I slide into one of the pews and smile at the other

228

members. The church is beautiful. A large wooden cross stands in front of the altar. Large, purple floral arrangements are placed beside the podium where the pastor speaks. I sit quietly, in thought, as the organ plays soft music.

The music speeds up, and a few people walk out with microphones. As they start to sing, the congregation stands to its feet. They sing beautifully, and I raise my hand to praise Him as tears fill my eyes. I'm filled with the Holy Spirit at what He's done for me these past few years. After the choir sings their last song, we take our seats as announcements are made. A man steps up to the podium and speaks into the microphone.

"Praise, God."

The congregation repeats it, and he smiles. "I don't know 'bout y'all, but He's been good to me."

The congregation shouts.

"Boy, do we have a word for you today. I've had the pleasure of mentoring this gentleman this past year, and let me tell you that he is *anointed*."

"YES!" the congregation yells.

"He was once lost, but he's been found."

"Yes, Lord!" a member yells.

"Please stand to your feet for our associate pastor, Pastor Sheldon."

I stay frozen in my seat at the sound of his name. Surely, they don't mean . . . I don't get to finish the sentence . . . because it *is* him. I see Sheldon every other weekend and every other holiday when I drop off the kids, and not once has he mentioned anything about church, let alone being a pastor. I'm confused, and my mind is blown. This can't be. My eyes must be playing tricks on me because there is no way the Sheldon I know would ever step foot inside a church. I remain seated, unsure of what I should do. Finally, he walks up to the podium and looks at the congregation. His eyes lock with mine, and he speaks while holding the stare.

"Praise God."

I repeat after him because this is truly a moment to praise Him. Sheldon, a man who never so much as touched a Bible, is now preaching the word of God? He continues to speak.

"You know, I had a different message to speak about today. But God has laid it on my heart to speak about something else. Is that okay with y'all?" The church fills with some loud yeses and umm-hmms. "Today, I want to talk about redemption and forgiveness."

He looks directly at me when he says it, and I shift in my seat. I feel someone sit closely next to me, but I can't tear my eyes away from him.

"Sorry, I'm late, girl." The sound of my coworker's voice fills my ear. "That's the pastor I was telling you about. Girl, ain't he fine?"

I don't answer her. I'm too busy seeing where Sheldon goes with this. He opens his Bible and speaks. He talks about the deliverance from sin and the grace and forgiveness of God. He looks my way occasionally, but not so much that it causes people to take notice. His sermon moves me. And not just because it's him. He really is *that* good. The church is on fire. People are out of their seats, shouting and calling out to God. As he winds down the service, he gives an altar call. He saves four souls and then closes us out with prayer. My coworker sees some people she knows and tells me she'll be back, and I stay glued to my seat as I watch Sheldon shake hands with congregation members. Finally, he reaches my pew and smiles.

"Eva, I'm glad to see you here."

I stand. "Sheldon, wow. I had no idea. Why didn't you tell me?"

"You don't speak to me much when I do see you. I honestly didn't think you'd be interested in anything I have going on."

He's right. When I drop off the kids or pick them up, we say hello, and that's it. Any communication regarding changes in plans or drop-off times is usually through text messages.

"Kam never said anything about coming to church."

"Yeah, I haven't brought them yet."

"Oh, why not?"

"Honestly, I don't know if I was ready for them or you to know. My mom watches them on my weekends if I have to preach."

"I'm sure she's not happy about this."

He smiles. "No. But she'll be just fine."

"You were wonderful up there."

His face lights up. "Really?"

"Yeah, really. I enjoyed the service a lot."

"Thanks, Eva. That means a lot coming from you."

The pastor approaches him, and I use that time to excuse myself. "I'm glad I came. I'll see you next weekend."

As I exit the pew, he calls after me.

"Eva?"

"Yes."

"Can we go somewhere and talk?"

SHELDON

It was nothing but divine intervention that Eva ended up in my church. I wanted to tell her on so many occasions that I was studying theology. I wanted to take accountability for my actions, my sin against God, and the way I treated her. I wanted to ask for her forgiveness. She was my wife—the mother of my two beautiful children, but I didn't treat her as such. As much as I wanted to lay this all on her, I also didn't want to burden her with *my* guilt. I'm the one who messed up, and it wasn't up to her to absolve the guilt

I was feeling—shame that I still feel to this day. As I got closer to God, He told me to wait. He told me that I would be able to air out everything in due time.

We sit on a bench at a park around the corner from the church.

"I have so many questions," she says.

"Ask away."

"When?" she asks.

"Honestly?"

"Yes."

"Before the divorce," I reply.

"But you're still a doctor."

"Yeah, because I won't be able to pay the child support on a pastor's salary."

Guilt crosses her face. "About that. I'm sorry. I was being spiteful."

I shake my head. "I deserved everything that happened to me, Eva. I was wrong. You were a good wife." She searches my eyes, and I lean closer to repeat myself. "You were a good wife, Eva. I was blessed to have you, but I messed it all up."

"I—"

"Listen. I've said it before, but I'll repeat it. I'm sorry. For all of it. I wasn't living right, and you and my kids were affected in the process."

"Sheldon, I . . ." She thinks for a minute. "I forgive you."

Finally, the weight I've been carrying has been lifted. I take a deep breath, put my head in my hands, and sob. She's at my side immediately.

"Are you okay?" she asks.

"You have no idea how much your forgiveness means to me, Eva."

Tears fill her eyes. "I wasn't perfect, Sheldon. I put the church before you and my family. I didn't listen to you when you said you needed intimacy. I was stubborn. I'm sorry for everything I did to hurt you."

She places her hands over mine and continues.

"I knew exactly what I was doing. I knew exactly how to hurt you and what to do to get under your skin. And I did it all out of spite. Regardless of whether you think you deserved it, I shouldn't have treated you that way."

I nod before I look at her. "I forgive you."

At that moment, the air feels fresher. The sun beams brighter. I say the last thing I've been holding before I lose my nerve. "I never stopped loving you."

Her eyes widen. "All this time?"

"All this time."

"But I thought . . ."

"What?" I ask.

"You told me you loved Amy. Then you said you weren't in love with me, and our marriage wasn't the same."

"I know. And I was an idiot. I didn't mean any of it. I *thought* I loved her. But it wasn't love at all. It was the urge to have something I thought was easy. And I've learned nothing worth fighting for comes easy, Eva."

"So, you and Amy—"

"Should have never happened."

She leans back and twiddles her fingers a little. "Sheldon, what are you getting at?"

"I'm not getting at anything. It's high time I was honest, and this is the time to do it."

I can see the wheels spinning in her head as she digests everything I just said. She looks beautiful in the sunlight, and the pain of losing her slams into my chest again.

"So . . . What now?" she finally responds.

I shrug because I don't know. I miss my wife. I miss my family. But I'm so nervous to ask her to give me another chance. Maybe because it's too late; that ship may have sailed. But as I stare into her eyes and she stares back, I swear I see her waiting for me to say it. I know I shouldn't use the word s*wear*, but she's waiting for me to make the first move.

"I want my family back," I say loud and clear.

The words blurt out before I have a chance to stop myself from saying them. At this point, I have nothing left to lose. The worst that can happen is that she says no. But now that we've forgiven each other, hopefully, she'll let me down easier this time. Her mouth opens, and she watches me to ensure I'm serious.

"Sheldon . . ."

"I know I have a lot to prove. I have a lot to make up for. But I promise you I will do the work, Eva. I will spend every day of my life showing you how much I love you."

She shakes her head slightly. "So much has happened."

"I know. But we can work through it. I *know* we can." She bites her lip and twiddles her fingers again. I keep talking because I'm afraid she'll say no if I don't. "Whatever it takes, Eva. Therapy. Counseling at the church. I'll even be a stay-at-home dad. Say it, and I'll do it."

"What about Lamar? The thought of you having a child with another woman broke me," she replies.

"I know. But Shanice didn't tell you? He's not mine. The DNA test confirmed it. I can do nothing about the past, sweetheart, but I promise I will make it all up to you if you let me."

A tear slides down her cheek. "I want to, Sheldon. I really do. But . . . I'm scared. I don't know if I can trust you again."

Her words break my heart because I'm the cause of her mistrust. I've ruined the safety and trust she felt for me when we first married. I grab her hand.

"I will build that trust back. You can have the passwords to my phones and emails. I don't care. Just . . . I love you so much, Eva."

The tears spill as she says it back. "I love you too, Sheldon."

I want to lean in and kiss her, but this isn't the place for that. I'll wait until we're off the church grounds and then make my move. For the first time in a long time, the passion I once had for my wife burns inside me. One may say I shouldn't be kissing her now that I'm a man of the cloth, but I beg to differ. Eva and I made a covenant before God. A covenant meant to last until one of us dies. She is still my wife technically, just not legally. I search her eyes anxiously, hoping I haven't scared her away with how forward I am.

"Talk to me, Eva."

"It's going to be hard."

"I don't care," I reply.

"What if we don't make it?" she asks.

"We will."

"I can't take another heartbreak, Sheldon."

"I won't break your heart."

She waits a minute, and then she nods. "Okay."

IRELAND

Austin Jr. laughs and runs across the living room as I try to catch him for his afternoon nap. "He's been busy all day."

He's playful like most toddlers, and my heart melts whenever I look at him. He looks like his father with his tan skin, brown eyes, and jet-black hair. He doesn't resemble me, but maybe one day he will.

"He's energetic like his mother," Mark chimes in. "Remember, she used to run all through the house, Amy?"

My mother chuckles. "Yes. She was always on the go. Even when she would fall, she would get right back up."

The two of them laugh, and I smile at the sight before me. I'm at my parents' house, and we're all sitting around like one big happy family. It took a lot to get here, but that's not important. What's important is that we made it here. I swore I would never speak to my dad again. Ever. I didn't want him anywhere near me or A.J., But that all changed when I gave birth. The day I had A.J. changed my life forever. I suddenly had the urge to be around family. I wanted my parents to know their grandson and vice versa. So, when Mom said my father had changed, I agreed to give him a chance.

Austin approaches me and holds his hands out.

"You look tired. Won't you rest your feet, and I'll take him?" he suggests.

I grab A.J. and hand him over to him. "It's time for his nap."

He nods. "Okay. I'll put him down. Then I have a call with my publisher."

Austin did it. He did exactly what he said he was going to do. He wrote a bestselling novel. It is so good it's sold millions of copies and has been optioned as a movie. We purchased a home and married with the money he received in royalties. I work as a decorating consultant. The flexibility allows me to work from home most days while caring for A.J.

Austin sits across from my father, and A.J. immediately settles down as he fixates on the book I give him. My father and mother exchange glances.

"Is that the book we used to read to you?" Mom says.

"Yes," I reply.

My dad pats Austin on the back. "There is nothing greater than the bond between a father and son, Austin. So whatever you do, make sure you hold onto it."

He glances over at Dylan when he says it and smiles at him before sipping his iced tea. My phone rings, and I pick it up.

"Hey."

"Sorry, I'm running late."

It's Camilla. Camilla and I are still best friends. She was also the maid of honor at my wedding, and she's not just A.J.'s aunt, but also his godmother. I know it's weird to designate that title to her since she's his aunt, but there's no other person I deem worthy enough to give that title to.

"It's okay. We haven't started dinner yet," I reply.

"Great. I'm on my way, and as soon as I get there, hand over my nephew."

I end the call and smile at Austin. "Your sister's on her way."

"Good. I feel like I haven't seen her in a long time."

"You haven't. We've been so busy with the books and A.J. that we haven't had much time for anything else," I reply.

Mom plops down beside Dad, and I take a deep breath before speaking. "I have news to share."

The room grows quiet, and everyone looks at each other nervously. Even Austin seems nervous.

"Should I go put A.J. down now?" he asks.

I shake my head. "No." I shift slightly when the room is quiet again and clear my throat. "I was waiting for Camilla to get here, but as usual, she's late. So, I'm just going to share my news. I'm pregnant."

Mom shoots to her feet. "Oh, sweetheart."

Austin smiles widely. "Baby, that's great news."

Dylan high-fives Austin. "This is exciting news. Congratulations, you two."

My father places his beer down on the coffee table and stands to his feet. He takes a few long strides toward me and stops when he's in front of me. He looks at me, and I look at him, then he embraces me. And I cry. I cry for all the times I wanted the affection of my father. I cry for all the times I wanted him to show me he cared. And he cries. Probably for the important times he missed. Probably for the times he can't get back. He pulls away, wipes a tear from my face, and smiles.

"Congratulations, baby girl. I love you."

I return the smile. "I love you too, Daddy."

DYLAN

My sister is glowing, and now I know why. She's going to be a mom again. I couldn't be happier for her and my brother-in-law. It took some time for me to warm up to Austin. I still thought he was too old to date my little sister, let alone sleep with her. But they were in love, the damage was done, and there was nothing to be done at that point.

"Hey, you." Hansh hands me a bottle of water as he joins me. "What did I miss?"

I jerk my head toward Ireland and Austin. "Ireland is pregnant. I'm going to be an uncle . . . again."

He throws his arm around me. "That's good news, baby."

My body tenses. I nervously glance at my father, who offers me a genuine smile before he turns his attention back to Ireland. I still get anxious around my father, but he and I are working on it. I'm grateful for our progress because, at one time, I thought I'd never see or speak to him again. I thought I'd never step foot in his house again as long as he lived there. But that isn't what happened at all.

At the suggestion of my therapist, I decided to sit with him and tell him how I felt about everything. Only much calmer and more detailed than when I yelled at him when I was in the hospital. I could tell him how his actions have affected me, how I had such a tough time growing up because of him. This time, he listened. This time, he apologized. It was a sincere apology, and for the first time in my life, I felt like my father did love me. For the first time in my life, I had confirmation that his actions had nothing to do with me and *everything* to do with him. And it felt good. So good that when I got home, I couldn't stop myself from crying. It was as if all the years of pain and anxiety were releasing from my body. We still have work to do and are doing our parts to rebuild our relationship. I have no doubt that if things continue as they have, my dad and I will become best friends. He walks over to us and extends his hand to Hansh.

"Nice to see you again, Hansh."

Hansh places his hand inside my dad's. "It's good to see you again, Mr. Carson."

My dad turns to walk away, but Hansh calls after him. When my dad turns around, Hansh reaches into his pocket.

"Mr. Carson, as you know, Dylan isn't much of a football watcher."

My dad nods. "Yes, I know."

"Well, I have two tickets to the Falcon's game next Sunday and was wondering if you'd like to come with me."

I'm shocked at his gesture but not surprised. His kindness is one of the reasons I fell for him. We both got accepted into NYU, and for the first time, I saw Hansh as more than a friend. We've only been dating for six months, but I honestly feel like he's the one, and I've even spoken to Mom about proposing to him before the year is out. My dad takes the tickets from him, and his eyes open wide.

"These are skybox seats."

Hansh smiles widely. "Yeah. My uncle is friends with the owner of the team."

My dad chuckles. "Hell yeah, I'd like to go."

"Great. I'll pick you up at nine a.m. so we can tailgate."

"I'm looking forward to it," Dad replies.

He pats him on the back before he walks away, and I fold my arms across my chest.

"So, when were you going to tell me you got football tickets for you and my dad?"

Hansh laughs. "I wasn't. I didn't want you trying to talk me out of it."

He's right. As I said, Dad and I still have work to do, and although we're trying, I still have that lingering feeling of disappointing him. I still sometimes think he's judging me when he sees me and Hansh together, even though he's been nothing but pleasant and respectful to both of us. Because of this, I would have been too fearful for Hansh and Dad to spend time together alone.

"You know me well."

He nudges me. "Are you jealous?" he teases.

I nudge him back. "Maybe a little," I tease back.

His expression turns serious. "I can get another ticket if you want to come."

I shake my head. "No. I hate football. Besides, remember, Dad and I are taking that father-son trip to the Grand Canyon in a few weeks. You know I've always wanted to go there."

"Yes, that's right. Speaking of the trip, I'm a bit salty I wasn't invited to that."

I grab his hand and lace my fingers with his. "There'll be plenty of other trips for us to go on."

He smiles before he takes a sip of his water, and I take a deep breath and relax my shoulders for the first time since I've been here. I look over at my mom, who looks much happier these days. She and my dad somehow worked through their marital issues, and she has her children back. But when I look at my father, he seems like he's aged. I don't know if it's from all the hate he carried for so many years or if it's from the stress of the news he shared with me and Ireland about his birth father. Maybe it's a combination of both.

My eyes float over to Ireland. For the first time, I don't see her as my baby sister. She's grown into a responsible, mature adult. Motherhood looks good on her. As we sit around and fellowship, I'm overcome with gratefulness. This is the type of family I wanted growing up. This is the type of family I want to come home to every day. And this is the type of family I want around my kids whenever I decide to have them. A close-knit, loving, and supportive family.

I can't change the past. I can't dwell on the fact that I once hated living in their home because my father made my life a living hell. Now, I choose to forgive and move forward. Although we went to hell and back as a family, I am thankful we are now in a good place. And right now, there is no other place I'd rather be.

AMY

My babies are home. I'm so happy I want to shout to the mountaintop and scream to the hills. I've missed them terribly. Ireland is in another state, so I would have to catch the bus or train to visit her. Dylan is literally down the street, but I would also have to take time to visit him. This put a strain on me, and I hated it. I hated having to see my children separately, under different roofs. I wanted my babies to come home. I wanted them to spend time with their parents in the home that they grew up in.

But I also had to be mindful that the home held many memories for them. Bad memories. Memories they didn't want to creep back to the surface every time their foot met the doorstep.

They hated that house. So, Mark and I did something we knew would benefit all of us. We sold it. We didn't move too far from it, but far enough to avoid driving past it. Mark and I have fallen in love again. But not without lots of accountability, forgiveness, and therapy. He's a different man now. A better man now. And I couldn't be prouder of him.

I hate how I hurt him. I hate how my selfishness helped drive a wedge between us. I'll admit that many other factors drove a wedge between us, but my affair deepened the wedge. Not only am I regretful for how I hurt my husband, but I also regret how I treated Sheldon. He was genuine in his feelings for me, and I used him as an escape. I didn't consider how it would affect him if Mark ever found out about us. As a result, I broke up a family. Although he and Eva had serious issues of their own, I contributed greatly to those issues and caused her pain. I regret it every day that I wake up. It had been in my heart to reach out and apologize to them. With all my work on myself and my marriage, I couldn't go another day without confessing how wrong I was. So, I reached out to Sheldon. Luckily, he hadn't changed his number. I apologized. He apologized. Then he asked me never to contact him again. He also said he would block my number after the call. I asked if there was a way that I could contact Eva, and he told me that he would relay the message to her himself.

It's probably for the best. Eva probably hates me, and there's no telling how the conversation would go if I contacted her. My phone rings, and I excuse myself to answer it. It's my sister.

"Hey."

"Hey, Sis. Sorry, I'm running late; my flight got delayed."

"Of course, it did. Where are you coming from again?"

"I was in the Caribbean for an undersea exploration."

I laugh out loud. "Jesus, Viki. You're such a daredevil. I hope you have life insurance."

"Yeah, well, they ask too many questions about my lifestyle. Most won't insure me because I'm considered a high risk. Hey, if anything happens to me, there's money in my safe to cover my cremation."

"Cremation?"

"Yeah. I *know* you didn't think I wanted one of those boring-ass church funerals. Set me on fire, Sis."

"I'm not doing this with you today. You've already missed the big news, so what time will you arrive?"

"About an hour." There's a minute of silence before she asks her next question. "How are you? How are the meetings?"

I won't lie and say I'm completely healed and cured of addiction. Some days are harder than others. And on those days, I can hear the pills calling my name. I can feel the urge to take a few to calm my nerves, but I don't. I remember my twelve steps and call my sponsor if necessary. The program is right. It works if you work it.

"I'm doing better. The program has been a lifesaver."

"Good. Okay, I'll see you soon."

We end the call, and I smile at how much closer my sister and I have gotten. She and Mark are getting along, and she's becoming closer with Dylan and Ireland. I look in the mirror, and for the first time in a long time, I'm not ashamed of the reflection staring back at me. I'm proud of myself. I'm proud of all that I've overcome. I've become a better woman. A better wife. A better mother. I've learned so much about myself in my meetings and therapy. I'm more vocal in my marriage now. I speak up more, and Mark listens and respects it. I've learned that I am in charge of my happiness. Not my husband and not my kids. After I decided to quit my job, I did something I'd always wanted to do. I got my real estate license.

I take one last look in the mirror before I exit the bathroom. I round the corner, and Mark approaches me with concern. I hold up the phone.

"Viki. Her flight got delayed, and she's on her way."

He smiles. "Let me guess. She was jumping out of someone's plane this time?"

I shake my head. "No. More like someone's ship."

He wraps his arm around my waist and stares into my eyes. "You look beautiful today, baby."

I blush. "Thank you."

He holds me close as he looks at our children, laughing and playing with A.J. He shakes his head in disbelief.

"If only I had been a better man sooner."

My eyes swing to his. "Hey. Stop. What matters is that you're a better man now. It's never too late, Mark."

He looks at me. "I guess you're right." His face softens. "I love you, Amy. Always have and always will."

I lean into him. "Ditto, baby."

MARK

I hug myself to warm my arms. My coat is layered but not enough to escape the cold winter air. "I'm going to be a grandfather again." My chest swells with pride as I say it. "A.J. is a character. You would have loved him, Mom."

I stare at the brick gravestone as I speak to my mother, wishing she wasn't buried beneath it. I think how nice it would have been for her to hold her first great-grandbaby. I think about how nice it would have been for all of us to sit around the dinner table and eat my mother's cooking. The thought of my dad sitting beside my mother creeps inside my brain. I look at the stone right next to hers. *Russell Carson* is engraved in it. I avert my eyes back to my mother's stone. "Anyway, so much has happened, Mom. You would be proud of me."

Tears swell as I think about how far I've come. They slide down my cheeks as I think about how grateful I am to be given